NEVER FALL FOR YOUR ENEMY

IT'S COMPLICATED

KATE O'KEEFFE

WILD LIME BOOKS

Never Fall for Your Enemy (especially not at Christmas) is a work of fiction. The characters and events portrayed in this book are fictitious. Any similarity to real persons, living or dead, is purely coincidental and not intended by the author.
All rights reserved, including the right to reproduce, distribute, or transmit in any form or by any means.
ISBN: 979-8494170057

Copyright © 2021 Kate O'Keeffe

Wild Lime
Books

🌸 Created with Vellum

ABOUT THIS BOOK

Three things I know for sure:
1) I hate Charlie Cavendish.
2) I hate Charlie Cavendish.
3) Oh, and did I mention I hate Charlie Cavendish?

Rich. Over-privileged. Smug. The guy's far too good looking or his own good and he's always got that smirk teasing at the edges of his mouth, telling me what he thinks of me.

And now, my worst nightmare has come true.

Charles Cavendish has moved into my building which means I can't avoid seeing him everywhere I go. He's always there, judging me, especially when I come in late at night. Hey, I can't help it if my "single American girl in London" writing gig means I've got to check out every new club in town. Charles is so tightly wound he goes to work before the birds have chirped their first good morning.

He needs to loosen up. Live a little. Actually, I don't care what he does, just as long as he does it nowhere near me. Because I hate him with the heat of a thousand suns. And I always will.

Only now I'm stuck in an elevator with him. On Christmas Eve. Alone. What's the worst that could happen?

ALSO BY KATE O'KEEFFE

It's Complicated Series:
Never Fall for Your Back-Up Guy
Never Fall for Your Enemy
Never Fall for Your Fake Fiancé

Love Manor Romantic Comedy Series:
Dating Mr. Darcy
Marrying Mr. Darcy
Falling for Another Darcy
Falling for Mr. Bingley (spin-off novella)

High Tea Series:
No More Bad Dates
No More Terrible Dates
No More Horrible Dates

Cozy Cottage Café Series:
One Last First Date
Two Last First Dates
Three Last First Dates
Four Last First Dates

Wellywood Romantic Comedy Series:
Styling Wellywood
Miss Perfect Meets Her Match
Falling for Grace

Standalone titles
Manhattan Cinderella
The Right Guy
One Way Ticket

PROLOGUE

Who likes blind dates? Anyone?
Yeah, that's what I thought.
They're super awkward and they rarely go well. I mean, you get your hopes up until they're jostling with the clouds, only for them to come crashing back down into the weeds when you find out the guy is an idiot, a psychopath, a jerk— or all of the above.

I guess the one saving grace of having Google at your fingertips is that you never have to go into a blind date truly blind.

The only problem for me right now is, the guy I'm about to meet is some kind of 90s throwback. No Instagram, no Tik Tok, no Snapchat. Not even an old person's Facebook profile.

I'm going in blind, people, and it does *not* feel good.

But still, here I sit, on a hard wooden chair in a quaint London pub, Celine Dion belting out that her heart will go on even when Leonardo di Caprio is long gone. And you know what I do? I do what I do every time. I get my hopes up.

This guy could be different.
This guy could be The One.

Not only will he look like Theo James's younger, hotter cousin, but he'll be kind and funny and intelligent and successful and totally *not* weird. Plus—crucially—he'll look at me and like what he sees, our chemistry so instant and strong you could slice it up and eat with a cup of hot tea.

Oh, yeah. My hopes have shot so high, they've reached the next galaxy by now.

"He's here," my friend, Emma says, her eyes bright.

Instantly my nerves kick up. I look up to see a man walking through the busy pub toward us. I trail my gaze over him, and heat prickles my cheeks. He's a classic heart throb through and through: tall and athletic, with broad shoulders, a square, stubble-lined jaw, and thick, dark-blond hair. His stride is purposeful, strong, and as his piercing Bradley Cooper eyes land on mine, my belly gives an involuntary flip.

Charles Cavendish is the full package.

So far, so amazing.

I flick my eyes to Emma and offer her a small smile. She and her husband, Sebastian, set this blind date up and I only agreed to it if they would come along for moral support. And yes, that's Emma and Sebastian from the famous *Dating Mr. Darcy* reality TV show, in which bachelor Sebastian chose Emma over me.

Which didn't bother me in the least.

Okay, maybe it did a little. But they're a great match and I'm super happy for them.

Really, I am.

Anyway, back to the hot man with everything going for him striding toward me.

I sit up straighter in my chair, thankful I'm wearing a cute dress that does wonders for my cleavage—meaning it *gives* me cleavage—smooth my long dark hair over one shoulder, and try to act as though I meet guys who look like they stepped off the pages of an aftershave ad every day of my life.

Which of course I don't because, you know, *real life*.

Charles Cavendish comes to a stop at our table and greets Emma and Sebastian like the friends they are as I sit and watch, my hopes still floating around somewhere in Andromeda Galaxy.

Those stark blue eyes land back on me, and he gives a small, extremely English bow of his head. "Hello. I'm Charles Cavendish. It's a pleasure to make your acquaintance."

He's so formal, like royalty, but in a totally endearing and sexy way.

"I'm Kennedy Bennet," I reply, doing my best to ignore the way his gaze makes my tummy think it's in some belly dancing competition.

He takes my hand in his. "A Miss Bennet?" he questions, a sexy smile teasing the edges of his mouth. It does nothing for the state of my cheek-to-body blood flow ratio. "With Mr. and Mrs. Darcy over here, does that mean you're all Jane Austen themed at this table?"

I let out a light laugh. It comes out like a girly, flirty giggle.

Smooth, Kennedy.

"It's my real name, actually. Nothing to do with the TV show. I've had it all my life."

"That's the way surnames usually work, I believe," he replies as he sits down in the wooden chair next to mine. "Unless you marry a lord, and then you get named after a large house in the country. Isn't that right, Emma?"

"Yup, although I prefer to be plain old Emma," my Texas gal friend replies. "Lady Martinston sounds super stuffy to me."

"Yeah. You're right," I reply. "Lady Martinston" sounds

more like a character from *Downton Abbey* than the name of my closest friend in London.

Charles leans closer to me and the hairs on my neck stand to attention, as though they're a hot guy radar. "So, tell me, Kennedy, do you get set up with strange men by your friends often?"

"Oh, I wouldn't call you *strange*, exactly."

His smile begins to grow, lighting up his handsome face. "Oh, I'm very strange, actually. You'll find that out soon enough."

"Not the run-of-the-mill hottie then, huh?"

Yup, I'm flirting. Sue me.

Wait. I just told him I think he's hot?

I suck in a sharp breath.

The guy doesn't miss a beat. "You think I'm hot?" he asks with a laugh, his blue eyes dancing.

Alert! Alert! Pull up! Pull up!

Oh, who am I kidding? *I* know he's hot. *He* knows he's hot. The girls at the table nearby definitely know he's hot, if the glances they keep throwing his way are anything to go by.

But I've only just met the guy. I can't blurt out something like that, two sentences into our very first conversation.

There is such a thing as being too eager.

"Oh, I, uh…it's an expression," I explain about as smoothly as a potholed road.

The heat in my cheeks has begun to burn my eyes.

His gaze doesn't leave mine. "I'm more than happy to be labelled 'hot' by a beautiful woman."

Was that cheesy? It felt a touch cheesy—but also a touch wonderful.

I almost chortle, but I manage to stifle it.

He's flirting with me, too.

Could this be going any better?

When I don't reply—because how do you reply to something like that?— he asks, "What?"

I shake my head. "Nothing."

"No, really. You had an odd look on your face. Is it because I called you beautiful?"

"I guess."

"You started it by calling me hot," he teases. "Which I appreciated, by the way."

"Did you now?" I ask with a laugh.

Wow. I've been reduced to a giggling, blushing mess in front of this guy.

I need to get a grip, perhaps steer the conversation to grown up lines. Something that won't have me melting into a puddle on the carpeted pub floor.

"Do you live here in London, Charles?" I ask him.

"I do, yes. And please, call me Charlie."

"Sure, Charlie."

More blushing. *Geez.*

"I've got a place not far from here, in fact. It's very handy. I use it all the time."

"Charlie's got a *pied-à-terre* in Mayfair," Sebastian explains, naming the most exclusive address in all of the city. "It's seen a few parties over the years."

"What's a *pied-à-terre*? It sounds like a French soccer player," Emma says.

Sebastian pulls a mock serious face. "Brady, we've talked about this before. It's *football*, not soccer."

"Three hundred and thirty million American people say it's 'soccer,' Seb," Emma replies.

"So, we're going with majority rules, are we?" Sebastian asks.

"Well, we do live in a democracy, so she does have a strong argument," Charlie replies with a laugh. He turns to me and adds, "*Pied-à-terre* is just a French expression for a small place in the city that isn't your main home."

"I'd hardly call your flat a small place, Charlie," Sebastian says.

Emma told me Charlie's family owns half of England. I size him up out of the corner of my eye. In his beautifully tailored navy jacket and crisp white shirt he definitely looks like he leads a life of privilege.

A single alarm bell tinkles faintly in the back of my head, reminding me of another man I once knew who wore jackets as finely and expensively tailored as his.

I push the uncomfortable feeling from my mind.

Charlie isn't *him*.

The conversation turns to some friend of theirs named Rupert, and my ears prick up when Emma calls him a 'party boy.' Pushing thirty, I've got no interest in dating a guy who likes to party too much. As hot and charming as Charlie might be—and he's definitely hot and charming—hearing he likes to live it up on a Saturday night could be the death nail for anything between us.

Guys like that aren't exactly known for their long-term monogamous relationship status.

"Are *you* a party boy?" I ask him, and hold my breath.

"I used to be a bit of one, but that was the version of me that thought he was invincible. It turns out, I wasn't. Just a bit of a fool."

Good answer, dude—good and intriguing.

"Well, that sounds like a story."

A brief shadow passes over his face before he rearranges his features. "Perhaps for another day," he replies evasively. "Tell me all about your life here in London. I believe you moved recently from across the pond."

"Yes, I escaped the unrelenting warm sun of SoCal to move to London," I reply with a smile.

Emma's phone rings, she glances at the screen, and immediately rises to her feet. "I'm gonna go take this," she says as she turns to leave.

"And I'll get us all some drinks. What'll you have?" Sebastian offers.

Charlie looks at me. "Ladies first."

"I'll have a glass of Chardonnay, please."

"Mine's a pint of lager, thanks, Seb," Charlie replies.

With the table now empty but for the two of us, Charlie asks, "SoCal?"

"It's shorthand for Southern California. I'm from San Diego."

"That's meant to be a great city. It's on my list, but I've never been."

"Oh, you should. It's a fun town, especially if you like beaches."

"Aren't there something like twenty beaches in San Diego?"

"Thirty-one," I correct. "All of them golden sand and gorgeous."

He studies my face for a moment before he replies, "You miss it there. Don't you?"

Suddenly achingly homesick for the wide beaches, easy lifestyle, and most of all for my family and friends, I reply, "I do miss it, but I moved to London for a new life."

"I know why."

My heart rate kicks up a notch. How could he possibly know that I moved here to escape the memory of someone who broke my heart?

I clear my throat. "You do?" I ask, my voice doing a pretty convincing cartoon character impression.

He nods, his eyes dancing with mischief. "You came here for the weather."

A surprised laugh bursts out of me. "Clearly. Rain is so much better than sun."

"Exactly. No risk of skin cancer from the rain."

"Or tan lines."

"Oh, I hate tan lines."

I'm powerless to stop my mind from imagining a tan line on his golden skin, somewhere around about where I imagine his six-pack hits his shorts.

Ahem. Let's keep this PG, Kennedy.

"Don't forget the unrelenting heat," he says, pulling me back to the room.

"You're never too hot in London."

"Not unless someone turns the heating up too high, anyway. And besides, isn't too much sun boring? At least here we've got a dozen different types of rain."

"A dozen?"

"Oh, yes. There's the big, plop-y rain, the freezing cold winter rain, the angled windy rain. To name a few."

"Don't forget the light rain that makes my hair go all crazy. That's a personal favorite of mine."

To my surprise, he reaches out and gently takes a strand of my long hair in his fingers. The light tug on my scalp sends a spark of electricity racing down my back. "I can't imagine you with crazy hair."

"Oh, I look horrendous. Believe me," I breathe. "Diana Ross on steroids."

He lets out a low laugh. "Now there's an image."

We share a small smile, and I know he feels it too, this instant attraction between us.

Sebastian returns to the table with our drinks and Charlie quickly releases my hair, our moment gone.

"Cheers," Sebastian says, as he raises his glass of red wine. "Here's to good friends."

"To good friends," Charlie echoes.

Can we get back to the hair fondling again?

I take a sip and return my glass of wine to the table. "How do you two know each other?"

"We go way back, don't we, Seb?" Charlie says.

"Right back to boarding school. Back then, Charlie was known as 'Sinatra' because of his blue eyes, and probably also because he was one of the illicit poker game organizers. Didn't you call it Little Vegas?"

"Vegas Lite, actually," Charlie replies, smiling at the memory. "We'd meet after lights out in the creepy basement. It was pitch black. The only light was from our torches."

"You had torches? As in, sticks with fire on the end? How old *are* you, exactly?" I ask with a laugh.

"As in plastic torches with batteries," Charlie explains.

"Oh, you mean flashlights," I correct.

He chuckles. "Remind me who invented the English language?"

I shoot him a grin, loving our easy, flirty banter. "Fair point."

"I get this all the time from Emma," Sebastian says. "Charlie, do you remember when we all nearly got caught by Dumbledore and had to stash both the cards and your dad's whiskey behind the boxed paintings?"

"And then the booze was gone when we went back the next night," Charlie says.

"We never found out what happened to it."

"Oh, it was definitely Jerry."

"What makes you say that?"

"He fell off his clogs at chapel the following evening, remember? Landed flat on his face and then promptly threw up all over Fincher's feet. He was lucky not to be expelled."

Sebastian laughs at the memory. "That's right."

My eyes dart between the two. "Clogs and Dumbledore? Did you two go to Dutch Hogwarts?"

"Nothing quite so exciting," Charlie replies.

"Just your regular, everyday boarding school I'm afraid," Sebastian adds.

Boarding school. Right. More evidence of Charlie's privilege.

"Charlie's a very good polo player," Sebastian tells me. "Are you still playing for the Seventh?"

"I'm getting too old and fat for all that carry on."

I sweep my gaze surreptitiously over him. He's neither old nor anywhere near fat. The guy's an Adonis. Period.

"Rubbish. The Other Charles played until he was in his mid-sixties. You're only halfway there, my man."

"The Other Charles?" I question.

"The prince," Charlie explains succinctly, as though I should just know.

I cock an eyebrow in his direction. "You know Prince Charles?"

"Not well," he replies.

"Doesn't your family have a house just down the road from him?" Sebastian asks. "You're neighbors."

"Well, yes, but I don't spend much time there."

I blink at him. The guy lives next door to the future king of Britain?

A sense of unease seeps through me, but I push it away.

"Let me get this straight. If you need to borrow a cup of sugar from your neighbor, it would be from Charles and Camilla?" I ask.

"Oh, no," he replies, and I begin to feel a little less like the low-bred, impoverished American imposter at this table, until he adds, "I don't bake."

I open my mouth to reply, then close it again.

Is he kidding me right now?

Sebastian is still not finished with his line of questioning. "I don't think you should give up playing for the Seventh."

"What's the Seventh?" I ask, still processing all of this.

"I'm sorry, Kennedy. I should have explained. It's a polo team," Charlie says. "You probably have zero interest in polo."

Hmmm, that was a little condescending.

"What makes you think that?" I ask, keeping my tone light. Because why would he assume I don't have any interest in polo? He knows nothing about me.

"What I meant is I don't imagine you know much about polo," he adds.

"I know all about polo," I reply, hearing the defensive note in my voice. Which isn't true, strictly speaking. I've never been to a match, let alone played the game, and couldn't tell you the rules if my life depended on it.

But he doesn't need to know any of that.

The sound of that faint alarm bell in the back of my head grows in volume. A wealthy, privileged man who thinks I don't know anything about his world?

For all his charm and good looks, is Charlie Cavendish just another Hugo Carter?

The man who made me feel like I wasn't good enough.

The man who chose someone else.

I paste on a smile. "Boarding school, polo, living next door to royalty. You're a regular Elon Musk," I joke.

"Only with significantly less wives," he quips.

"As in none?" I question.

"As in none," he confirms with a grin, his eyes dancing.

But I'm not feeling it. There's something about his flippant reference to his obvious wealth and status that gets my back up.

"Enough about me. Tell me about you, Kennedy. Emma tells me you were on the dating show with her. What made you want to do a thing like that?"

I tighten my lips. Judging much?

"My sister, Veronica applied after, well, after she decided it would be good for me."

His grin spreads. "What had you done to your poor sister to deserve something like that?"

"Thanks a lot, Charlie," Sebastian replies with a laugh, as I quietly seethe. If he wasn't so darn handsome and charming...

No. I'm not going to sabotage this. It's hard enough being single at twenty-nine, with a married sister with two kids who reminds you about it at every turn, without sabotaging this date.

So, instead, I make light of it. "Isn't it obvious? She hates me."

Charlie lets out a hearty laugh. "What was Mr. Darcy over here like on the show?"

"He was too busy falling in love with Emma to bother much with us contestants."

"Is that true, Seb?"

"I did try to be a gentleman with everyone," he replies. "But Kennedy's right. It wasn't exactly easy to 'date' the contestants when my heart was otherwise engaged."

"You were a total gentleman, Seb. You and Emma are the perfect match," I say to him. "And if it wasn't for the show, I wouldn't be living here, and I love living here. London is awesome."

"I can tell you're new here. Wait until you've had to deal with Tube delays and all that rain and endless queues," Charlie tells me.

"The English do love to line up, that's for sure." Feeling more relaxed I ask him, "What do you do for a living?"

"Oh, you know. This and that," he replies elusively.

"Don't play coy," Seb says. "Charlie runs the family business."

"You do?"

"Well, my father's the boss. I'm the group C.O.O."

"Sounds important."

"It keeps me off the streets."

"Off the streets? I'm amazed you have time for anything else. You see, Kennedy, it's more of an empire than a business," Sebastian says. "How many companies are there?"

"A few," he replies modestly.

"Wow. So, you were just given this business empire, huh?" I ask with a laugh, even though I'm only half joking. Because it sounds like this guy has had everything handed to him in life on a great big silver platter.

He shakes his head. "Not 'given' exactly."

"Did you have to interview?"

"Well, no, but—"

"Right. Got it." I say it with a smile that masks the growing gulf between us.

Me? I've had to fight for everything I have. From going to college, to getting my first job, to finding my dream job as a writer for *Claudette* magazine here in London.

It's becoming increasingly hard to block out the chime of that bell.

Charlie's eyes narrow. "What are you saying, exactly? That I'm just some poor little rich guy who's never had to work for a thing in his life?" His features are soft, but there's a new edge to his voice.

"Of course she's not," Sebastian says. "Isn't that right, Kennedy?"

"All I'm saying is that we don't all start out in life with a silver spoon the size of Texas in our mouths. That's all," I say.

"That sounds awfully uncomfortable," Charlie replies with a laugh. "In fact, I'd go so far as to say it's an anatomical impossibility."

"It's a metaphor." I cross my arms and set my mouth, challenging him with my eyes.

My hopes have returned to Earth with a disappointing thud.

Emma arrives back at the table, reads the tension, and shoots me a questioning look. I'm not sure how to convey *I liked this guy until I found out he's an over-privileged jerk who's been handed everything his whole life*. But I can't quite work out how to say that with just one look.

"Hey, did you two know that you've got a bunch of things in common?" she asks, as she sits back down. "Kennedy grew up in San Diego and loves the beach. Right, Kennedy?"

"The beach. Sure," I reply. I don't want to be drawn into conversation with this guy again. I know his type. Heck, I dated his type.

And it did not end well for me.

"And Charlie, you like to race motorboats, right?" Emma continues.

"I have been known to dabble," he replies in a haughty way.

I've been known to dabble? Who is this guy?

I leap on it right away. I'm not proud, but I do. "You see that's where we differ once more: I like to surf and paddleboard and swim, whereas you like to create noise pollution and *actual* pollution in a speedboat." I smile at him, but it's more of a challenge than a wish to be polite.

He cocks his head to the side. "So, you're at one with nature, and I'm some ignorant petrol head, is that what you're saying?"

Caught: hook, line, and sinker.

I broaden my smile. "I didn't say that."

He shakes his head. "You're impossible, did you know that? Oh, what am I saying? Of course you do."

I widen my eyes. "*I'm* impossible? I'm not the one ruining the serenity of the ocean and spilling gas onto the poor sea creatures below, destroying their delicate ecosystem."

Wow. Who knew I was such an eco-warrior?

"It's not like I get a tin of *petrol*," he says pointedly, as though it's the correct word for gas and not the stupid British version, "and drain it overboard every time I take a boat out."

"You might as well."

He drains his beer and places the empty glass back on the table. "Well, this has been an excellent evening. Thank you, Sebastian and Emma for the drink."

He has clearly decided he's had enough.

Am I sad about that?

That would be a *heck, no.*

He rises from the table. "Such a pleasure, Kennedy. Let's *not* do this again."

I simply glower at him.

Good riddance.

He turns on his heel and leaves, trailed by a confused Sebastian.

"What the heck, Kennedy?" Emma says, once the guys are out of earshot.

"What? The guy's a jerk."

"You liked him. You were flirting with him."

"That was before I knew he was an overprivileged speedboat racer who thinks he's God's gift to women."

"He's not like that. Sure, he's wealthy, but he's a regular guy. He and Seb are really good friends."

"Lucky Seb."

She pushes out a breath. "Okay. I get it. Charlie's not the guy for you."

"Nope."

"Got it."

"Great."

"But you *did* like him."

"He's a jerk."

"Good to know."

A moment later, Sebastian returns to the table. "Well, that went well," he says sarcastically. "I'm sorry it didn't work out between the two of you."

I give a shrug. "You win some, you lose some."

"And I think that signals the end of our matchmaking career, Brady," Sebastian tells Emma.

"What about Rupert?" she has the audacity to suggest.

Is she kidding me right now?

"No!" is both Sebastian's and my firm response.

"No more blind dates, Em. Promise me," I warn.

She gives a reluctant nod. "Promise."

I, for one, will be quite happy to go through the rest of my life without ever having to go on a blind date again, especially with someone like Charlie Cavendish.

CHAPTER 1

Christmas in London is simply magical—busy, cold, and overrun with pushy people bundled up in their winter warmers who won't look you in the eye, but definitely magical. The Christmas decorations stretch overhead from one side of the broad street to the other, gleaming against the cold, dark gray sky. Angels, stars, Christmas trees, ornaments, the works. They sparkle and they twinkle, little rays of light in the gloom of mid-winter.

As I said, it's simply magical.

So, here I find myself with my three London best friends, Zara, Lottie, and Tabitha, standing on the usually traffic-clogged Regent Street as we wait for the Christmas lights to be officially switched on for the season.

"Ow!"

I pull my attention from the soon-to-be-illuminated overhead lights to Lottie. She bounces up and down on one foot, complaining loudly. "You got stood on again?" I ask and she gives a grim nod, making a face at me.

"There are so many people here, and they're all pushing and shoving and generally being extremely rude. Whose brilliant idea was it to come to watch the Regent Street lights get switched on, anyway?"

"Kennedy's," Tabitha and Zara reply in unison.

Lottie rolls her eyes. "The American tourist. Figures."

"What? It's Christmas and we're in London. *Of course,* we had to come to this. It's magical."

"Tell my foot that," Lottie replies.

"I'm not a tourist, either," I sniff. "I live here, which makes me a Londoner."

"Ow!" Lottie exclaims once more and a short, wide, bald man with a pair of eyes tattooed on his neck turns and glares at her.

"Watch where you're going, will y*aaaaa*?" he spits at her.

He extends the final vowel so long, it needs its own zip code.

"Watch where *she's* going?" Tabitha scoffs, incredulous. "*You're* the one who stood on our friend's foot."

"What are you talkin' about? I ain't got no big feet. You're the one with big feet," he says, as he leers at her.

"Is that so?" she asks. "Well, my friend here has small, dainty feet." She gestures at Lottie, whose feet are indeed small and dainty. "But somehow, you and your allegedly non-big feet managed to step on hers."

"Yeah? What's it to y*aaaaa*?"

More unnecessary syllable stretching from Mr. Friendly Neck Tattoo.

Lottie places her hand on our feisty friend's arm. "Tabitha, don't. It's fine."

"Yeah, leave the girl alone, mate," one of the man's equally bare-headed and tattooed friends says to him. "They're birds. You don't wanna pick a fight wif no birds."

Birds? Do we have feathers and beaks now?

Mr. Friendly Neck Tattoo looks tall, slim Tabitha up and down before offering her a sneer. He returns his attention to holding his phone up as we all wait for the "on" button to get pushed and the overhead lights to flash to life.

"Friendly guy," I mutter under my breath.

"Tabitha, you really shouldn't have said anything," Lottie scolds. "You need to just let things go."

"All I was doing was standing up for you," she protests. "The guy's an idiot."

"Shhh!" all three of us say, in case he's still listening. Idiot or not, none of us want to antagonize him further. He wasn't what you'd call charming.

"There are literally almost a million people here right now," Zara says, as she consults her phone. "A million people. That's insane."

"I think every single one of them has stood on my foot," Lottie complains, as she rubs it against her other leg.

I look down at her painted toenails poking out of her high heels. "Maybe you should have worn some closed-toe shoes. It's freezing cold. I'm surprised you haven't gotten frostbite already."

"Aren't these shoes darling?" She ignores my point. "I've got a work thing afterwards and I need to look cute."

"For Dreamy Matt?" I question, and she grins at me.

"I'm sure he's going to see me in a new light tonight. I've got on a sexy new dress in his favorite color under my coat, too."

"What's his favorite color?" Zara questions.

"Black."

Zara makes a face. "That's a weird favorite color. It's like saying my favorite food is cauliflower."

"How exactly are you equating the color black with cauliflower?" Lottie asks.

"They're both bland. Nondescript," Zara, our interior designer friend explains.

"Zara's right. Black is actually the absence of color, so technically, Matt can't have it as his favorite," Tabitha says.

"I'm not going to tell him that because that's weird," Lottie replies. "Anyway, the plan is that he sees me in these killer heels and cute dress tonight and falls in love with me."

"Good luck, girl," I say, although I think she'll need more than luck with this guy. From what she's told us, Dreamy Matt hasn't seen her as anything other than his work colleague for the past three years. I'm not sure a new dress in the absence of all color and hypothermia-inducing footwear is going to change that anytime soon.

The countdown begins and suddenly the lights above us erupt into an explosion of light and a brass band bursts into a well-known Christmas tune. The crowd around us cheers excitedly and I gawk at the beauty above our heads. Rows and rows of angels, their wings stretched from one Georgian building to another, across the full width of the four-lane street, stretching down and around the corner toward Piccadilly Circus, fill the dark night sky.

"This is amazing!" I shout over the cheering crowd, as I hold my phone up to film. "My family back home is going to be so jealous I got to be here for this."

"It's so beautiful," Lottie agrees.

Fireworks flash overhead, their accompanying bangs booming through me. The atmosphere is electric, and I forget about the rude strangers with eye tattoos calling us "birds," the throngs of people jostling for position. I forget about the cold. I gaze at the breathtaking beauty of the lights floating above me and let out a contented sigh. You see, where I'm from we've got nothing like this. The coldest it gets in San Diego at Christmas is a balmy 65 degrees, and although it's a sizeable city, it's not packed to the rafters like London with its 13 million inhabitants. Sure, we have Christmas lights, but nothing as majestic as this.

I pan my camera, recording the scene. From the beautiful architecture to the lights and fireworks, for me it's nothing short of Christmas perfection.

I feel a tug on my coat sleeve.

"Come on, Kennedy. Haven't you had enough of being a tourist? Let's eat," Zara pronounces.

"I booked us into a new tapas place a couple of blocks from here and we need to get there now if we want to keep our table," Tabitha adds.

"I've got to get to my office party to dazzle Matt," Lottie says.

I shake my head at them all. "You three are such jaded Londoners. Where's your sense of wonder? Where's your sense of the magical? We need to be little kids again, seeing all this through new and excited eyes." I open my arms in an all-encompassing gesture to make my point, and immediately whack Mr. Friendly Neck Tattoo with one arm and a middle-aged woman in a fluffy leopard print jacket with the other.

"Sorry, sorry," I say to them both.

"That's all right, love," the woman in the leopard print jacket says.

Mr. Friendly Neck Tattoo predictably responds with a different approach. "What is it wif y*aaaaa?*" he says, followed by a list of expletives that would make a rapper blush.

"I said leave it, mate," his friend warns, throwing me a gap-toothed smile and a beady-eyed wink. "You all right?" he asks me.

"Great. Good. Thanks," I reply.

Lottie nudges me with her elbow. "You said you were ready to fall in love. How about this guy?"

I shoot her a look.

Zara's eyes flick to the men. "Now would be the right time to go, don't you think, Kennedy?"

I let out a defeated sigh. "I guess. Hold on a sec." I lift my phone above my head once more as I finish my full three-sixty-degree turn, capturing the whole scene. I flick my camera off. "Done."

My friends don't waste another moment. Tabitha hooks her arm through mine and pulls me through the crowd.

"Aw, don't leave. You lot are right good-lookin' birds," Mr. Friendly Neck Tattoo's friend calls after us, which only serves to quicken our pace through the throngs of people and down a side street.

"Are you sure you don't want to go back? He was gorgeous. I especially loved how economical he was with both his hair *and* his teeth," Tabitha says with a smirk.

I shake my head at her. "Tempting, but no thanks."

We walk for another couple of blocks until we reach a busy, hip-looking restaurant. Very Tabitha's style.

"I'm going to love you and leave you now, girls," Lottie says, as she gives each one of us a quick hug. "Wish me luck with Matt!"

"Good luck," we all say, before she trots off down the street in her heels.

"That girl is going to get frostbite and lose a toe," Zara pronounces with a shake of her head.

"All in the name of love, babe," I say. "Let's get inside. It's freaking freezing."

"*Now* she notices," Tabitha replies, with a good-natured eye roll.

We push through the door into the tapas bar and are immediately hit by the warmth, chatter, and delicious aroma of the place. My mouth begins to water, sending messages to my tummy, that growls at me to be fed immediately.

The hostess takes us to our table, where we unravel ourselves from our winter layers. I had to buy a whole new wardrobe when I arrived in this city just over a year ago.

Coats, scarves, gloves, hats, boots. Wrapped up in all that, this SoCal girl feels like an oversized burrito.

Mmmm, burrito.

Yup, I'm hungry.

"What looks good to you?" Zara asks, as she peruses the clipboard menu.

"All of it," I declare. My eyes land on a line item. "Except for the octopus and their little suction pads."

"What's wrong with that? They're yummy with potatoes and tomato sauce," Tabitha replies.

"You get them. I'm going with e-very-thing else." I put my menu down on the table just as my phone beeps. I turn it over and notice it's a message from Candice, my roommate—or "flat mate" as it's called here in the UK.

I'd like to say I'm happy to see a message from her, but I'm not. It's never good news when I get a message from her.

I met Candice when I replied to a "flat mate wanted" ad. She owns a cute two-bedroom place in a building not far from Zara in Fulham, and she was looking for someone to help her pay off her crippling mortgage. It was a cute place and, newly arrived in the city and knowing only two people in all of England, neither of whom even lived in London, I was delighted to find the place so easily.

So, I moved in and started to hang out with Candice after work and on weekends.

Which was great until the crazy set in. And by crazy, I mean boundaryless, rude, and generally difficult to be around.

I let out a groan as I read the screen, a lump of clay forming in my belly.

"What's up?" Zara asks.

"Candice."

"Why you're still living with a person who steals your

clothes and returns them with pit stains and BO is beyond me," Tabitha tells me.

Zara's eyes widen to saucer size. "She does that?"

"Oh, yes," Tabitha replies for me. "Didn't she tell you that as your landlady it's fully expected that she have access to all your stuff and that's just the way it works in England?"

I pull my lips into a thin line at the memory. "She's got some challenges with boundaries."

Tabitha shakes her head. "I'm not sure she'd know a boundary if she was fighting at the front in World War I."

"I decided to give her the benefit of the doubt. She was really sweet about it all," I reply, not sure why I'm defending the girl.

"And?" Tabitha leads.

"And I needed a place to live."

Tabitha and Zara both shake their heads at me.

"You can always come and crash on Lottie's and my sofa. You know that," Zara offers.

"Or mine," Tabitha tells me.

"That's sweet of you."

"Read Candice's message," Tabitha instructs.

"Yeah. I want to know what she's done now," Zara adds.

I unlock my phone and scan her message, my heart sinking with each word I read. "She's just told me she's having an impromptu party tonight and I shouldn't be surprised if a few people decide to crash for the night." I pause for dramatic effect before I add, "On the floor in my room."

"Seriously?" Zara guffaws. "Kennedy, you need to move."

I let out a sigh, the effort of looking for a new place sucking the energy from me. "I guess."

Tabitha says, "I have an idea. I've got a friend who's got a fabulous place. Apparently, she has to go away for six months for work, and she told me only yesterday she's looking for a flat sitter and still hasn't found one."

"Where?" I ask.

"Portugal or Spain? Or was it Norway? I can't remember."

"No," I reply with a giggle, "I mean whereabouts is her place?"

"Notting Hill. The fancy part."

"Isn't all of Notting Hill fancy?" I ask.

"Tabitha, your friend must be loaded," Zara says.

"Oh, she is. She's a big YouTube star. She's got this cute channel about, well, about her. I've been to her place. It's nice. You'd love it, and you'd have it all to yourself." She picks up her purse to pull out her phone. "Want me to ask her if it's still available?"

"Is the Pope Catholic?" I ask excitedly.

"Yes, Kennedy, I believe he is," Tabitha replies, in her typically droll manner.

I wait impatiently as she taps out a message.

Once done, she places her phone back on the table. "Done. Now, let's order."

We get the server's attention and order enough food to feed a roomful of hungry toddlers.

As we eat, we chat about our lives. Tabitha and I bemoan the fact we're still single at almost thirty, and our loved-up friend, Zara, tells us she's gotten almost too many new interior design customers since I talked my boss into featuring her designs in *Claudette*, the fashion and lifestyle magazine I work for.

"I simply cannot thank you enough, Kennedy. You have turned my business around."

"Well, it wasn't just me. Your boyfriend told all of his clients about you, too, remember? How is Asher, and why's he not here tonight?"

"He had to go away to Prague for work, but I'm going

there to meet him for the weekend." Her face lights up in a massive grin, and a pulse of envy pumps through me.

It must be wonderful to be in love.

"Oh, you'll love Prague, Zee. Have you been?" Tabitha asks as she forks a tiny octopus, suckers and all. "Mmmm, yummy. You should try some, Kennedy."

I raise my hands in the air. "I told you: I'm an octopus-free zone."

Zara shakes her head. "I went once, years ago with my family, but I have a feeling it's going to be a lot more romantic this time."

"With your *loverrrrr*," Tabitha teases, and Zara's face colors.

Tabitha's phone beeps on the table and I tell her, "Pick it up. It might be from your friend about the flat."

A moment later, Tabitha's finished reading the message and looks back at me. "Can you meet her at her place at nine tomorrow morning?"

The Candice-induced lump of clay in my belly vanishes in a flash. "Absolutely."

"You can crash on my sofa for the night," Zara says with a mouthful of tapas, so it sounds a bit like "You dan brad on my doba bor da nib."

"Good idea, babe. You don't want to wake up to a roomful of strangers on your floor," Tabitha tells me.

I beam at my London friends. "Thanks, girls. You've saved my life."

"It's a Christmas miracle," Tabitha says sardonically.

"I'm serious. *You* are the Christmas miracle. Thank you," I reply with a grin, the thought of having my own place far, far away from Candice placing a grin firmly on my face.

CHAPTER 2

After spending an uncomfortable night on Zara and Lottie's two-seater sofa—not an easy feat when you're five foot eight—I borrow a fresh blouse to wear with yesterday's skirt and catch the Tube to Notting Hill.

As I make my way up to street level, I consult my phone. Tabitha's friend's name is Delphine Fox, which sounds like an entirely made-up name to me. She insists it's not. I googled "Delphine" because I'd never heard the name before, and apparently it means dolphin in Greek. So, I'm going to see a Greek dolphin fox.

Should be interesting.

I follow my phone's map through the affluent streets until I find myself standing on an elegant road with pastel-colored buildings lining each side. I look up at a four-story building, complete with wrought iron balconies and imposing columns. It's grand and expensive looking, like it could form the backdrop on an episode of *Bridgerton*, and I half expect to see a horse and buggy swing by, filled with ladies in hats and Empire line dresses.

I check the address and check again.

I knew YouTuber Delphine was wealthy, but this place is next-level.

Just as I locate the intercom and am about to press the button for flat number 5b, my phone rings. I glance at the screen. It's my sister, Veronica, with her regular check-in communication.

"Hey, Ronnie," I reply. "I'm just about to see a new apartment. Can I call you back later?"

"You're moving again? You're like a gypsy. Put that down. We don't eat coasters. They're not food." The last part is aimed at one of my nephews, who is evidently sampling a coaster.

I wait patiently.

There's some rustling and then she continues with, "Why are you moving? What happened to your place?"

"It didn't work out."

"But I thought you liked the girl you were rooming with. Candy or Caitlin. Mommy needs that back, please. We don't eat flowers, either. They're not food, honey. Well, we can eat some flowers like nasturtiums, but that's beside the point."

"It was Candice, and no, I didn't. She was a total nightmare. But things are looking up for your little sister. This new place looks amazing." I gaze up at the elegant building looming over me, as a dapper-looking man in a tweed jacket and tie walks by with a black poodle on a leash.

"Sweetie?" she asks, and I'm not sure it's to me or one of her kids until she says, "Kennedy, are you still on the line?"

"Yup, but I've gotta go. I'm meeting the girl who I'm gonna flat sit for in about a minute."

"Flat sitting? As in looking after someone's apartment while they're away? Oh, sweetie. That's so impermanent. You know Mom is super worried about you."

I feel a stab of homesickness. I brush it quickly away.

"I'm doing great. I've got my dream job, a great group of

friends, and I've got a good feeling about this new place. So, tell Mom I'm fine and I'll call her soon, 'kay?"

"Okay," she replies begrudgingly, "but you can come home anytime. You know that, right?"

"I'm coming home for a few days at Christmas, remember?"

"You know what I mean. For more than just a visit. Gosh, I wish I'd never entered you into that stupid dating show. Then you'd never have left us, and I wouldn't have to deal with Mom's anxieties about her baby girl on the other side of the world."

"Ronnie, personally, I'm glad you entered me in *Dating Mr. Darcy* because it forced me to get out of a bad situation."

"He broke you. I hate him for that."

I press my lips together in a vain attempt to squash the pain in my heart.

Which is ridiculous. *Beyond* ridiculous.

Sure, Hugo Carter broke my heart. Sure, he's now happily married to the seemingly perfect woman he replaced me with. But it was almost two years ago.

Two *years*.

But I can't help my insides clenching at the thought of him.

He was Mr. Country Club to my Ms. Works at a Burger Joint. Mr. Well Bred to my Ms. Wrong Side of the Tracks.

They say opposites attract, but what they don't add is that when a more appropriate version comes along, you get kicked to the curb.

Look, I'm not saying I'm still in love with the guy. I'm not. That's something I know for sure. But he hurt me in a way I didn't see coming.

He made me feel *less*.

He made me feel like I wasn't good enough—not for him or his lifestyle, and definitely not for his family.

I know what I should have done. I should have changed my hair and had an ill-advised fling with the wrong kind of guy. Got it out of my system. Instead, I let my sister enter me onto a reality TV dating show where I had less than zero chemistry with the bachelor, and spent the whole time wondering what I'm going to do with the rest of my life.

So fun.

But then, I spotted a writing job at *Claudette*, the British women's magazine I grew up loving. I applied, and got it. It felt like the stars were finally aligning for me.

And just because those stars were aligning in another country—far from the one where Hugo and his new perfect wife lived in wedded bliss—was mere coincidence.

Or at least that's what I told myself.

"Ronnie, I'm happy here in London. It's a super fun place. The Christmas lights alone are enough to stay for. You've got to bring Dan and the kids over."

"The flight sounds like a nightmare. Sweetie, put your sister down. No! Do as Mommy says. Put. Your. Sister. Down."

"Ronnie? I've gotta go," I say, but she's too involved in managing her kids to hear me. "Bye." I end the call and open my Instagram app, flicking immediately, as I always do, to Hugo's page. The same image as yesterday stares back at me. Him and his wife skiing in Aspen in their matching designer snowsuits.

Ugh.

I slide my phone back into my purse.

Adjusting my hair and pasting on a smile, I press the button for 5b and peer at the camera. My nerves jangle as I wait.

This just has to work out.

"Hello?" a female voice says.

"Yes, hi. I'm Kennedy Bennet. Tabitha mentioned you're looking for someone to housesit"

"You're American? Tabby Cat didn't mention that."

Tabby Cat? I bet Tabitha loves being called that. I try not to let a giggle escape from my lips, as I freeze my smile in place and stare at the camera.

"I hope that's okay?" I ask as if being American is 1) a bad thing, and 2) something I could change on the spot.

I'm about to offer to put on my best English accent—which I've been told is laughably bad, at best—when she says, "You're here now and you look nice enough, so you'd may as well come on up. Fifth floor. Flat 5b. You can take the lift if you like."

I smile at the British word, "lift" for elevator. "Sure thing. Thank you."

The door makes a buzzing sound and pops open. Once inside the lobby, I take in the high ceiling, the glossy floor, and the stunning chandelier. Everything is white except for the black-rimmed mirrors that line the walls, and the deep red carpet underfoot.

Having put on a few pounds lately, I forgo the elevator, taking the stairs instead. I was told that there's such a thing as the "Heathrow injection" when you move to the UK. At first, I thought it was something to do with a vaccination, but I've since learned it refers to the ten-plus pounds people put on here from the fast pace of living—and all the eating out.

I need these stairs.

I reach the floor and notice there are only two doors: 5a and 5b. I knock on 5b, and a moment later the door is swept open by a girl my age. She's wearing a long, floaty Boho dress with rows of bangles around her wrists, her sandy blonde hair piled up on her head in a messy knot that would take me hours to perfect.

"Hello. You must be Kenny," she says with a smile, her

bangles jangling as she kisses me on both cheeks. Well, they're cheek-adjacent kisses, anyway. "Come in. Come in."

"Thank you. It's Kennedy, actually. Not Kenny," I say as I follow her into the flat and look around the room. By London standards, it's absolutely massive, with gracious high ceilings, large windows, and a beautiful, ornate fireplace, in front of which are comfortable cream sofas, and a red Turkish rug over hardwood floors. The room is welcoming yet elegant, and my eagerness to get to live here shoots right through the roof.

"Wheat grass?" she offers, as she pads toward the open-plan kitchen in her toe-ringed bare feet. Considering it's cold enough to snow outside, it's like a furnace in here and I begin to peel off my London burrito layers.

"No, I'm good. But thank you." The idea of drinking wheat grass isn't exactly appealing.

"You know you really should drink it," she says, as she sucks some gross-looking, dark green liquid through a metal straw. "It lowers your cholesterol, boosts your immune system, and pushes toxins right clean out of your body."

Sounds painful.

"Wow. Amazing."

"I'm not taking no for an answer, Kenny. Here." She pours some of the green liquid into a glass and hands it to me.

I search my brain and land on a way out. "Actually, I'm gluten intolerant," I fib, "so I'm not sure I should have wheatgrass because, you know, allergies."

I have no clue whether wheatgrass has gluten in it, and I hope she doesn't, either.

"And it's Kennedy, not Kenny. Kenny's a guy's name."

She eyes me as she sucks on her drink. "No wheatgrass?"

"No wheatgrass."

"You're missing out on all that goodness." She places my untouched glass back on the kitchen counter. "You know,

Kenny's an awfully odd name for a girl. Is it short for something? Or is it just one of those odd American names, like Chip and..." she pauses as she searches for another "odd" American name.

"Dale?" I offer.

"Yes, or Dale. Chip and Dale. Hmm, that does sound familiar."

"It's an old cartoon."

"Oh, I don't think so."

"It is for sure. They're two little chipmunk brothers. Chip is the cunning and clever one, Dale is a bit slower off the mark."

She looks at me blankly.

"They eat a lot of nuts?" I add, as though that fact would be the clincher.

"I have absolutely no idea what you're talking about, Kenny."

"Actually, my name's Kennedy. Not Kenny," I repeat for at least the third time.

"Like the President?"

"Sure."

"He was awfully dishy, wasn't he? Shame he got himself shot. Such a waste. And his poor wife. Mind you, he'd be about a hundred now if he were alive. Wouldn't he?"

"I…guess so."

"Do you have brothers and sisters?"

"One sister."

"Is she named after one of your presidents, too?"

I think of the well-meaning but overbearing Veronica, and smile at the thought of her being called something like Eisenhower or Roosevelt. "No, and I'm not named after a president, either. Kennedy's a girl's name, like Dolphin." I shake my head at my mistake. "Err, I mean Delphine."

She regards me through narrowed eyes as she sucks the

dregs of her drink up through her straw. "Do you know who I feel sorry for? Jackie O. She looked so lovely that day, didn't she?"

Annnnd we're back to presidents.

"The day President Kennedy was shot?" I ask.

She nods. "She's one of my style icons, actually. That pill box hat? Stunning."

I sweep my eyes over her long, floaty, floral dress, bare feet, and toe rings. Delphine's style couldn't be further from Jackie O's buttoned up aesthetic if she tried. "I agree. Jackie O was a total style icon."

She leans her elbow on the counter. "What do you mean 'was?'"

"Well, you know."

She pulls her eyebrows together. "No, I don't know."

I've got to break the news to this woman that her supposed style icon, Jackie Onassis is dead?

"I'm afraid she died. A while back, actually."

"Gosh. Well, that's no good. Are you sure?"

"Yeah. Pretty sure. It was quite a long time ago, too. In the nineties, I think."

"Oh, so sad," she agrees, her hand flying to her chest, her face crumpling as though she might cry.

"Yes. It's very sad."

"You know what else is amazing, though? This new Instagram filter I discovered this morning."

"Ok*aaa*y." I shoot her an uncertain look.

This sure has become one free-ranging conversation.

Delphine collects her phone from the kitchen counter, holds it up in the air as she presses her cheek next to mine, and snaps a shot of us. She plays on her phone before she turns the image around. "See? We look simply divine."

I flick my attention to the photo and see myself gazing back. I look like me, only a flawless version, with sparkling eyes and an unblemished, rosy complexion. "Wow, that *is* divine."

"I'll send you the info on it. Do you want to see the flat?"

"I'd love to. I'm so excited to live here. It looks absolutely beautiful."

"I'll show you around." She flicks her wrist at the living room and says, "You've already seen this room, and this is the kitchen. Dining room is down the hall."

I follow her as she takes me from room to room. First is the dining room with its long oak table and chairs, then the white tiled bathroom with a black and white checked floor, and then on to the spare room that looks like a boutique hotel room, with a plush cream comforter and welcoming pillows, and black and white pictures of cows lining the walls.

Finally, we arrive at the light-filled master bedroom. Like the rest of the place, it's decorated in cream with hints of green. There's another fireplace at one end with a photo of a black and white cow gazing out at us, and a massive bed with a padded linen headboard at the other, positioned so you could sit in bed and gaze out over the treetops of Notting Hill.

The only thing that looks out of place in the room is a large stuffed Winnie the Pooh on a child's stool in the corner. It must be a childhood favorite, which she's kept for sentimental reasons.

"Your place is so gorgeous, Delphine." I say to her. "I absolutely love it."

"Wait, there's more. This is my favorite part," she says, as she pulls a set of double doors open. I walk through, expecting to find another bathroom, and instead am met with the most wondrous sight. A walk-in closet, lined with shoes and purses and racks of clothes. There's an ottoman in the middle of the room, under a chandelier that hangs from the high ceiling, and a floor-to-ceiling mirror in which to gaze at your reflection in your outfit of choice for the day.

I stand and stare. It's like angels are singing to me, telling me I've officially arrived in closet heaven.

"It used to be another bathroom, but I had Eddie pull it out and build this. I saw the design on an episode of the *Real Housewives*, and I knew I had to have it."

"Who needs a second bathroom when you can have all this. It's absolutely perfect."

"I knew I'd like you," she says, as she pulls me into a hug.

I blink at her in surprise. "You did?"

"Almost from the moment we met. So, would you like to flat sit for me? I'll be gone for at least six months, so right through to the start of summer."

Happiness rushes through me. "I would love to flat sit for you, Delphine."

She smiles her pretty smile at me. "Good. That's settled then."

I scrunch my nose. "One thing, though. Tabitha didn't mention how much you're charging, and looking at this place, it might be out of my budget."

She regards me with a blank expression. "I'm sorry. I don't understand."

I'm not sure how else to put it.

"What's the weekly rent on this place?"

"Oh, I own it. There's no rent."

She's making an awkward conversation even trickier.

"No, what I mean is how much are *you*," I point at her to make it clear, "going to charge *me*," I point at myself, "to live here?"

Her features morph into a smile. "You think I'm going to charge you *money*? Oh, you are silly, Kenny. I mean Kennedy. Kennedy, I need to remember that. Like the president." She taps the side of her head. "Oh, that reminds me of poor Jackie O." She pulls her face into a frown.

I ignore the random train of thought spilling from her lips. "Are you saying you're not going to charge me to live here?" I ask.

"Of course not. I mean, you'll need to pay the bills."

I let out a puff of air. I can't believe my luck! "Of course."

"Things like the electric and the Wi-Fi thingy. Oh, and the Harrods's bill, too."

"The Harrods's bill?"

She looks at me as though I've asked her if the sky is blue. "For the weekly shop. Every Monday morning it arrives at my door and the only annoying thing is, I've got to put it all in the fridge. I wish they'd send someone to do that part. Don't you?"

"You get your groceries from the most expensive department store in London?"

"Is Harrods the most expensive department store in London?"

"I think so."

"Well then the answer is yes, I suppose. I do love their macarons though. Don't you? To die for."

"Oh, their macarons?" I question, never once having had one. "I'm sure they're totally delicious."

I make a mental note that the Harrods delivery will clearly need to stop as soon as I move in. I don't have that kind of money. A regular old supermarket will do for non-You-Tube star me.

"Oh, and you'll need to look after Lady Moo, of course. But I'm sure Tabby Cat told you all about her."

I glance at the oversized cow photo above the fireplace. Surely Delphine doesn't own a cow. Not in Notting Hill, anyway.

"Lady Moo? Is she a fish or something?" I chance, because

this is Notting Hill, not rural England. "I don't remember seeing a tank."

"A fish?" she asks, her voice raising an octave, as she lets out a laugh. "Who would call a fish Lady Moo?"

"Someone who likes cows?"

She squeals with laughter, as though I've said the funniest thing ever. "Oh, you're such a hoot. Tabby Cat didn't mention you're a hoot."

"Sure."

"No, Lady Moo is my precious little poochie-woochie. She's out right now, but she should be back any moment."

"Poochie-woochie? As in a dog?"

Before she has time to reply, there's a knock at the front door. "Oh, what a coincidence. That'll be Lady Moo right now."

I arch an eyebrow. "She knows how to knock?" I ask in jest.

Another laugh from Delphine. "A hoot! She's been out and about, you know. Doing her poochie-woochie business." She breezes past me out of the closet, and I follow dumbly after her.

Poochie-woochie business? I press my lips together to stifle a laugh.

I knew there had to be a catch for this place to be this gorgeous and rent-free. Looking after a dog can be a big responsibility. Don't get me wrong, I love dogs. I grew up with dogs. But being a single girl, living on my own with a full-time job, and having a dog to care for at the same time? Not so easy.

Particularly as any dog named after a cow has to be pretty freaking huge. Right?

Delphine pulls the front door open with a jangle of bracelets and declares, "Lady Moo! Oh, I missed you! You are such a darling. Isn't she such a darling?"

Expecting a dog at waist height, I look down as a small black and white dog bursts into the room and immediately leaps on Delphine, her little stub of a tail doing overtime, swinging her body from side to side. Delphine pets her, cooing what a good girl she is, before the "poochie-woochie" sets her dark eyes on me.

The next thing I know, she's abandoned Delphine and rushes at me, making the weirdest squealing noise I've ever heard from a dog. It's a cross between something a banshee would make and a drunk *Real Housewife*, bent on exacting her revenge on a fellow cast mate.

"Isn't Lady Moo just such a gorgeous girl?" Delphine asks, as she scoops the wildly excited dog up in her arms. The dog immediately begins to lick her face, the squealing noise reducing a notch to something less ear-piercing. It's still equally weird. "I call her Lady Moo because she's just like a little canine cow, don't you think?"

I smile at the exuberant dog in her arms. Her markings are cow like, for sure, but that's where the similarity ends. "She's very...cow-ish," I reply.

"She had a great walk and did six deposits, four liquid and two solid," a voice says beside me.

I've been so busy watching the dog—and feeling grateful she's not cow-sized, as I'd originally feared—I hadn't even noticed she arrived at the door with a human. She's a teenage girl, probably about fifteen or sixteen, wearing jeans and tennis shoes, a bright yellow dog leash covered in pink heart-shaped diamantes in her hands.

"Hey, I'm Kennedy," I say to her with a smile.

"I'm Esme." She adds unnecessarily, "I'm the dog walker."

"I figured as much." The possibility of being able to take this place just got a major boost. With Esme walking the dog, I can go to my job without having to worry about her during the day. "Do you live locally?" I ask.

"Right downstairs, actually. Flat 1a."

Better and better.

"Ouch! Oh, Lady Moo, you are so naughty!" Delphine snaps, drawing our attention. She's trying to untangle her dog's front paws from her top knot, although how Lady Moo managed to get up that high is beyond me.

"Here, let me help," I offer. I get a hold of one of the dog's paws and work on unraveling Delphine's hair, while the dog does her level best to lick my face. With one paw free, the other one is a cinch, and I hold the little dog at arm's length before popping her down on the floor. She scampers away, her paws darting in all directions on the slippery hardwood floor, and disappears into Delphine's bedroom.

"Thanks awfully. That hurt, Lady Moo," Delphine scolds, even though she's nowhere to be seen. Her once-stylish top knot now looks like, well it looks like she's had a dog tangled up in it.

"I'll be back at two to take her out again, if that works?" Esme asks.

"Oh, thank you, darling," Delphine coos as she smooths out her hair. "This is Kennedy, by the way. Not named after an American president, in case you're wondering. She's going to be living here when I'm away."

"Cool. I'll see you 'round then," she says to me.

"I will. Nice to meet you."

Esme closes the door behind her.

"Is Lady Moo always like that?" I ask Delphine.

"She's very spirited, but I encourage it. I think it's part of her charm. She's from a long line of pedigreed Boston Terriers, you see. She can be a little…stubborn."

"How?"

"Oh, you'll see. I'm sure you'll adore her before long, just as much as I do."

I hope so.

I run through dog care practicalities in my mind. "Will you be able to give me instructions for Lady Moo's care? Things like her vet clinic and what food she eats?"

"Of course. I'll leave you a note. She's very easy to look after. Oh, but she doesn't like men. Well, bad men anyway."

"What does she do when she sees a 'bad' man?"

"She barks, like, a lot. She's amazing when I'm going out with a new guy. She can weed the good ones from the bad ones for me."

"Huh. Useful."

There's an odd whining sound, followed by growling and yapping coming from down the hall.

"What's she up to?" I ask.

"Oh, I imagine I know," Delphine replies as she makes her way down the hallway toward the master bedroom.

I trail behind her, not sure what to think.

We arrive at the bedroom, where I spot Lady Moo tearing into the Winnie the Pooh stuffed toy that was sitting on the kid's stool before. There are bits of fluff flying, and I spot a discarded ear on the floor.

I flick my eyes to Delphine. She's smiling at Lady Moo as she disembowels the toy, like it's perfectly fine for her dog to be destroying what I'd assumed was Delphine's childhood treasure.

"Do you want to stop her?"

"Why ever on Earth would I do that?" she asks, as though I've suggested something completely outlandish.

R*iiii*ght.

"The only thing you need to do when she's in one of her moods is make sure she doesn't swallow the eyes. Otherwise, you'll need to scoop them out from her little doggie poops and put them in here."

Scoop them out from her little doggie poops? *That'd be a hard no.*

She pulls a drawer in her nightstand open and pulls out a plastic tub. Inside there are at least two dozen plastic eyes, all staring up at me.

It's beyond creepy.

"Have they all been, you know, digested?" I ask, incredulous.

Delphine gives me a solemn nod. "I'm sure they can't be good for her, so I collect them all to reassure myself that they're not still stuck inside of her little body. There's an even number here. That's how I know."

"Got it," I say with a forced smile, because there's no way I'm rifling through a dog's poop to find Winnie the Pooh's eyes.

And those are words I never thought I'd think in my lifetime.

"Couldn't you just *not* let her chew the toy?" I suggest, which seems like the most logical thing to do here.

"Not let Lady Moo chew her favorite toy?" There's a look of wonderment on her face.

"Well…yeah."

She blinks rapidly a few times before she lifts her lips in a smile. "There's no need to worry about the toy. I have plenty." She waltzes over to the hallway closet and pulls open a door to reveal a collection of at least thirty identical Winnie the Pooh stuffed toys, stacked on top of one another, all staring out at us. "See?"

Thirty sets of eyes gaze back at me, misplaced smiles on their teddy bear faces. They don't know their fate, but I do, and it ain't pretty.

"All of these are for the dog?"

"She's obsessed, what can I say? And if she runs out, I've got an account at Hamleys so you can go and get some more."

"Hamleys is that huge toy store on Regent Street, right?"

I'd been there once before, when I first arrived in London. With its red awnings and bright toy displays that remind me of childhood, I couldn't resist.

"Now, let me get you the keys," she says, as she glides out of the room. "I'm flying out in the late afternoon tomorrow, so will it be all right if you come over tomorrow night? That way Lady Moo will have company."

I take the offered key. "Of course. Thank you so much for this, Delphine. I'll take good care of the place for you. And Lady Moo, of course."

"Don't thank me, Kenny. You're doing me the favor. Not the other way 'round."

I don't bother to correct her.

Ten minutes later, I trip down the gracious tree-lined street toward the Tube stop. I cannot believe that I get to live in such a beautiful place *rent-free*. No more Candice, no more tiny bedroom. The whole place is mine, mine, mine.

Sure, there's a Winnie the Pooh-destroying, mildly insane Boston Terrier to deal with, but really, this whole thing has come at the perfect time for me. I cannot wait to get my new life here in Notting Hill underway.

What could possibly go wrong?

CHAPTER 3

"I cannot believe this is where you get to live," Lottie exclaims, as we dump a new pile of boxes on Delphine's living room floor.

"I know, right? I feel so grown up." I straighten up and pull my UC San Diego hoodie over my head before I wipe my forehead with the sleeve of my gray long-sleeve T-shirt.

"Well, you *are* turning thirty soon, so you should be feeling grown up," Tabitha replies as she places a suitcase against the wall and stretches out her back.

I roll my eyes, the thought coalescing into a heavy lump in my belly. "Don't remind me."

Thirty. The idea is not appealing. There's something about that number. Something solid. Something serious. Thirty's the age I should be when I've got my crap together. It's when I'm supposed to have met my Big Love, perhaps even gotten married, my eye on motherhood. It's when I'm meant to have my life mapped out.

Right now, I'm like a newborn deer, trying to stand on wobbly new legs, and falling flat on my face with every step I try to take.

Yup, I'm a twenty-nine-year-old Bambi.

Lottie looks around the plush room with its high ceilings, tall windows, and fancy furniture. "I really should start my own YouTube channel."

"Yeah, because I'm sure it's that easy. Deciding to be a YouTube star and then *bam* you are one." I offer her a sardonic smile.

She lets out a sigh. "Good point. But a girl can dream."

I eye the boxes and take a quick tally. "One more load and I think we're done."

"Thank goodness for that lift is all I'll say. Can you imagine having to carry all these boxes up the stairs otherwise?" Tabitha says.

"Nightmare," Lottie agrees.

"Where do you want these?" a low voice says behind us, and I turn to see a long pair of legs with a stack of boxes in the doorway. A mop of black hair and a pair of dark eyes are visible over the top box.

"Is that you, Asher?" I move across the hardwood floor toward him.

"Sure is."

Zara appears in the doorway, holding a bottle of champagne in one hand and one of my duffle bags slung over her shoulder. "Surprise! We thought we'd come and help you move in." She greets me with a hug before she plunks the cold bottle in my hands and drops my bag to the floor. "Champagne is always helpful for unpacking boxes, don't you think?" she says with a glint in her eye.

"You're the best. Thank you," I coo. "Isn't this place gorgeous?"

"Oh, it so is!" she declares, as she makes her way into the room. "Where's the crazy dog you told us about?"

"She's at Esme's, the dog walker. I thought it would be

better not to have her tearing things to shreds as I try to unpack."

"You're not just a pretty face," Zara replies.

"I'll put these down here, shall I?" Asher says pointedly, as he lowers the boxes to the floor with a *thud*.

"Sorry," I reply hurriedly. "I was too busy greeting my girl here. Thanks so much for helping out." I do another quick tally of the boxes and luggage. "I can't believe you brought up the last of it. Thanks, guys."

"That elevator is like something from Medieval Europe," he adds, referring to the building's old-fashioned elevator. I think it's charming, but it's definitely not from this century.

Or possibly even the last.

"Yeah, because they had a lot of lifts in Medieval Europe, Ash," Zara ribs.

Asher shakes his head. "You know what I mean, Zee. It's freakin' old."

"They did have lifts back then, actually. Right back as far as the Romans, in fact," Lottie explains from over by the window. "I learnt all about it on one of my super fascinating museum visits, you know."

"I bet you did, babe," Zara replies with a good-humored eye roll.

Lottie organizes regular trips for us to London's weird and whacky museums. We've been to the city's first operating room, which completely creeped us out, the much more palatable Natural History Museum, and the Sherlock Holmes Museum to name a few.

Asher lets out a laugh. "You are a font of useless knowledge, Lottie."

"That's not useless knowledge. It's interesting. You should spend more time exploring your adopted city and less time being all lovey-dovey with your girlfriend," she huffs, although we all know she's not actually offended. Lottie's so good-natured and easygoing, I can't imagine her being offended about much at all.

Except her mom. Definitely her mom.

"Well, if that's all the boxes and bags, let's crack open this bottle and toast your new place," Zara says. "Where are the glasses?"

"I have no idea. Let's try the kitchen." As I rifle through the cupboards, there's a knock at the open door.

Esme steps inside, holding Lady Moo. "Hi," she says, looking awkward. Her eyes flick to Asher and her cheeks instantly color. Asher's a great looking guy, and dressed in his form-fitting white shirt and jeans that show off his physique, he's enough to raise most women's heart rates, let alone a teenage girl's.

"Hi, Esme. Come on in," I say, as I move across the floor and collect Lady Moo in my arms. "Lady Moo. Were you a good girl for Esme?"

"She was. Well, as good as she can be, anyway," she replies. "She did three water deposits and two solid," she reports in a solemn tone.

I scrunch up my nose. Do I really need that level of detail?

"You know what? You don't have to tell me that. Just walking her is enough for me."

"But Delphine always likes to know. I think she keeps a tally."

"I'm not Delphine."

"Okay."

"This is Esme, everyone," I say, as my friends all greet her, and she waves at them, her blush deepening.

"I need to go. I've got an essay due," she tells me.

I thank her and close the door behind her, placing Lady Moo on the floor. She immediately rushes over to greet my friends, trying to scale their legs and bouncing around like a basketball on caffeine, making that same weird whining sound.

"Wow, enthusiastic dog," Asher comments.

"You must be a good guy," I tell him. "Delphine says she barks at the bad ones. It's gotta be a pretty useful screening tool for dates."

"I cannot tell you how relieved I am to hear I have the approval of a dog named after a cow," he replies.

Lady Moo tears off down the hallway to the master bedroom.

"Where's she off to in such a hurry?" he asks.

I shake my head, pulling my lips into a line. "Don't ask."

"Why?"

"She's got a thing for Winnie the Pooh. As in a destructive thing. She basically murders him on the daily. It's not pretty."

"She murders Winnie the Pooh?" Lottie asks, appalled. "But I love Winnie the Pooh. He's a national treasure."

Tabitha giggles. "It's just a stuffed animal. No biggie."

"Lady Moo has no qualms about destroying a national treasure. Delphine is super organized though. Look." I pull open the hallway closet door to expose the rows of yellow bears with red shirts staring back at us. Their facial expressions tell us they've got no clue what their fate will be.

"OMG," Zara mutters, as all three of them gaze at the sight.

"It's like a toy store that exclusively sells yellow bears," Asher comments.

Zara takes a few steps to the left and then back again. "Their eyes watch you as you move. It's creepy."

"You can't call Pooh Bear creepy," Lottie protests, as she pulls one off of a shelf and hugs it. "I had one of these when I was little. I adored him."

"So does Lady Moo," Tabitha replies with a sly smile.

"Stop!" Lottie complains.

Zara asks, "I wonder if you gave her a generic teddy bear whether she'd murder that, too?"

"Just Winnie here, apparently," I reply.

Zara shakes her head. "Weird."

"So weird."

Tabitha shrugs. "The dog's got standards, that's all. No second-tier dog toys for her."

Lady Moo arrives back in the room with the most recent Winnie the Pooh clutched tightly in her jaw, tripping over the much larger toy every few steps. Undeterred, she makes it into the living room, where she places her front paws on the toy's belly and growls as she tugs on its fur, yanking off one of the toy's ears and discarding it.

"That dog is intense," Asher comments.

"I'm gonna wean her off Pooh," I state, and Tabitha and Zara both begin to giggle. I raise my eyebrows at them.

"What? It sounds funny," Tabitha replies.

"Wean her off Pooh," Zara repeats, and both girls' giggles turn into fully-fledged laughter.

I shake my head at my friends. "I'm not sure I'll ever understand the British obsession with toilet humor."

"I'm with you on that," Asher agrees. "Hey, do you think we should introduce her to Stevie?" he asks, referring to Zara's Jack Russell.

Zara gestures at the Winnie the Pooh fragments now dotted around the room. "As long as she doesn't try to do *that* to my precious baby."

"Let's hold off until I know she can be trusted around other dogs," I reply. "You guys watch the sick display if you can stomach it. I'm gonna get the champagne in some glasses."

A few moments later, Lady Moo is still working ferociously on disemboweling the poor toy, and we clink our glasses together and toast my new place.

"You are going to be so happy here, babe," Lottie declares.

"How could she not be? This place is wonderful," Zara agrees.

There's another knock on the door.

"That must be Esme again. Maybe she forgot to tell me something." I make my way over to the front door and peer through the little peep hole. To my surprise, there's a group of people in the hallway, not just the solitary Esme. "Hello?" I call out, my dad's London security training kicking in.

"Hello," a female voice replies. "We're your new neighbors and we thought we'd pop in and wet the place for you."

I shoot my friends a questioning look. "Wet the place? That doesn't sound like something I'd like to let these people do."

"It means have a drink with you to welcome you to the building," Zara explains.

"Right. Gotcha." I pull the door open and am met by a group of five grinning people, all women, and all in their seventies or eighties. Some are dressed in skirts, some in smart slacks. All of them have a minimum of two rows of pearls around their necks and each and every one is wearing glasses.

One is clutching a bottle of champagne in her hand.

"Hello, dear," an elderly woman with bright white hair and a pair of pink-rimmed glasses with little bows at each edge says. "Delphine told us her flat sitter was a lovely young lady, but she didn't tell us just how pretty you are."

I like her already.

"Thank you so much," I reply, blinking at the crowd of women as they very obviously look me up and down.

"She's slim."

"She's young."

"She's got a nice face."

"You're American," Pink-Rimmed Glasses exclaims.

I smile. "Sure am."

"She didn't mention that," one of the other women says, this one with straight gray hair and a pair of tortoise shell glasses.

"That's certainly information we should have had," another agrees.

"But we're still going to come in, aren't we?"

"What's happening?"

"We're going to wet Delphine's place with her new flat sitter," Pink- Rimmed Glasses explains to the woman in a loud voice.

"Oh, I know that," she replies.

"Well?" Pink- Rimmed Glasses says to me. "Aren't you going to invite us in?"

I regard the group. They're all looking at me in expectation.

Possibly against my better judgment, I say, "Sure. Of course. Come on in. Sorry for all the boxes." I stand back for them, and they crush through the door and into the living room, chatting among themselves like an excited bunch of ducks.

I name each of my friends to introduce them. "It would seem these ladies are the building welcoming committee," I explain.

"That's right," Pink- Rimmed Glasses says. "We decided long ago that we were going to buck the trend in this neighborhood of not being friendly to new people, so here we are. Loud and proud."

"I think that's a London thing rather than just a Notting Hill thing," Lottie says, and I've got to agree with her. Londoners seem to want to look anywhere but at you, especially on public transport. My New Zealand work friend, Shelley, said it took her weeks to get used to not greeting everyone she saw out on the streets—something everyone in her small town of Ranfurly does every day, apparently.

"Oh, Lady Moo. I see you're up to your old tricks," Pink-Rimmed Glasses says as she regards the dog, who is now lying prostrate on the rug, chewing on Winnie the Pooh's only remaining arm. The rest of the poor toy is strewn across the living room floor like a massacre has just taken place. Which it has, really—of the stuffing variety at least.

"It's gonna take me some time to get used to this habit of hers," I say.

"I always told Delphine to train her not to attack poor Pooh, but she wouldn't listen."

My two mature friends, Tabitha and Zara, snort giggle at the toilet humor.

"She wouldn't," chimes a couple of the others.

"It's barbaric, defiling a treasured toy like that," says the smallest one.

"You're so right," Lottie agrees.

"But how rude of us not to introduce ourselves properly," Pink-Rimmed Glasses says. "I'm Barbara Burt," she continues before pointing at each of her fellow neighbors. "This is Gertie, this is Evelyn, this is the spring chicken of the group, Elsey, and last but not least, this is Maude. She's a little hard of hearing, so you need to speak up."

She points at the smallest, roundest member of the group, who lifts her hand in a wave, a broad grin on her plump face.

"She's rather opinionated, aren't you, Maude?" Barbara continues.

"What did you say?" Maude asks.

"You're rather opinionated," she repeats louder.

"Me? Oh, yes. If you can't have your opinions, what can you have?" Maude replies.

It's a good point.

Everyone in the room shakes hands and says hello before

Barbara offers to pop open her bottle of champagne. Before long, the Ducks, as I'm calling them in my head, join us with a mixture of glasses and mugs in their hands, and we toast my arrival in the building.

"How are you finding the place?" asks Elsey, the alleged spring chicken of the group.

"It's gorgeous. I think I'm going to love living here. Which flat are you in?"

"I'm immediately below you," Elsey explains. "I've got my Simeon but we're empty nesters now, I'm afraid to say. Our darling Petra went off to Oxford a few years ago, and, well, that's that. All I can say is this group is just wonderful. They got me through my darkest days. You're very lucky in your neighbors, you know."

"I can tell. They're all very welcoming."

"Oh, there are more to come."

I blink at her. "There are?"

"Oh, yes. We're simply the advance party. I don't mind telling you now: we wanted to see what you were like before we allowed the others in. They can be a bit sticky beak, you see. Always pushing their noses in where they're not wanted. We wanted to ensure you were the type to handle yourself, and you certainly appear to be one of those."

"Nosy neighbors, huh?" I ask, shooting an amused look at my friends, because if these ladies aren't the nosy neighbors, what the heck are the others like? "That old cliché."

"They're harmless, really, but not much gets past that Winnifred in flat 3a. Speaking of which, I might send out a message to the WhatsApp group and let them know to come on over."

"Oh, you don't need to do that," I protest, but it falls on deaf ears. She's already pulled her phone out and is tapping away, calling in the rest of the building.

Barbara sidles up to me. "Now, tell me all about yourself, Kennedy dear. Are you single?"

Talk about getting down to the nitty gritty.

"I am single."

"Do you want to be?"

"Well, I suppose," I reply uncertainly.

"How old are you?"

"Twenty-nine."

"Oh, the dreaded thirty is upon you. Well, you'll need to find someone quick-smart, you know. Are you seeing anyone? And is he the marrying type? I do hope he is the marrying type for your sake."

And *Winnifred* is the nosy one?

I force a smile. "Uh, no. I'm not seeing anyone."

She pats me on the arm. "Never mind, dear. I'm on the case now. Gertie? I say, Gertie?" she calls, and Gertie, who has been speaking with Zara and Asher about who knows what, looks over at us and raises her eyebrows.

"What is it, Barbara?"

"Kennedy says she's single at twenty-nine and looking for love."

Her face lights up. "Is she now?"

Barbara turns back to me and asks, "When are you thirty?"

"In a couple weeks," I reply, wishing this whole thing wasn't happening.

Barbara sucks in air as though I'm the captain of the Titanic and I've just informed her we're all going to die. "For shame! Thirty and single? Oh, darling. We *must* do something."

"Yes, we must," Gertie confirms, and the other Ducks nod their agreement.

Awesome.

I shoot my friends a startled look. "It's fine. You don't have to do anything. I'm fine the way I am. Really."

"Oh, no you're not. Do you like boys or girls? Or are you one of those newfangled types? What do they call it?" Elsey questions.

"Bilingual," Gertie says assuredly.

"It's not bilingual," Elsey protests. "It's the opposite. It's non-bilingual. Isn't it?"

"You mean non-*binary*, you silly old goats," Evelyn, the one in a pair of beige slacks and cashmere sweater says. "Bilingual means she speaks more than one language, and who knows what non-bilingual means."

"Not speaking two languages. Clearly, Evelyn," Barbara says, her tone pointed.

"That's just lingual then, isn't it?" Elsey asks.

"I don't think it is. What is it called when you speak just one language?" Maude asks.

"English," Elsey replies, and all five of the Ducks titter with laughter.

"Very funny, darling," Barbara pronounces.

"What are you talking about?" Maude asks.

Lottie and I share a look as we both press our lips together to stifle a giggle.

"So, Kennedy? What is it then? Boys or girls, or both?" Elsey questions.

"Or none," Barbara adds. "That's always a possibility in this day and age."

"Well, that wouldn't be any fun," Gertie says.

"What wouldn't be any fun?" Maude asks.

"Not wanting to kiss anyone," Gertie explains loudly.

"Even I want to kiss someone, and I'm 91. That Colin Firth. Delicious," Maude pronounces with a grin.

Evelyn shakes her head. "This generation has made it all so jolly complicated, haven't they?"

Barbara brushes her off. "That's a conversation for another day. Kennedy? Do tell us. Who do you like to kiss?"

All ten bespectacled eyes turn to me.

I glance at my friends, who are all watching me too, with looks of glee on their faces. "I...err...I like to kiss boys, I guess," I pronounce reluctantly, and they burst into excited chatter as my friends chortle.

"You're in for it now," Asher tells me.

"Oh, the possibilities," Barbara declares, her hand over her chest. "What's Doreen's son called again? The one who went to York and made a lot of money with horses?"

"Doreen doesn't have a son," Elsey replies.

"Yes, she does. He's tall with a rather large bottom," Barbara explains.

"Because she's a girl," Evelyn replies.

"Oh. Well, not that one, then," Barbara says.

"What about that lovely man who lives on the next street over. The one who always wears a beret," Elsey suggests.

"Not him. He's bound to be French." This from Gertie.

"Good point," Elsey agrees.

It's Evelyn's time to make a suggestion. "Oh, I know. What about that dishy young man who moved in upstairs?"

"The one who's been doing the renovations?" Elsey asks.

"You mean the one who refused to have us welcome him to the building?" Barbara states.

"That's right. What was his name again?" Evelyn asks.

"I'm not sure he's right for our Kennedy. He might be handsome, but he's too rude. Who doesn't want a welcome party?" Barbara asks with a shake of her head.

"And he doesn't want to come to our wonderful building events, either. He's a curmudgeon," Gertie states.

I've been listening to the Ducks try to decide who they're going to set me up with for long enough.

"Look, it's fine," I say, cutting them off. Because really,

enough is enough. "No one needs to set me up with any man, whether it's the one a couple of streets away or the one doing the renovations. I'm perfectly fine the way I am."

It falls on deaf ears. I try once more, and then give up, instead joining my friends over at the kitchen counter.

"This sure is gonna be interesting living here," Asher comments to me, out of earshot of the chatting Ducks.

Zara laughs. "They'll have you married off before the end of the week, babe."

"Not if I can help it," I reply.

"Oh, they're harmless," Lottie declares. "I'm sure they'll be lovely neighbors, and considering most Londoners go their entire lives without meeting the people who live right next door, I think you're very lucky."

"That's a good point," Tabitha agrees.

There's a knock at the door, and I stroll past the plotting ladies and swing it open. This time, I'm greeted by an even larger crowd of people. They're of varying ages, including Esme and what looks like her younger sister.

I blink at them all in disbelief. "Are you all my new neighbors?" I ask.

"We certainly are," a man in his seventies with a thick grey mustache and a walking stick replies. He juts out his hand and we shake. "Oscar Peabody."

"Well, come on in. The more the merrier." As the words leave my mouth, Lady Moo appears at my feet. Her eyes land on Oscar Peabody and she begins to growl and back away before she bursts into frenzied yapping.

"I say, settle down there, little dog," Oscar says.

Lady Moo isn't listening. She gnashes her teeth and barks and barks.

"I'm so sorry," I say over the racket. "Delphine said she dislikes men." I don't specify "bad men," because that wouldn't be very neighborly. I scoop her up in my arms, but it does nothing to stop the barking. "I'll take her to another room."

I rush down the hall and into the bedroom with her. I glance at the carpet and think better of it, so I put her in the bathroom instead. If she has any accidents, at least they'll be easy to clean up.

I return to the living room and Barbara and Gertie corner me. "That little dog is a very good judge of character, you know," she says in a conspiratorial tone. "That Oscar Peabody is bad news."

"He is?" I ask.

"Oh, yes. He's been married five times and has twelve grown children, none of whom are on speaking terms with him," Gertie tells me.

"And he trails dirt through the hallway from the communal garden," Barbara complains.

"I'm sorry to hear that. About the wives and kids and the dirt, too."

Before long, between the boxes and the sheer number of people in the place, my new living room is jam-packed, everyone sipping their drinks out of whatever cups and glasses I can find, chatting and laughing and generally having a nice time.

There's another knock on the door, and Barbara calls out, "I'll answer it for you Kennedy, dear," before circumnavigating the throng of people to the front door.

I follow her, but Barbara has already reached the door. She pulls it open, and I come to a crashing halt as I gawk in disbelief at who's standing in the doorway.

"Oh, it's you," Barbara says, her tone telling me she's not exactly thrilled to see him.

"Hello, Mrs. Burt," the man replies. As his gaze shifts from Barbara to me, his intense blue eyes widen in surprise before the edges of his mouth lift into a smile.

"You?" I manage to say, in shock.

"I could say the same thing," he replies all too smoothly.

"Wh-what are you doing here?" I stutter, taking in his beautifully cut, dark navy suit with his white open neck shirt, a winter coat draped over one arm.

Suddenly my beat-up old tennis shoes, jeans, and long-sleeve T don't feel quite as cute as they did a moment ago.

"It's nice to see you, too, Kennedy," the man replies, his tone telling me he's gotten over the initial surprise of seeing me here in Delphine's flat.

Because this guy is over-privileged, over-wealthy, over-confident and over here.

Charlie Cavendish.

His face morphs into a smirk, as though he's a cat who has 24-7 access to a cream factory, rendering his face annoyingly handsome. "Welcome to my building."

CHAPTER 4

I blink at him a few times, my mind scrambling to comprehend this new, horrible information.

Charlie Cavendish lives in my new building.

Seriously now?

Come on, Universe! What did I ever do to you?

"*Your* building?" I ask, a potent mix of bewilderment, shock, and disbelief completely replacing the blood in my veins.

"Well, not *mine* exactly. I don't own the whole building, just the top two flats, which I've renovated into one larger place," he replies.

He must be the rude renovator the Ducks were talking about.

Figures.

His lips lift in a smile, showing just how much he's enjoying the wind being sucked from my sails.

The sadist.

"So, *you're* Delphine's flat sitter, it would seem."

"I didn't know you lived here." I narrow my eyes at him. "You've got a place in Mayfair."

He cocks an eyebrow. "Have you been checking up on me, Kennedy?"

"Checking up on you? Of course not," I sniff. "You mentioned it, that's all."

"Well, now I live in Notting Hill. Right above you, in fact." He raises his eyes to the ceiling. "Your ceiling is my floor," he muses.

Kill me. Kill me now.

I lift my chin and lock my gaze onto his to show just how little this new information bothers me.

Inside, I'm seething.

Of all the gin joints in all the towns in all the world...

He tells me, "I'll try not to be too noisy for you, although I do warn you, I'm an early riser."

Of course he is.

"So am I," I reply.

"Five am?"

I'm tempted to reply that I get up way before five, but that would be an outright lie. "About then," I huff.

Seven is almost five, right?

"I'll be seeing you in the lift, then."

"You bet."

"Great."

"Great."

The edges of his eyes crinkle in an annoyingly sexy way as a full smile claims his face.

I don't crack a smile.

How can I smile when I've just found out Charlie Smug Cavendish lives above me? I mean, the chances of us bumping into one another can't be high if he gets up at some ridiculous hour, but still. I'll *know* he's there.

If Delphine's flat wasn't so gorgeous and if I wasn't in such desperate need of a place to live, I'd move out, immediately.

"You obviously got the note about the welcoming party," Barbara says to him, her tone cool.

I've been so wrapped up in the *Charlie Cavendish lives above me* bombshell, I'd totally forgotten Barbara was at my side.

"I did. Thank you, Mrs. Burt."

"We invited everyone, so don't go feeling special or anything," she quips.

I suppress a small smile. He calls her Mrs. Burt, but she's told me to call her Barbara. I've been here five minutes and already I'm more popular with the neighbors than he is.

Figures. He *is* a horrible person.

"I'll try not to feel special," he replies, those blue eyes of his shining.

A blur of black and white catches my attention out of the corner of my eye, and I turn to see Lady Moo hurtling toward us. She comes to a crashing halt in front of Charlie.

Oh, this is going to be good.

"Hello there, little dog," he coos.

I wait for her to burst into the yapping, growling frenzy she threw at Oscar Peabody, but instead all she does is sniff Charlie's shoes, her stub of a tail shaking as she tries to leap up, placing her front paws on his legs.

What the—?

"Is your dog always so friendly?" he asks as he leans down to pet her.

I narrow my eyes at her. *Lady Moo, you traitor.*

"She's not my dog," I say.

"Oh, she's Delphine's. Of course," he says, as he rubs her behind the ears.

I lean down and pick her up, bringing the dog petting session to a sudden halt. "How did you get out of the bathroom," I ask her.

"Well, that's unexpected," Barbara comments, her eyes

wide behind those huge pink frames of hers. "Lady Moo doesn't like certain men." She shoots me a meaningful look.

Lady Moo's clearly not the bad man soothsayer she's reputed to be if she doesn't bark at the worst of the worst.

"How do you two know one another, then?" Barbara asks.

"Kennedy and I dated," Charlie replies smoothly before I have the chance to say anything.

"You did?" she guffaws. "Kennedy, you dark horse."

"I'd hardly call one terrible blind date when Charlie left early as 'dating,'" I reply.

"You left a date with Kennedy early?" Barbara questions, and I'm beyond pleased when she gives him the stink eye. "Why does that not surprise me?"

I think I love this woman.

I smile at him. "Yes, Charlie. Why does that not surprise *Barbara*?" I ask pointedly, emphasizing her name.

"Mrs. Burt, I feel that's between Kennedy and me," he replies.

That doesn't go down well with the boundary-challenged Barbara. She purses her lips and looks him up and down. "I see."

"Now, I brought you a welcome gift," Charlie says, proffering an exquisite potted orchid. "Delphine assured me 'Kenny' would love orchids, by which I assumed you would be a man."

"Well, I'm not."

"I can see that."

I take the orchid in my hands. "That was kind. Thank you." It physically hurts to be nice to this man, but he bought me a gift and it's only right to be polite. Plus, I adore orchids, but there's no way I'm telling Charlie Cavendish that.

"I suppose you'll want to come in," Barbara says to him with as much enthusiasm as a kid faced with an algebra lesson.

"This is a brief visit. I only wanted to welcome Delphine's flat sitter to the building. I have a lot of work to do."

I harrumph.

"Charlie?" Zara appears at the door. "What are you doing here?"

His face lights up in a genuine smile.

"Zara," he says, as she wraps her arms around him and plants a kiss on his cheek. "I live upstairs."

"This is where your London *pied-à-terre* is?" she asks in wonderment.

"I bought here a few months ago."

"Wow, Charlie, it's quite the address."

"I like it," he replies, in that modest way people who could drown in their own cash a hundred times over say.

My eyes roll like they're taking a ride on a Ferris wheel. *So* typical.

"I'm finishing up some renovations right now, but I'd love to have you and Asher over once it's all done."

She beams at him. "That would be so nice."

Asher appears behind Zara, wrapping his arms around her waist. "Charlie?" he asks, and then shoots me a questioning look.

"Charlie lives upstairs," Zara explains, as the two men do an awkward handshake. Awkward because Zara's literally caught in the middle.

"Well, that's gonna be interesting." Asher flicks his gaze to me and waggles his eyebrows.

"No, it's not," I grind out through gritted teeth, heat rising in my cheeks.

"Do all of you young people know this man?" Barbara demands.

"We do," we reply with varying degrees of gusto. Well, mine varies. Asher's and Zara's are positive. Mine? Not so much.

"Well, your work can wait, Charlie. You'll need to come in and join the party," Barbara declares flatly.

I open my mouth to protest and close it again. I can hardly refuse him entry, not when my living room is filled to the brim with neighbors I've only just met.

"Thank you, but as I said, I do have a lot of work to do. I'll leave you all to it," Charlie protests.

That's the first thing he's said that I can get on board with.

"Nonsense," Barbara replies. "You can come in and ingratiate yourself to your neighbors. You spend all your time skulking around that flat of yours, never coming to the potluck dinners or the parties or the quiz nights. We pride ourselves on having a lot of social engagements in this building, and you never come to anything! The least you can do is make Kennedy feel welcome."

I twist my mouth and raise my brows at him.

Did I mention I love this woman?

"I didn't even know your name was Charlie until a moment ago. All your post is addressed to 'C. Cavendish,'" Barbara continues.

He blinks at her. "You look through my post?"

"Well, not *through* it of course," she concedes. "That would be a violation of your privacy."

He fixes her with his gaze. "Yes. Yes, it would."

"So, Charlie," I begin, to pull the conversation away from mail, "Feel free to go get your work done if you want to."

He flicks his eyes to mine. "Actually, I'd love to come in and meet everyone. It's high time, isn't it Mrs. Burt?"

"It is indeed, Charlie."

"Seriously, don't trouble yourself," I say through gritted teeth.

"It's no trouble," he replies, with that patronizing smile of his teasing the edges of his mouth. The one that tells me exactly what he thinks of me.

I harrumph as he walks through the door and into the crowded living room. He's immediately pounced on by the Ducks, who furnish him with a drink and pepper him with a stream of questions. He shoots me a bewildered look and I smile sweetly back at him.

You reap what you sow, dude.

Zara crosses her arms and watches him. "Charlie Cavendish lives in your building. How's that going to work?"

"It'll be fine. Barbara says she never sees him, and from what I've seen of her, I'm sure she's in everyone's business. Plus, he's already told me he gets up super early, which I do not. I'll hardly ever see the guy."

"I hope so. For your sake. I know you're not his biggest fan."

I glance over at him. He's still surrounded by the Ducks, all of whom have invaded his personal space to such a degree he looks like he'd rather be anywhere but here. Maude is clutching onto his arm and saying something serious to him, and he's nodding along, his body rigid.

He must be hating this.

My face breaks into a grin at the thought.

"I think it's going to be fine. None of them like him."

"Oh, I'm sure they just don't know him."

"They're good judges of character, as far as I can see."

She turns to me. "Tell me something. Why do you hate him so much?"

"I never said I hate him."

"It's obvious, babe. Emma told me that when she and Seb set you up on that blind date you were totally into each other, but then she turned her back for five seconds and things went horribly pear-shaped."

"It wasn't five seconds. She was gone forever."

"Not the point. So? What happened between you two."

I shrug. "He's not my type, that's all."

"He's hot, he's loaded, and he's really nice. That's not your type?"

"Yes, he's hot and loaded," I concede, "but nice? If you think a guy who rubs his privilege in your face is nice, then you and I are very different people."

"I can't imagine he would do something like that. Sure, he's more Seb's friend than mine, but I've known him for years and he's been nothing but lovely."

How can I explain to my friend that it's not like that for me? Zara's from an aristocratic family with a house the size of a long line of school gymnasiums stuck together. I know her family isn't exactly wealthy these days, but she went to the country's best schools, and until recently, she didn't even need to take her interior design career seriously.

Me? I came from a very different place. My dad worked construction, and my mom cleaned motels. They're good people, but they've never had two dimes to rub together. I sure as heck didn't have some trust fund to pay for college, and I can't name anyone in my social circle back home who came from money.

"All I know is that's how he comes across to me, anyway."

Zara narrows her eyes. "How did you find my brother when you met him on the show?" she asks.

"He was fine."

"He's not exactly from the wrong side of the tracks, but he didn't bother you the way Charlie does."

"That was different."

"How?"

"It just was, that's all."

She studies my face before she declares, "Interesting."

"What's interesting?"

"Nothing."

I cock an eyebrow in her direction.

"It's just that Sebastian's wealth and social position didn't bother you, but Charlie's does. There's got to be something in that."

"Yeah, the fact that Sebastian is a good guy."

She lets out a laugh. "I'm not going to change your mind on Charlie, am I?"

I shake my head. "Nope."

Lottie makes her way through the crowd to us. "These people are divine. Did you know Evelyn volunteers at a women's shelter, Barbara runs a knitting circle, and Isla, your dog walker's sister, is studying to be a ballerina?"

"You sure have been chatting," I comment.

"You'll have to go to the Christmas potluck dinner. They tell me it's the social event of the year. I think you're going to love living here, babe."

"Especially with Charlie Cavendish living upstairs," Zara teases, her dark eyes dancing.

"Charlie Cavendish lives in this building? That's why he's here?" Lottie asks, her eyes wide. "That's going to be interesting."

Again with the 'interesting?'

"Actually, I think it's going to be very boring," I reply, ensuring the tone of my voice communicates just how boring it's going to be for me.

"Why did you invite him in if he's so boring?" Lottie asks.

"He got dragged in by Barbara. She complained that he didn't come to any of their building functions," I explain. "I think he was trying to make a point."

"Well, they certainly don't want to let him out of their sights right now," Lottie comments, and all three of us look over at him, still surrounded by the throng of bespectacled, pearl-wearing elderly ladies, two of whom are clutching onto his arms.

Appearing to sense our eyes on him, he glances over at us, and mouths *help*. I shoot him a look that says *no way,* but my traitorous friends take pity on him.

"We need to save him," Lottie declares.

"Oh, we do," Zara agrees. "Poor Charlie. I nominate Kennedy for the job."

"Not me." I shake my head. There's no way I'm going to "save" a grown man from a bunch of elderly women, especially not if that grown man is Charlie Cavendish. "He's a big boy. I'm sure he can take care of himself."

"He needs us. Look at him," Zara says.

I flick my gaze back to him and watch as Barbara continues to berate him for something. I'm sure he deserves every word.

I cross my arms. "Be my guest. I'm gonna go talk to some of my other new neighbors. The nice ones who don't look down their noses at me."

"Oh no you don't. Come with me." Lottie begins to pull me through a throng of teenagers to the edge of the Duck group. "Be a good hostess and save your hot neighbor," she instructs.

"Do I have to?" I whine, sounding exactly like one of my sister's kids.

"You do," is her solemn response. "And don't think for one moment I didn't notice the fact you didn't say he wasn't hot." She nudges me. "Go on. Save the guy. Tell him you need to talk about something."

"About what?"

"I don't know. Hot neighbor stuff."

"What the heck is 'hot neighbor stuff?'"

"Make it up." She lifts her brows and fixes me with her stare. "Now."

I let out a defeated sigh. Lottie's not going to let me get

away with not doing this, so I'd may as well save him from the Ducks. Then I can go talk to someone else.

"Go on." She nudges me once more, this time with completely unnecessary force, so that I end up stumbling into the group.

"Kennedy," Charlie says, as he regards me in surprise.

I take a deep breath to brace myself for having to talk to him for the second time tonight—cruel and unnecessary punishment in my opinion—and say in a loud voice, "Can I talk to you about something? It's, err, super important."

He doesn't need to be asked twice.

Leaping on his chance to escape the interrogation, he replies, "Super important, you say? Of course. Ladies, this has been an absolute pleasure, and I do take your point on board that I should come to more building events, but I am needed by our lovely hostess. So, if you'll please excuse me."

Barbara places her hand on his forearm. "Promise you'll come to Maude's Christmas potluck dinner. There will be mulled wine."

"I promise."

"And croquet on the lawn in the New Year," Elsey adds. "It's a winter tradition. You'll need to wrap up."

"Of course."

"And our knitting circle. We meet every Tuesday," Gertie says.

I almost feel sorry for the guy.

But not quite.

Charlie raises his hands in the surrender sign. "I will do my very best to come to all the building events for the foreseeable future, my work schedule allowing," he states. "Will that do?"

It seems to please the ladies, who remove their hands from his arms. They part like the Red Sea to allow him to leave.

Once free of their—literal—grasp, his features relax. "Thank you for that. I thought I was never going to get away from them. They're rather insistent, aren't they?"

"I've only just met them, so I can't really say, although they seem just wonderful to me."

His lips twitch. "Do they, now? So, I can only assume I'll be seeing you at the Christmas potluck dinner, the croquet, and their knitting circle soon?"

"You're going to their knitting circle?"

"I wouldn't miss it for the world."

I scoff. The idea of someone as arrogant, self-interested, and pompous as Charlie Cavendish sitting in someone's living room, gossiping over his knitting, brings a smile to my face.

"What?" he questions.

"Nothing. I just didn't see you as a knitter. It's not very *polo*. Is it?"

He pulls his lips into a line. "Do we get to relive that conversation from the blind date?"

I look away to show him just how little our date means to me. "I'm just sayin'."

He falls silent, and I can feel his gaze on me. "Perhaps I will go to the knitting circle," he says eventually.

"Sure. You knit. I can totally see that."

"I might."

"You don't."

"I could."

"You won't."

"I get it, Kennedy. You don't like me."

"And you don't like *me*," I rebuff.

"I've never said that."

"You didn't have to. It's obvious."

"I think you'll find *you're* the one who greets me like you're going in for a colonoscopy."

I let out a laugh. "No contest between you and a colonoscopy, dude. Believe me."

He presses his lips together to stifle a smile, his irritatingly iridescent blue eyes shining bright. "Is that so?"

"Don't you go pretending you like seeing me, either. We'd may as well be honest about this, now that we're going to be living in the same building."

"*My* building."

"Whatever."

"We're being honest with each other now, are we?"

"Well, at least *I* am. You're still sticking to the fiction that you're joining the building knitting circle."

He lets out a deep belly laugh, throwing his head back to show a row of straight, orthodontically perfect teeth. Naturally. "Well, thank you very much for a pleasant evening. It's been…educational."

"I'm super glad you learned something tonight," I say in my most saccharine voice. "Should I see you to the door or do you think you can you find your own way there?"

"I'm certain I can find the door on my own." He turns to leave, thinks better of it, and turns back. He leans toward me, a little too closely, so I get a lungful of his aftershave—a mixture of woodsy citrus and musk that would be appealing on anyone other than him—and says quietly, "You know what? This is going to be fun."

I pull back from him, and mutter, "No it's not."

His response is to flash me with a cheeky smile before he strides confidently away, pausing only to wave at the Ducks and the rest of the neighbors, before he disappears out my door.

I expel a breath of air, thankful he's now gone—and wondering why the fact he thinks it's going to be fun with me living in the same building as him makes my belly do a little flip.

CHAPTER 5

I reach the office the next morning, and as I hang my winter coat and scarf over the coat stand, I notice Sandra, my boss, banging around in her glass-walled office. I wander over to her doorway and knock on the glass wall.

She looks out at me through the glass, a wild look in her eyes, gesturing for me to come inside. "Kennedy. Where have you been?" she snaps.

"It's 2 minutes to 9. Technically, I'm early."

She pulls her brows together. "Well, you're here now. And none of it matters anyway."

"Why? What's going on?" I ask, as I glance around the room. Her ordinarily organized Executive Editor office is littered with files and magazine merchandise, a couple of boxes balanced on the blue-gray sofa. "Are you getting your spring cleaning done super early or something?"

She shoots me a tight-lipped look and brushes past me to close the door.

"Sandra? What's going on?" I ask.

"They're gunning for me," she states in a low voice.

"Who's gunning for you? The new owners?"

She gives a grim nod, her blonde curls bouncing. "They've been asking a lot of questions. Like a *lot*."

"That's normal, isn't it? I mean, they just bought the publishing house. I'm sure it's only natural that they have questions."

"Call it a sixth sense, but I know my days here are numbered."

"But you do a great job. Why would they want to get rid of you?"

"Because maybe they've got someone who does an even better job than me. I'm collateral." She picks up a rubber stress ball and flings it into one of the boxes. "You'd better watch your back. That's all I'll say."

Fear grips my stomach and gives it a sharp twist. "Why do you say that? Do you know something? I can't lose my job. *Claudette* sponsors me to be in this country. I got my British visa because of it."

Sandra regards me with a pinched expression. "Get a back-up plan. Fast."

"But—" I begin, only to be interrupted by a sharp rap on the closed door, making both of us jump.

"Come in," Sandra calls out, as she shoots me a meaningful look.

The door pushes open, and I hold my breath. Could it be the Grim Reaper, here to send Sandra and I both to our doom?

It's Eric, the fashion editor's snarky assistant. Dressed immaculately, if loudly, in a purple tweed three-piece suit and pale lemon shirt and tie, his eyes glide over my pencil skirt and white blouse combo with obvious distaste. If Eric were the Grim Reaper, we'd all go to our doom dressed fabulously with an espresso martini clutched in our perfectly manicured hands.

He scans the room before he eyes the boxes on the sofa. He arches a brow, but doesn't mention them, instead choosing to purse his lips.

"What do you want, Eric?" Sandra asks in a clipped tone.

Eric is not one to ingratiate himself to anyone outside of the fashion department, and even then, he's only ever nice to his boss.

"There's a meeting in the conference room, starting now. Senior management only." He shoots me a look that tells me I'm not important enough to attend, which is fine by me. I'm still reeling from Sandra's suspicions.

"Who called it?" Sandra asks. "It's not in my schedule."

"Upstairs," is his ominous reply. One floor up from us is the management floor. Recently vacated by a group of high-powered execs and decision-makers who I seldom saw, a new crowd has taken up residence in the last few weeks, throwing the magazine into a frenzied state with the word "restructure" bandied about with sickening regularity.

"Upstairs. Right. I guess I have to go to the meeting then."

"That was the general idea." Eric's voice drips with gooey sarcasm.

Sandra collects her tablet from her desk and plods past me.

I give her arm a quick squeeze. "Good luck."

She harrumphs, already deciding that her fate is sealed as she follows Eric from the room. I trail after them, my stomach twisting some more as I reach my desk.

I plunk down heavily in my chair.

What if I do lose my job? What then?

I'd have to move back to San Diego, that's what. I'd have to move back to what I escaped from.

A blonde head pops up over the cubicle wall. "How's it going, Kennedy?" says a New Zealand accent.

I smile up at my fellow writer's bespectacled face. "Hey,

Shelley. Did you know there's a big meeting going on right now?"

"Yeah, I heard."

Her head disappears from sight, reappearing a moment later in my cubicle, attached to her body. She leans her pink-clad butt against my desk and lets out a puff of air. "I heard a rumor."

"What did you hear?"

"Sandra." She makes a neck-slashing movement with her thumb across her neck.

"How do you know?"

"My cousin's friend is one of the EAs upstairs. She told me after work yesterday."

I slump in my chair. "Poor Sandra."

"I know, right? I feel bad for her, but it was inevitable, really. She's the big boss. They're bound to want to get rid of her. You and me? We're lowly enough to be safe, I reckon."

"Sometimes being a writer minion has its benefits?" I suggest.

"Exactly."

We hear a noise, and both stand and peer over the top of my cubicle to see Sandra being marched off the premises, holding a box with the top of a pot plant I recognize from her desk poking out the top. She catches my eye and lifts her brows at me, and I raise my hand and mouth *I'm so sorry* as she disappears around the corner.

I slump down in my chair.

"That was brutal," I say.

"Cutthroat."

"Who's next, I wonder?"

"Could be anyone. Hey, I'm going to back to my desk. Don't want to be seen skiving off work."

Shelley disappears behind the cubicle, and I flick my attention to my screen, the half-written first draft of my feature on vaccine hesitancy, that I'd been researching for the last week, staring back at me.

How can I work at a time like this?

I play around with sentence structure and do a little research online, but it's hard to focus. About ten minutes in, Grim Reaper Eric appears at the entrance to my cubicle, a look of distaste on his face. "You. Meeting in conference room 3 now. You, too, Shelley," he adds.

"Us?" I ask. "But…but we're not management."

"Yeah. We're just the worker bees around here," Shelley says, her head appearing over the partition once more.

"It's a full magazine meeting, you Muppets. Don't make me tell you twice," he replies, his tone accusatory and harsh. When he first called me a Muppet, I thought it was cute and endearing. It's not. It basically British speak for idiot.

Eric's not exactly the warm fuzzy type.

I force a smile. Antagonizing Eric isn't high on my list, particularly when my job is on the line.

A handful of minutes later, every employee—bar the now departed Sandra—crowds into the conference room. The atmosphere is tense to say the least. No one is smiling. No one is chatting. We await the new management to tell us our fate.

My heart jangles in my chest like a rattlesnake.

I could lose my job.

A tall, thin woman with thick, curly auburn hair, dressed in a pale blue shirt and a pair of slim-fitting pants makes her way through the employees to the front of the room.

"Ladies, gentlemen, and nonbinary members of staff. Thank you for being here this morning," she begins, smiling out at us all as though our world isn't about to be turned on its head.

"Like we had a choice," Shelley mutters to me under her breath.

"For those of you who don't know me, I am sorry for your loss," she says.

I crease my forehead. What the—?

"Ha! Just kidding. I'm Edina Harrop, your new editor-in-chief, your new boss, your new reason for being." She grins out at us, her hollow eyes maniacal.

I shoot Shelley a concerned look, and she pulls her lips into her mouth as she catches my eye.

"Today is the beginning of something new, something exciting, something *amazing*," Edina continues. "You see today, we're taking this magazine and we're turning it on its head. Yes, *Claudette* has performed well since its inception some forty-seven years ago. But we've got the opportunity to make it perform better than just 'well.' Performing well is not enough for us. We want incredible!" She slaps the table with her long, skinny hand, making us take a collective jump. "We want magnificent!" Another slap. "We want the impossible!" A slap that must reverberate up her arm and make her teeth chatter.

This woman sure likes talking in threes. And slapping tables.

A group of people at the front of the room burst into spontaneous applause, but I don't recognize any of them.

"They must be the new management from upstairs," I say to Shelley. "No one else is clapping."

"Why would we? We could all be about to lose our jobs."

My belly performs another twist. "Don't say that."

The rest of us watch in stony, apprehensive silence. We liked *Claudette* the way it was. Turning the magazine on its head sounds vertigo-inducing.

"Now, you may be wondering what changes we're making because, as the Dalai Lama says, the only constant is change. The first thing I can tell you is the changes we are making are fierce. They are exciting. They are now. We have a vision, and I think you are going to love where we're going. It's a brave new world, people!" She slaps the table once more, her small eyes wild, and even though this is her fourth attack on the tabletop, my hand still flies to my chest in shock.

"I wish she'd stop doing that. It's not good for my digestion," Shelley mutters.

"With a new vision comes change, as I'm sure you are aware," she continues.

I hold my breath. *Here it comes.*

"Our vision did not align with some members of the team. It's unfortunate, but there it is. So, some of the old team have had to be moved on. We say farewell, and we hope they find new, fertile pastures."

An image of Sandra and her cardboard box flashes before my eyes.

"The good news for everyone in this room is that you are still part of this new, fantastic team. All of you are here for the ride!" She opens her arms and grins out at us.

I let out a relieved breath of air. My eyes lock with Shelley's and we share a smile.

"Thank eff for that," she says.

"However," Edina continues.

Uh-oh. I don't like a *however*. Following good news, a *however* is never good.

"Some of you will find your roles have changed. We are stepping it up, people. We are making things new and exciting. We are bringing passion to this magazine."

I chew on my lip, alarmed. I like having the scope to choose my topics, to research things beyond the latest hair and beauty products. To educate our readership. I don't want that taken away from me, no matter what this alleged new vision is.

"So, each and every one of you is going to get the opportunity to embrace our new vision if you choose to. If you want to. If you feel it." She slaps her chest, which is a nice change from the table. "I want to spend time with each team member today, so I'll be calling you in to see me to discuss where your piece fits in this new *Claudette* puzzle. Oh, and one more thing: there will be morning tea." Her smile is magnanimous as her eyes sweep the room, as if the lure of morning tea—as the Brits like to call a mid-morning snack and coffee break—is so great that we'll forget that she's just told us that our jobs are about to change, probably for the worse.

Eric elbows his way through the crowd and pulls a piece of white cloth from the center of the large oak table to reveal plates of mini muffins, cookies, and cake slices.

Edina looks down to consult her tablet, then looks up and says, "Kennedy Bennet. Where is Kennedy Bennet? Gosh, I do like that name. It just rolls off the tongue."

I regard her in surprise as I hesitatingly lift my hand. "Here."

"You are the lucky first to have your one on one with me," Edina tells me. "So, let's do this. Everyone else, eat. Enjoy. You will be called for your one on one with me in due course."

As I get up to leave, Shelley squeezes my arm and says, "Good luck."

"I think I'm gonna need it."

I make my way out of the room and across the office floor, to what was Sandra's office a mere hour ago. Edina is already behind the desk, her long, slim figure looking out of place in the familiar office.

I knock on the door that sits ajar. "Hi, there. I'm Kennedy Bennet."

"Kennedy Bennet. Great to meet you," she says, as she gives me a firm handshake. "Take a seat. Let's chinwag."

"Chinwag. Gotcha." I force a smile as I settle into one of the chairs.

"I've seen your work. I like what I see. It's smart, it's punchy, it's fresh."

"Thank you."

"What I want you to focus on now is a new perspective on the city. I want London at its sparkling, glamorous best. London at its most exciting. London as it is right now."

"But I've been writing a feature on vaccination hesitancy, and I've already—"

"Switchover, turn around, do an about-face."

I pull my brows together. "You want me to just trash my feature?"

"Of course not. We don't want you to trash anything."

I relax my face. "That's good to hear."

"Just do it on your own time, for your own purposes."

"As in write it and not submit it to the magazine?"

Her lips lift in a smile. "You cotton on quickly. They told me you would."

"That's…good," I reply, wondering who "they" are, and recovering from the fact that the article I've put a lot of time into is now no longer going to be published.

She pushes a piece of paper across the table toward me. "Here's your brief for a new column. We want you out there on the streets at night, reporting back on what's hot, what's happening, and where to next."

I skim my eyes across the title: *Single Girl in London*. "What exactly do you want me to write about?"

"The latest things to do, the latest trends, what's hot right now," she replies in her *speak by threes* approach.

"When you say trends, do you mean fashion? Because I'm not a fashion writer."

"I'm talking about where to go that's off the beaten track, that's fun and new and out of the ordinary. What can be more important to our readership than knowing where to go to get the best mojito in the city on a Saturday night?"

Uh, a lot of things?

"Judging by the column title, you want me to write about the latest places for single people to go. Right?"

"You've got it."

"You know I'm American? I'm not exactly local."

"Which is why you're prefect for this. You can see the city through fresh eyes." She slides the piece of paper back and scribbles on it. "*Single* American *Girl in London*. What do you think of that? Amazing, isn't it?" Her eyes are wide, her face lit up with excitement.

I try to muster enthusiasm, but my heart has sunk to my toes. "Yeah. Amazing."

She slaps the table with her bony hand. "I *knew* you'd agree. Come up with a list of places for me by close of day today and then let's do this. Nothing run-of-the-mill. I want interesting, unusual, though provoking." She stands to indicate our meeting is now over.

I blink at her in alarm, as I rise to my feet. "You want a list today?"

"Today," she confirms. "Can you ask Shelley Macintosh to come in next?"

"Sure thing." I slink back to my desk.

Well, I guess that's it then. If I want to keep my job, I've got to write the new *Single American Girl in London* column, and I have no clue where to begin.

CHAPTER 6

I wake with a start. Hugo's wife is chasing me through Hyde Park, yelling something in French I don't understand as my feet crunch over leaves and twigs. She's trailed by a hammerhead shark and my sister, Veronica, neither of whom are happy with me.

What the—?

Well, that's a dream you don't have every day.

The room is bathed in darkness, so I roll over and push the imagery from my mind. I let out a deep breath and snuggle back against my pillow. I begin to drift back off to sleep.

There's a loud bang.

I ping my eyes open. Did I dream that?

I lie in bed and listen. Silence. Well, London's version of silence, anyway, which means a constant hum of traffic, garbage collection trucks, and the occasional helicopter, among many other city noises.

I let out a sigh and snuggle back into my pillow, pulling my comforter up around my ears.

Sleep, blissful sleep.

Is there anything nicer than being warm and snuggly in your bed when it's Friday morning and you know you don't have to get up until your alarm goes off.

Okay, *not* having to get up when your alarm goes off would top that, but knowing I've got more sleep to enjoy right now is a close second.

I begin to drift off.

And then it happens again. A loud bang, this time followed by a strange scraping noise. Lady Moo leaps out of her dog bed by the window and launches into frenzied barks.

That was definitely not a dream, and I've got zero chance of getting back to sleep now that the dog's been triggered.

I sit boldly upright in my bed and glance at the red lit numbers on the clock on the nightstand: 4:52.

4:52 on a Friday morning! That is way too early for loud disturbances in my book.

I glare up at the ceiling, as though it's making the noises and not the human upstairs.

A human named Charlie Cavendish.

"It's okay, Lady Moo," I say over the yapping. "Come here, girl." I pat the bed and she leaps up onto it, her barking momentarily forgotten as her short tail does double time at being allowed onto the bed. I twist my mouth as I pet the dog, glaring up at the ceiling as I wait for the next cluster of noises.

I don't have to wait long.

When the scraping, banging noises come, I whip the comforter off me and swing my legs out of bed, touching my toes to the cold hardwood floor. Lady Moo gets such a shock, she immediately begins to bark once more.

I slide my feet into my slippers and throw on Delphine's thick, fluffy robe from the back of the bathroom door to keep me warm against the freezing morning air. The heat is scheduled to kick on at the very reasonable hour of 7 am, but until then it's like an icebox in here.

"Come on, Lady Moo," I say, as I scoop her up in my arms. "Aunty Kennedy has some selfish British butt to kick, and you get to have an early breakfast." I pad out of my bedroom and down the hall to the kitchen, where I pour some kibble into one of Lady Moo's bowls—a white bowl with cow-like black spots. Shocker.

There's another series of loud noises from upstairs.

With Lady Moo happily chomping away, I wrap the robe tightly around myself, grab the keys from the hallway table, and stomp up the flight of stairs to the top floor.

It's not hard to locate Charlie's front door, what with his flat being the only one up this high. I rap my knuckles on the door and lock my jaw, ready to confront the man who thinks it's okay to disturb the peace so rudely on a Friday morning.

The door swings open, and there, standing before me, is the noisemaker himself. Holding a mug in one hand, he's wearing a pair of shorts and a sports T that make him look handsome and athletic, but in that totally smarmy way of his.

His gaze lands on me and his eyebrows lift in surprise. "Kennedy Bennet, the girl next door. Literally." He slides his eyes over my clothes before he lifts them back to mine. "And wearing a fetching outfit, too. Are those…udders?"

I glance down. I notice for the first time that although Delphine's dressing gown looked inoffensive enough while hanging on the hook, now that I'm wearing it I can see it's covered in a cow motif of black and white patches.

But that's not all.

My eyes slide further down to the front of the dressing gown.

Oh no.

There's a padded pair of pale pink udders that appear to hang from my waist.

Great choice, Kennedy.

I make a quick mental note: *when confronting unpleasant neighbors, remember not to wear a cow-like dressing gown, particularly one with udders.*

I pull the belt tighter and raise my chin in defiance. "It's a robe, Charlie. Get over it."

"Well, I'll give you one thing. You've certainly got interesting taste."

"It doesn't matter what I'm wearing. What matters is you're making a lot of noise and it's extremely early," I reply, as prickly heat claims my cheeks.

His lips twitch.

"And anyway, it's Delphine's robe. She's got a thing for cows. If you must know."

"But *you're* the one who's wearing it in my doorway."

I lock my jaw.

"Tell me something. Is this outfit your subtle way of asking me to call you Moo Moo?" he questions.

"What? Why would you do something like that? It's a comical dressing gown, Charlie. Seriously, get over it."

He takes a slow sip from his mug and then gestures at my chest. "It's just that's what it says: 'Love Moo Moo.' That's all. I assumed it was your subtle way of asking me to call you that nickname."

I lower my sight and notice the words "Love Moo Moo" embossed on the dressing gown.

Terrific, Delphine.

I lift my hand to my chest, hoping to hide the words. The damage is already done, of course. "I would prefer it if you refrained from commenting on my appearance, thank you," I retort. I smooth my hair behind my ears, wishing I was wearing something else—*anything* else. Why didn't I throw on some sweats like a normal person?

"Of course. My apologies." He gives a brief incline of his head. "Name preferences aside," he begins.

I interrupt with, "Kennedy. That's my name preference."

"Not Moo Moo?"

I glare at him. "Not Moo Moo."

"All right then. To what do I owe the pleasure, *Kennedy?*" he asks, his smooth-as-silk voice deep and very British in his upper-class way.

"It's no pleasure," I reply sweetly. "Not at this time of the morning. You are making a lot of unnecessary noise."

"I am?"

"Oh, yeah. It's loud and it's early and it's unreasonable. Plus, it's disturbing the entire building."

"Oh, you mean when I was moving the furniture just now? Look, I'm having the floorboards polished today and I needed to clear the space for them. You understand."

"Couldn't it have waited until after six, or better yet after seven?"

"Seven?" he repeats as though it's the most outlandish suggestion he's ever heard. "Seriously? Who's in bed at seven on a weekday?"

Uh, me? Particularly when I've been up past one writing an article.

I square my shoulders. "Seven is a completely reasonable time to still be in bed. I don't know why you wouldn't think it was."

"You're right. It is completely reasonable—"

I lift my brows in surprise. He's agreeing with me?

"—for people who don't have any commitments or a job to get to," he adds.

Right. He hadn't finished his sentence.

"I have commitments and a job," I huff.

"Of course you do."

"What does *that* mean?"

His smile spreads. "Nothing. Look, I had to move the furniture now because I've got to get to the gym before work. So, there's that." He shakes his head as though he's genuinely full of regret.

He's going to the gym. Figures. Without my brain giving me permission, I sweep my eyes over his outfit. His legs are long, muscular, and toned. His shirt is loose around his waist, and the thin material clings to his broad shoulders, showing the outline of his impressive pecs and hinting at taut abs beneath.

My belly flutters.

As I lift my eyes to his, the edges of his mouth are curved upwards in that characteristic smile of his. The way that tells me I'm an object for derision.

I clear my throat. "Your living room must be immediately above where I sleep. It's not at all considerate to make that level of noise so early in the morning. Even *you* have to admit that."

"Even me, eh?" His piercing blue eyes are dancing with amusement like they're in some kind of dance troupe. "Because you know me so very well."

I cross my arms. "I know enough about you to know your type."

"And what is my type, exactly?"

"I don't need to tell you your type. You already know."

"But I'd like to hear it from my new neighbor who's currently standing outside my door wearing a pair of udders."

Exasperated, I reply, "Enough with the robe already."

I itch to tell him what I think of him. That he's smug and arrogant and a total product of his privileged background. Of course, he won't be able to see it. None of them can. They're so wrapped up in their elite world of polo and country clubs and super yachts, they don't even notice the little people. People like me.

"Look, I'm asking you as a courtesy to your neighbors. Please refrain from making noise early in the morning. I was up late last night, and I need my sleep."

"In that case, would you have preferred it if I did it late at night when I got home from work instead?"

"I'd prefer you didn't do it at all, actually."

"You're saying you want the floor polishers to work around my furniture so I get unappealing, patchy floors? That doesn't seem at all reasonable to me. These people are here to do a job. Who am I to stand in their way?" He pauses before he adds, "Kennedy."

"I couldn't care less about your floors, *Charles*," I reply pointedly. Two can play *that* game.

His hand flies to his chest. "On behalf of my floors, I'm offended."

"No, you're not."

"How do you know I'm not?"

"Because you're a grown man and that would be weird. That's why not." I glare at him.

He takes a sip of his coffee, his eyes trained on me like we're in a staring competition, which I'm determined not to lose.

Mature, I know.

After a beat, he raises his free hand. "All right. I'm sorry to have disturbed you."

"The whole building," I correct.

He takes a step toward me and glances up and down the hallway. "Is that why everyone in the whole building is here with you? Because I disturbed *everyone*?"

I pinch my lips together. "Maybe they're too shy to come up and confront you."

"Have you *met* Barbara and the Ladies' Committee?"

He's got a point.

"You call them the Ladies' Committee?"

"Among other things. It depends on my mood."

"You see that attitude is why they don't like you."

"I thought it was because I don't go to their multiple monthly events."

"Well, that too. Still haven't been to their knitting circle, I assume?"

"What makes you say that?"

I allow my eyes to sweep over him once more. "You're not the knitting type."

"You're very quick to judge. Aren't you?"

"I don't need to judge. We both know you had no intention of ever going to go to their knitting circle."

He shrugs. "Think what you like."

"Oh, I will. You don't need to tell me. Just keep the noise down, please."

By now his face has creased into a full smile. "I'll do my best to move my furniture in silence in the future."

I lift my chin. "Thank you."

"You're welcome."

"Good. That's settled then."

He pushes his fingers through his hair. "Was there anything else? Because I've got to get going to the gym. My PT gets cranky if I'm late, and then he punishes me with extra burpees, and I'm sure you wouldn't want to be responsible for me having to do extra burpees."

An image flashes before my eyes. He's all hot and sweaty as he does a series of exercises, his muscles glistening, his body lithe.

I blink the image away.

I've got no business picturing Charlie Cavendish doing anything that makes him hot and sweaty.

"I didn't think so," he says smoothly.

"Of course not. I...thank you for that."

He presses his lips together to stifle a fresh smile. What is it with this guy and smiling? Am I really that amusing to him?

"Was there anything else?" he questions, when I don't move.

"No. Just the noise."

"Okay. Well, bye, Kennedy."

I nod, letting out a puff of air. "Yup. Bye."

I return to my flat. I got my message through. That's all that matters. And I've learned something very useful. Between working late and working out, he clearly doesn't have a life at all, and I, for one, am glad he's not going to any of the building's social events.

That way I'll never have to see the guy.

CHAPTER 7

I tape up the box and write 'Delphine's stuff' in permanent marker on the side. With my hands on my hips, I survey the room. Delphine left the place as though she'd gone out for the morning, the shelves filled with her ornaments and vases and books. This is the final box, which includes the large collection of ceramic cows on the mantelpiece above the fireplace.

I pick up the box and stack it on top of the others in the hallway closet, under those disturbing rows of Winnie the Pooh toys, to replace before she returns.

Although I have a fraction of what Delphine has, I've displayed my meager collection of possessions in the vacated spots: a snow globe from a trip to Stockholm Zara, Tabitha, Lottie and I went on last winter; a couple of Sophie Kinsella novels I bought when I first got to London; a blue and gold blown-glass vase I bought at Camden Market last summer that reminds me of the blue sea and golden sand of home; and a collection of photo frames, filled with shots of my friends and family, including one of me with my London besties standing next to Prince William and Kate

Middleton at Madame Tussauds' on one of Lottie's museum trips.

I let out a contented sigh. This place might be a whole lot fancier than I'm used to, but it's starting to feel like home.

I make myself a cup of herbal tea and plunk myself down on the sofa. I pull my phone out. Lady Moo is snoring peacefully in her dog bed by the fireplace, and I grab the chance of what feels like rare quiet with her, to catch up with my family.

I open my laptop and dial. A moment later, Mom's face appears on the screen. Well, part of her face. She never seems to know how to hold her phone when I videocall her. I should count myself lucky, though. Today she's clearly talking on her computer, so I can see her face from her eyes up, rather than an extreme closeup of her ear.

"Hi, sweetie. It's so good to see you," Mom declares.

"Mom. Lower your camera. It's too high."

"Like this?" she asks, as she adjusts it so I can see even less of her head.

"The other way, Mom."

"Okay. Give me a second."

I sit and wait as she adjusts her screen, until finally, I can see her whole face. It takes four tries. "You got it," I tell her. "What have you been up to?"

"I've been to visit your nana in the retirement village. She sends her love."

"How is Nana?"

"She's doing fine, sweetie. Super busy with all the activities they've got going on there. Movie nights and dinners. Retirement never looked so good. She can't wait to see you at Christmas. She made me promise to make traditional turkey this year with all the trimmings instead of my Mexican extravaganza I did last year. Apparently, turkey and cranberry fajitas isn't festive enough."

Mom is adventurous with food. She always has been. That doesn't mean she's a good cook, though, which is probably why Nana wants to avoid the Mexican disaster of last year.

"I've got good news on that front. I land at two-fifty in the afternoon on Christmas Eve. I'll send you my flight details."

"You'll be here in time for dinner with your Uncle Jim and Auntie Louisa. They'll have both the boys and their wives and kids back this year, and you'll never guess what just happened."

"What?"

"Susie got engaged to that nice Duncan Whatshisname. The one you knew in high school."

"Who's Duncan Whatshisname?"

"Brad and Jill's oldest."

"Oh, Duncan Chesterfield. They're getting married? Huh."

Another member of my family tying the knot, while I'm still single with not even a glimmer of a prospect on the horizon.

"June wedding next year. You'll have to come back for it."

"Of course."

"You'll be thirty by then. I can hardly believe it. My baby, a thirty-year-old woman."

"Don't remind me."

"I am so sad we won't see you on your birthday."

"It's not a big deal."

"Kennedy, you're turning thirty. That *is* a big deal."

I do an internal groan. Thirty, single, writing about things I don't care about, and dog-sitting a dog who massacres toy bears.

My life has turned out *exactly* as I'd planned.

"What are you doing for your birthday? I hope you're at least having a party? Of course, we'll dedicate the day after

Christmas to you when you're back home. I have a whole thing planned."

"Don't, Mom. I kinda wanna fly under the radar with this one."

"Oh, don't be silly. You've achieved so much in your life already and your dad and I are so proud of you. We want to celebrate our youngest daughter."

I smile despite myself. "You're the best. And don't worry, I'm gonna mark the day. I'm not sure what I'm gonna do. I'm thinking I'll spend it with my friends, drowning my age-related sorrows."

She laughs. "Wait until you're my age. You can drown your sorrows plenty when you're pushing sixty. Now, I thought of you last Sunday when I went to the Aldridge for lunch with Bree Green. You know, that super wealthy woman who sometimes volunteers at the shelter? Well, she suggested it and I thought, why not? I've only been there a couple of times before, and even though I know it's so fancy, I figured it'd be fun. We had the most delicious salmon and those new potatoes that taste like little balls of heaven. You know the ones. You worked there long enough. So delicious."

"You went to the Aldridge Country Club?" I ask, my heart rate rising.

"Yes, as I said. I...well, I might as well come out and say it."

"Say what?"

"I ran into Hugo. He was there with his wife, Fleur, and his parents."

My body tenses. "Oh."

"They asked about you."

"Who did? Hugo or his parents?"

"His mom, Genevieve, actually. She wanted to know all about your new London life, so I told her what a success you're making of things over there. She was impressed, sweetie. Real impressed."

I swallow, my throat dry. "That's nice."

"If I'm completely honest, I think it did Hugo some good to hear how well you've been doing since you broke up."

"Since he dumped me for Fleur because I wasn't from the 'right kind of family,' you mean." I try to keep the bitterness from my voice, but I know I fail. "Mom, you shouldn't be so nice to him. To any of them. They think they're better than us."

"I don't care what they think. I know my worth, and if Genevieve thought that she certainly didn't let on."

"Did she call you sweetheart?"

"Now that I think of it, yes, she did."

"What did she call Bree Saunders?"

"Well, 'Bree' of course."

"And the servers?"

There's silence as she thinks about it. "I can't remember," she replies, and I know she's bluffing.

My stomach twists in a knot. "She wasn't being nice, Mom. The only people Genevieve Carter calls 'sweetheart' are people she looks down on, like the help. She called me sweetheart for the first six months of my relationship with Hugo before he had to tell her I wasn't just a waitress; I was his girlfriend. She then switched to 'darling,' until we broke up. Then it was right back to 'sweetheart.'"

"Well, I'm not worried about it."

I smile, despite the sense of unease the memories evoke. Mom has always had a high degree of self-worth. It's something I admire about her. She knows who she is and she's good with it. She has never been dazzled by the Carters like I was. Their lifestyle, their expectations of life, their privilege.

But then, she was never in love with their son.

Lady Moo wakes up and stretches, doing downward dog

like a pro. Which figures. She spies me on the sofa and bounds across the floor on her little legs, then stops and stares at me.

"Mom, I think I might need to feed Lady Moo."

"I cannot believe you're looking after a dog named Lady Moo."

"I know, right?"

She bounces her front paws onto my leg, her tail wagging.

"She's actually kinda cute, even if she can be a bit crazy. I better go feed her. Send my love to Dad and I'll catch up with him soon, 'kay?"

"Of course. He's out in the garden putting a swinging chair together from a kit. It's a battle, that's for sure."

"Let's hope it's it. Bye, Mom. See you in a few weeks." I hang up and smile down at the dog. "Is it snack time, Lady Moo, is that what it is? Actually, you know what? I'm gonna call you Lady M. It has a hint of mystery to it, don't you think?"

All she does is wag her tiny tail at me, her skinny pink tongue sticking out of her mouth.

I pad across the floor to the kitchen, expecting Lady M to follow me. When she doesn't, I walk back to the hallway to see her bouncing up and down in front of the closet—the one filled with rows of Winnie the Poohs.

"I don't want to give you one of those. It feels wrong."

Her reply is to do a full three-sixty turn in the air, and land back on her feet as she emits a high, excited whine.

I pull the door open and gaze at the shelves filled with the stuffed toys peering out at me, a happy smile on their teddy bear faces. Lady M goes into overdrive at the prospect of getting one of the toys, twisting and turning and making the weirdest noises.

Really, I should be filming her for Instagram right now. It could go viral.

I reach for one of the toys and pull it off the shelf. It's soft to the touch, bare but for a little red T-shirt with the word "Pooh" embroidered on its chest. I glance down at the world's most excited dog, then back at the toy. "I can't do this to you, little bear. I just can't."

Without another word, I set the toy back on the shelf and close the door. Lady M whines and barks at me, demanding to know what I think I'm doing.

"You and I are gonna take a trip to the local pet store, Lady M. No more Winnie the Pooh for you."

I throw on my boots and my winter coat, slip one of Lady M's cow-patterned woolen sweaters on her—Delphine has really taken this whole cow thing too far—and head out the door. As we glide down in the elevator, I do a search on my phone for local pet stores. I find a couple within walking distance, and we make our way there, with Lady M stopping to sniff and pee and bark at things on the way.

We reach a line of stores two blocks away, including a pub, a mini-mart, and a couple of boutiques. The sign above the small pet store shouts *Pets! Pets! Pets!* and an old-fashioned bell chimes as I push my way inside. I'm immediately struck by the warmth and the smell of hay as Lady M strains on her leash to sniff out her new surrounds.

"Heel," I say to her, as she tries to bolt in the direction of a glass cabinet full of rabbits, almost pulling my shoulder out of its socket.

She doesn't listen.

Instead, she tries again and again, jerking my arm with each attempt. First, it's the rabbits, then it's the dog food, and then it's some poor, unsuspecting customer who I had to apologize to when she got scared. I tighten the leash, but it doesn't deter her.

I have no choice but to pick her up and hold her firmly against me.

A man with graying hair and a friendly, smiling face sidles up to me. "How can I help you...Oh." His eyes land on Lady Moo, poking her head out from my firm *you're not getting anywhere near those rabbits* grip. "Is that who I think it is?"

Is Lady M famous? It must be from Delphine's YouTube channel.

I should have grabbed a hat and pair of sunglasses for her before we left the house. Keep her incognito.

I smile at the thought.

"I guess that depends on who you think she is," I reply with a light laugh.

"She's Lady Moo. Isn't she?" he replies, watching her warily.

"That's right, but don't tell anyone else, okay? I want to keep this outing on the downlow. You know: fans."

"Fans?"

"From Delphine's channel?"

"I don't know anything about a channel, but you can't bring that dog in here, love. She's banned. That's what she is. Banned for life."

"So, she's not famous?"

"More like infamous."

I blink at Lady M. She's given up wriggling in my arms and has chosen instead to stare at the man, a low growl emitting from her mouth with every short breath.

"Now, leave. Both of you." He makes a shooing gesture at us.

"Are you serious?" I only half joke, because who's ever heard of a little dog being banned from a pet store?

"You'd better believe it, missy," he sniffs.

"But...but all I want is a chew toy for her, to stop her from destroying the Winnie the Poohs because it really freaks me out," I protest, possibly giving the guy too much information.

His features soften a fraction. "She's still doing that, is she?"

I nod.

"Where's her owner? The dippy one with the cow obsession."

I stifle a giggle. That sums Delphine up perfectly. "She's away for six months and I'm dog-sitting Lady M here. I'm kinda new to this."

He sizes me up before he replies, "All right. As long as you hold on to her, you can have a quick look-see. They're over 'ere."

"Thank you so much," I gush, relieved I get to find a toy to replace poor Pooh.

He leads me to the dog chew toy section, and I pick up an appropriately sized toy—a rubber duck with a huge grin—and offer it to Lady M. She turns her little black nose up at it. Literally. I try another. This time it's a fluffy yellow hippo wearing a basketball hat. Again, her nose is lifted.

This process continues until I've been through every small dog chew toy in the store.

The man comes up behind me. "You almost done 'ere? 'Cos I've got a couple of dogs over by the fish tanks and I don't want no trouble."

"I'm not having any luck. She doesn't like any of these."

"That's because she's the devil dog," he states as though this outlandish statement is a commonly held fact.

"Lady M isn't the devil dog," I reply with a surprise laugh, offended. "She's just feisty and has a weird penchant for one particular bear. That's all." I raise my chin in defense of the little dog in my arms and sniff, "She's misunderstood."

He snort-laughs. He doesn't mean it nicely.

He glances over his shoulder and then leans in toward

me. "Look, missy, buy something or leave. I need to keep me other customers happy. Know wha' I mean?" He eyes Lady M, held firmly in my arms. "She's un unpredictable bitch, that one."

He's calling Lady M a bitch? I mean, I know technically it's the correct use of the term, what with her being a female dog and all. But I'm offended on her behalf all the same.

Lady M's growl increases in volume.

"She doesn't like anything here, anyway, so I guess we'll leave," I sniff.

"The right choice."

I stride out of the store and back into the cold winter air. It's begun to snow, and light flakes are floating down around me. With the Christmas lights and festive store windows, it's magical, and as I put Lady M back on the sidewalk and we begin to make our way to the next pet store, my spirits lift—despite learning my new canine charge has been banned from a store for being "the devil dog."

I'll unpack that later.

A few blocks' walk through the cool wind and snow, and we reach the next store. We go through the same process: me offering every chew toy in the store, Lady M turning her little black nose up at them all as she shoots me a look that says *get that thing away from me*.

When a woman in a bright green, long-sleeve T-shirt with the words *My dog thinks I'm cool* spots us and asks if my dog is Lady Moo, with concern etched on her face, I already know how this is going to play out.

I carry the growling dog out of the store.

Admitting defeat, we trudge back through the snow toward home.

"You have quite the reputation, Lady M," I tell her, as she trots along beside me as though she hasn't been blacklisted by every pet store in Notting Hill.

We've just walked across the street toward our building when I notice the front door swing open and none other than Charlie Cavendish step outside.

Oh, great.

I do not want to see that guy right now. Or at any time.

But it's too late.

As he walks down the stairs and onto the sidewalk, his eyes land on me, and I watch as they widen in surprise. He glances down at Lady M at my side, and then back up to me, his face creasing into a smile.

"Hello, neighbor," he says.

"Hey," I reply through gritted teeth, as I try not to notice how good he looks wearing his suit and expensive looking overcoat, his stubble emphasizing the squareness of his jaw. The blue of the scarf draped around his neck brings out the color of his eyes.

My tummy does a weird little flip.

I ignore it studiously.

"No udders today?"

I shoot him a look. "Clearly."

"Pity," he replies, with a smirk on his face. "How are you settling into your new place?" he asks me, as though my well-being is of any interest to him. Which we both know it's not.

"Fine, thanks," I reply pleasantly and begin to move past him—and put an end to this conversation, *STAT*.

"Are you and the dog getting on well?" he asks.

I stop and turn to look back at him. "Of course. Lady M is an angel," I bluff, pushing the whole *banned from local pet stores slash devil dog* thing from my mind.

"You're an angel, are you?" He leans down and pets Lady M, who wags her short tail in glee.

Canine traitor.

He straightens back up and fixes me with those intense eyes of his. "Well, I'll leave you to it. I have a plane to catch."

"Where are you going? Nowhere too far away, I hope." My tone oozes sarcasm. I'm not proud.

He lets out a low laugh. "I'm going to Vienna, Berlin, and then onto Dubrovnik. So not too far, no."

"Wow, that sounds amazing," I reply before I can stop myself.

Living in London has meant it's been so much easier for me to travel to the famous European cities on my bucket list. So far, I've been to Paris, Barcelona, Dublin, and Stockholm, but there are so many more places I want to visit. My list may be big, but my bank account is not, so it's a work in progress for me.

One city at a time.

His face lights up. "You like to travel?" he asks me.

I do a thumb gesture at myself. "Duh. American in London?"

"Of course. Your whole life is a travel adventure right now."

"Well, I wouldn't put it quite like that."

"But you're from San Diego, and you're living here in London, a city thousands of miles from your home. That must be an adventure."

I shrug. It is an adventure, and one I am absolutely relishing, but I'm not going to tell him that. "Sure. I guess."

"You guess?" he asks. "You get to discover a new city and all its secrets. That's pretty exciting in my book."

"It's okay," I reply noncommittally, my tone purposefully flat.

"What's your favorite city you've visited?"

"Paris."

"Oh, I can see why. The Seine, the architecture, the food and wine. The sheer romance of the place. It's the whole city package, in my opinion."

I open my mouth to respond and then close it again. Paris

is all those things. The words may have come from his lips, but they are my sentiment exactly.

"You know, I went to this incredible restaurant there recently, just near my hotel. It was in the Latin Quarter on one of those small, cobbled streets." He gets a faraway look in his eyes as he speaks, his face bright. "Totally charming and Gaelic. The food was out of this world, of course, and afterwards, I walked along the Seine as lovers strolled arm in arm, music playing, the evening air so much warmer than here."

I smile at the image. It was like that when I visited, too, and I remember thinking how wonderful it would be to spend time in the city with someone I was in love with someday. "Sounds romantic."

"Well, as romantic as it can be when you're there on your own, I suppose," he replies with a self-deprecating laugh. "I was there for work, so…"

The word "so" hangs in the air between us.

The idea of him eating alone in the most romantic city in the world strikes me as so very sad.

Without my permission, I find my heart squeezing for him.

Nope. I'm not going to feel sorry for Charlie Cavendish. He's rich and arrogant and smarmy.

"Right. Not so romantic then," I reply.

"It was still special. Funny, we've found something we have in common, Kennedy."

"Paris? Right."

"Isn't there a famous movie line about that?"

"*Casablanca*. 'We'll always have Paris.' Humphrey Bogart to Ingrid Bergman."

His face creases into a smile, and I find myself smiling back at him. "I love that movie." With his eyes still on me, his features soften, and I'm struck by the depth of color in his eyes, and the frown lines forming an eleven between his brows.

I clear my throat, breaking whatever moment it is we're having here.

This is Charlie Cavendish, the guy who looks down on me from a great height. I don't want to go having any moments with the guy.

"Don't you have a flight to catch?" I ask him.

"My flight. Of course. I must get going."

"Have fun."

"It's work. It won't be fun."

"Working in Vienna, Berlin, and Dubrovnik doesn't sound too shabby to me. I guess you can at least get your fill of Wiener Schnitzel and apple strudel while you're there. Maybe buy a pair of lederhosen?"

He laughs. The sound is low and rumbling and warms my belly. "I think I could really rock some lederhosen."

My laugh ends in a snort before I catch myself. "I'm sure you could."

"What should I get you in Dubrovnik?"

I pull my brows together. "You don't have to get me anything."

"I'd like to."

Weird.

"Okay," I concede. "What do they have in Dubrovnik?"

"A lot of things. How about I bring you back some Arancini?"

"What's that?"

"Candied lemon peel. It's a Croatian sweet."

"Really, you don't have to."

"I'd like to. I can bring a little part of Croatia to you, my travel-loving neighbor."

"Ok*aaa*y," I reply uncertainly. "But…why?"

He flashes me his grin. "Why not?" he asks. "Take it as an apology for disturbing your sleep the other morning."

I regard him through narrowed eyes, taken aback. Charlie Cavendish is apologizing to me? Well, that's one for the books.

He glances at his wristwatch, and I notice it's a Rolex. Of course. Looking back at me, he says, "It was a pleasure to see you again."

I bite my lip. "Yup. Have a good trip."

His gaze lingers on me for a beat before he says, "Good bye, Kennedy," turns on his heel, and walks away.

I watch him make his way down the street, discomfited. Charlie Cavendish mocking me and being rude is what I expect. But buying me foreign candy as an apology and bonding with me over our common love of travel is a whole other thing. A thing that doesn't fit with my image of who the man is.

I push it to the side. He's a smug, privileged man who looks down his nose on the likes of me. The last thing I want to do is bond with a guy like that. Or worse yet, *feel* something for him.

Wait, what? Me, having feelings for Charlie Cavendish?

No way. Uh-uh.

Never.

Gonnna.

Happen.

I lift my eyes to his receding figure. To my surprise, he looks back at me over his shoulder and holds my gaze for a beat, maybe two, before he flashes his smile and disappears around the corner.

And before I even know what's happening, my belly flutters.

CHAPTER 8

"This place looks like a normal, everyday restaurant to me," Tabitha says as we take our seats on a hard bench at the long, chunky wooden table.

Lottie peruses the black leatherbound menu. "It's meant to be amazing food here, as well as entertaining."

"What's the haps for tonight, Kennedy? You're the one writing the article on this place, Ms. Single American Girl, so tell us what you need us to eat and drink," Tabitha says.

Lottie consults her menu. "I know what I'm having already. I'm starting with a *Coppélia*."

"What's a *Coppélia*?" I ask, as I flip my own menu open.

"It's some sort of drink. I just love that it's named after the ballet *Coppélia*."

Tabitha shakes her head. "You are such a romantic, Lottie. Why not choose a drink based on what you actually want to drink, rather than on the name?"

She shrugs. "Where's the fun in that?"

I scan the drinks list. "Look at all these names for their drinks. They're all from ballets, right? Odette from *Swan*

Lake, Cinderella from, well *Cinderella*, Prince Desirée, Giselle, Romeo."

"Ooh, the Sugar Plum Fairy looks nice, and very festive," Zara exclaims.

"Each night's entertainment is supposed to compliment the menu, and they have different themes for each night of the week," I explain. "I read online that tonight is the *Ballet de Fureur*. Whatever that means."

"The Fuhrer? As in Hitler?" Lottie asks, aghast. "I don't like the sound of that. I'm not sure I can take goose steps and hail this and hail that while I'm trying to digest."

Tabitha shoots her a sardonic smile. *"That's* what you don't like about it?"

"It's spelt f-u-r-e-u-r. I think it's French," I explain.

"Ooh, I did French at school," Zara tells us. *"Fureur* means something like...furry, I think. Yes, I'm pretty sure that's right. Maybe it's a furry animal ballet?"

"That would be hilarious," Tabitha says.

I shrug. "I'm not sure I want to eat my dinner with a bunch of woodland creatures dancing around us, but it is what it is."

A normally-dressed server in a white shirt and black pants arrives at our table, and we place our drink orders: an Odette for Lottie, a Sugar Plum Fairy for Zara, a Prince Desirée for Tabitha, and I order a Giselle, mainly because the review I read online said it tastes like a gin and tonic and I'm not feeling overly adventurous in the drinks department tonight.

"How's the new place?" Tabitha asks me.

"It's awesome. I love living there. It's so spacious and comfortable and unbelievably quiet."

"And there's no Candice," Zara adds.

"Exactly. No Candice means my life is so much less

complicated, and there's zero chance of waking up to some randos sleeping on my floor."

The server delivers our drinks, and we take our first sips.

"Oh, that's delicious. Here, try mine." Lottie offers Zara her drink, and we all take a sip of our own before we pass them around the table. The drinks are sweet and tasty, the Sugar Plum Fairy easily the sickliest.

"How's the crazy dog?" Tabitha asks, as she takes her original drink back.

"Cute but weird. She continues to massacre the poor Winnie the Poohs, even though I took her to some pet stores to find her something less unsettling to chew on."

Tabitha gives a flick of her wrist. "You'll be fine. You've got a whole cupboard full of them."

"One time, before I had the wherewithal to remove the eyes before I let Lady M have her way with it, I had to scoop them out of her poop." I shudder.

Zara makes a face. "Ugh."

"You're so weird the way you don't want to have to fish eyes out of dog poop," Tabitha says, her eyes dancing with mischief.

Lottie grins. "So weird."

"I can recommend some great dog toys," Zara says. "Ones that she can chew on until the cows come home."

"Was that a joke?" Tabitha asks.

"No."

"Lady Moo? Cow?" Tabitha leads.

Zara giggles. "Ha! I hadn't thought about that. Totally intentional. Kennedy, I'll take you to Penelope's Pooches."

"The place you got Stevie from?" I ask, referring to her Jack Russell puppy. "Aren't they certifiable in there?"

Zara shrugs. "Yeah, but they've got the best stuff."

The server arrives back at the table and informs us that the evening's entertainment is about to begin, so we need to put in our dinner order. A quick skim of the menu and we've all ordered dishes called A Nutcracker, Sylphide, and Don Quixote, all of which we are informed are names of famous ballets.

"I can't believe your new job is to get to go to these places, eat for free, then write about them," Zara says.

"You know what? I didn't like the idea all that much to start with, especially since it means I can't pursue the more serious topics I'm interested in. But now that I'm here," I look around the room with its black walls, minimalist decorations, and soft lighting, "I'm starting to get on board with the whole thing."

"What's not to love? London has so many exciting restaurants and bars and clubs and you get to go to a stack of them on the company ticket. You'll have a ball, babe," Zara tells me.

"And you have to bring us to all of them. No excuses," Tabitha adds.

I grin at my friends. "Of course. It wouldn't be as fun without you girls."

"What about Charlie Cavendish?" Lottie asks, once our meals have been delivered to our table.

"What about him?" I reply in my breeziest voice.

"Have you seen him since your first night?"

"Twice."

"And?" she leads.

"He was making noise early one morning and woke me up. I had to go tell him to keep it down." I don't mention the cow robe attire. "And then I bumped into him with Lady M the other day. He was…weird."

"Weird how?" Lottie asks.

"He told me he's gonna bring me back some candy from Croatia as an apology for having woken me up."

"That's so nice of him," Lottie declares.

Zara raises her eyebrows at me. "Did he, now?" She shares a look with our friends.

"What?" I question. "It's just candy."

Tabitha gives a slow nod, her lips pressed together. "Candy. Right."

"He owes me that apology. He woke me up super early," I tell them.

"He could have just said 'sorry,'" Tabitha points out, and I know she's right.

Why *is* he buying me Croatian candy?

"I think it's sweet of him," Lottie declares. "He's showing you he's not the condescending plonker you thought he was when you first met."

"He's still a condescending plonker," I reply, using the unfamiliar British term. "And by 'plonker' I assume you mean jerk. He laughed at my outfit the other day. It was very rude of him."

"What were you wearing?" Tabitha asks.

"A plain bath robe," I fib.

"What's to laugh about with a plain dressing gown?" Tabitha questions.

I think better of lying to my friends. "Okay, it was Delphine's robe and it had a cow pattern on it with some padded udders."

My friends laugh.

"Udders?" Tabitha questions. "Anyone would laugh at that, babe."

"Yeah. You can hardly blame the guy," Zara says.

I let out a puff of air. "I guess. But I still don't like him."

I really don't need my friends teasing me about a guy I've got an ill-advised attraction to, a guy I'm supposed to hate. Because I do hate him. He's Charlie Smug Cavendish, the person who looks down on me with that smarmy smirk of his, finding me and my life endlessly amusing. He's the king, laughing at the poor peasant, the great unwashed.

"Did you know everyone in the building hates him? They all know what an arrogant jerk he is, too." I load my fork up with a slice of roast beef and Yorkshire pudding, the perfect British roast.

"They don't hate him. He just hasn't put in an effort with them, and they've taken offence. That's all," Lottie replies. "Gertie told me all about it at your welcome party. Charlie has promised to go to their events."

"Good for him," I deadpan.

Tabitha leans back in her chair, her eyes on me. "Personally, methinks the lady doth protest too much."

"We're talking like we're from Shakespeare's time now, are we?" I question. "Because that sounds like fun." I put my hand over my heart and say, "Romeo, oh Romeo. Wherefore art thou, Romeo?"

Tabitha raises her brows at me as though I'm being a child she has to tolerate. "Don't change the subject. You know what I mean."

"I'm not 'doth protesting too much.' All I'm saying is other people in the building agree with my perspective on the guy. That's all."

"Uh-huh," Tabitha replies, unconvinced. She shares a look with Lottie and Zara.

What is it with my friends? Can't a girl hate a guy for the very good reason that he was arrogant and rude to her on their blind date and not think there's some unspoken attraction for him?

Sure, I do think he's hot, but anyone would. He's tall and broad, and with the muscular forearms the Ducks were pawing the other night, he's clearly no stranger to the gym. Then there are those Bradley Cooper eyes of his, that I'm sure have made many a female heart flutter. Not mine. No way. They're probably colored contact lenses, anyway. The cheat.

But a guy can be handsome and sexy and all those things and I can feel...*things* for him and he can still be a complete jerk. More so, in fact.

"Look, there's nothing between me and Charlie Cavendish and there never will be," I protest.

Tabitha smiles at me. "Of course not."

"Absolutely," Lottie agrees.

"Mmm-hmm." This from Zara. "You're going to keep running into him, you know. It's unavoidable when the guy lives in the same building as you."

I push out a breath. "I'll smile and say hello and carry on with my business, just as I'm sure he will. Now, let's drop it, 'kay?"

"Okay."

"Speaking of carrying on with your business, I've got a great idea for your birthday," Zara says.

"You want to talk about me getting old, now? How cruel can you be?" I ask with a laugh.

"We're all hitting thirty. Some of us are already there, right Zara?" Lottie says.

"It's not so bad," she tells us.

"Says the girl who runs a super successful business and is in love with a great guy," I reply.

"Lottie and I are both single and pushing thirty, and we're okay about it. Right, Lottie?" Tabitha asks.

"Right. Although, having a husband would definitely get my mom off my back."

"She's still giving you a hard time?" Tabitha asks.

"I'm letting the whole family down by not giving her grandchildren, apparently."

Tabitha makes a face. "Your mum is the worst."

"Can I tell you my idea for Kennedy's birthday?" Zara questions.

I chew on my lip. "Look, I don't want some big fancy party. Not like yours, Zee. Low key, easy. That's more my jam."

"I know. I'd thought we could go to your new local. We could all get dressed up and check out the talent for you."

I cock an eyebrow at her. "You want me to find a man at my local pub on my thirtieth?" I think of the pub a street across from my new place with its green tiles and Christmas lights in the window. It's called The Black Cat and has a cute wooden sign hanging out over the street, complete with a drawing of a black cat with a smile on its face. It looks welcoming in that quaint and charming British pub way I've grown to love while living here.

Zara lifts her shoulders, her hands palm up. "Why not? It's as a good a time as any," she replies. "And besides, if you meet a nice guy at your new local, he's likely to live in the neighborhood, which makes it easier to date."

"Which makes him harder to avoid when you break up," Tabitha adds.

"What do you mean? Kennedy might never break up with him. He might be her Big Love," Zara quips.

"He might not be, too," Tabitha replies.

"How do you know?"

"I don't. All I'm saying is, don't be too optimistic about her meeting some hot guy at her local."

"What's wrong with being optimistic?"

Tabitha taps her chin. "Where do I begin?"

"You're so cynical, Tabitha."

"I'm a realist."

I flick my eyes between my sparring friends. "You do realize you two are arguing over a fictitious guy?"

"Yes," they both reply.

"Kennedy, do you like the idea of having your birthday party at your new local pub? Hot local guy or not," Lottie asks.

"I'll check it out," Zara offers. "Asher and I can be the scouting party." As the final word leaves her mouth, there's a deafening crash of cymbals from over by the entrance, and we all look up, startled.

"What the—?" Zara mutters.

"I nearly choked on my gnocchi," Tabitha complains.

Classical music begins to play, and I lean closer to my friends. "This must be the furry creature ballet. I'm excited about this. I bet it's super cute."

We sit in expectation as a beautiful ballerina in a lilac-colored tutu, a wreath of lavender in her hair, dances into the room. She moves through the tables to *oohs* and *aaahs* from the assembled diners until she reaches a small stage near our table. She leaps elegantly up onto it and lands as soft as a mouse, and then proceeds to twirl and pirouette and plié and generally do all the things my ballet teacher Madam Wasillew tried and failed to get me to do with any grace when I was seven years old. She's absolutely beautiful to watch, and we happily munch on our meals as another ballerina and then another and another arrive and join in the perfectly synchronized dance.

"This is so pretty," I say to my friends. "I am so glad we came."

"Imagine being able to dance like that," Lottie says wistfully.

"I know, right? Gorgeous," I agree.

"I wonder when the furry creatures are going to arrive? I bet they'll be so cute," Zara tells us.

Just as I've taken a sip of my drink, the music comes to a sudden stop and the dancers turn to face one another. "Maybe the furry dancers are about to turn up?"

Lottie grins. "I hope so."

We watch as the ballerinas' body language changes. They hunch their shoulders and stomp their slipper-ed feet as they glare at one another like a collection of starved Sumo wrestlers.

And then, the one dressed in lilac lets out a blood-curdling scream. It comes as such a shock, I spit my drink out over the table.

My friends and I dart concerned looks at one another.

"What's going on?" Lottie whispers once the scream stops and we're thrown into surprised silence.

"I don't know, but I'm not sure I like where things are heading," I reply.

The blissful silence in the room doesn't last. Soon enough, all four ballerinas are yelling at one another, stomping around in circles as though they're about to attack, *Cobra Kai* style. The lilac one stomps her foot like an angry bull and then yells something in what sounds like a completely made-up language before the ballerina in yellow darts between the tables, yelling back at her. The music starts up, a frenetic classical piece, as the ballerinas run around the restaurant, ducking and diving between tables, yelling and screaming at one another.

"This is beyond weird," Tabitha exclaims. "I need another drink. Anyone else?" She waves the server over, who is now wearing a pair of pale blue fluffy earmuffs.

Smart girl.

"What can I get you?" she asks over the noise and lifts one of the earmuffs to hear our reply.

One of the ballerinas crashes into her, and the server rights herself and smiles at us as though this is all in a days' work.

Which I guess it probably is.

"Another round, please," Tabitha says as she pastes on a

smile as the yellow ballerina yells loudly beside us. "And make it quick."

Yellow Ballerina grabs another by the bun and wrenches it in a classic wrestling move, eliciting another ear-piercing scream.

Really, the whole thing is quite delightful.

And then, blissfully, the music changes to the soothing sounds of earlier, and the ballerinas stop their shrill yelling and bun-grabbing and instead begin to dance, gliding through the restaurant elegantly and effortlessly, as though they hadn't just gone all WWE on each other only moments ago.

"What the heck just happened?" Tabitha says, her mouth gaping as they dance toward the exit and disappear from the room.

"I know, right? That was just so unexpected," I reply.

"Unexpected and totally, totally crazy," Lottie agrees.

"I thought you said this was going to be cute woodland creatures," Zara complains. "I want cute woodland creatures."

I shake my head. "I never said that."

Zara flicks through her phone and then looks up at us. "Sorry girls. I put you wrong. *Fureur* means fury, not furry. One wrong letter and we get that."

"So, these were furious ballerinas?" Lottie asks.

"They sure seemed like it to me," I reply.

"Did you know this was going to happen?" Zara asks me, and I shake my head.

"I'm so glad we were here for it. My night feels complete, because I really did wonder what was missing. Now I know it was missing crazy-angry ballerinas," Tabitha says and as her eyes flick to mine, we begin to giggle.

Before long, Zara and Lottie join in, and we melt into laughter together, marvelling at the absurdity of what we just witnessed.

"That ear-piercing screaming!" Tabitha declares with a shake of her head.

"The bun grabbing!" Zara adds, incredulous.

"What about how the pink one got a hold of the yellow one's tutu and ripped off a chunk? I'm not sure that was in the choreography," I reply.

By the time we finished our next round of drinks, a man in a penguin suit—as in a tux, not a guy dressed up as a creature, unfortunately—has explained that we have witnessed the angry ballerinas and thanks us for coming tonight.

I leave knowing I've got a great topic for my first *Single American Girl in London* column, and have had an experience I need never repeat.

CHAPTER 9

As I arrive at the office, I say good morning to the magazine receptionist as I make my way through the office to my desk. I stayed up late last night to write my article, and now I wish I'd managed to grab more than just a handful of hours' sleep before I have to face Edina.

"Hey, Shelley," I say, as I stroll past her and into my cubicle.

"How's it going?" she asks me in her cute Kiwi accent, as she sidles around our partition and leans up against my desk. "Ooh, you look tired. What's his name?"

"There's no guy. I went out to this insane place last night and I was up half the night writing an article about it. Edina wants to see the first draft today."

"What was insane about it?"

"Don't ask." I rise to my feet, my notepad and pen in hand. "Wish me luck."

"Into the lioness's den, huh?"

"Are you gonna tell me she's really a pussycat in disguise?"

Shelley shakes her head. "Nope. She's a lioness for sure. She told me to completely rewrite my article on lipstick trends to 'be more blue sky.'" She uses air quotes with her fingers. "What the heck is blue sky lipstick?"

I chuckle, anxiety darting around my belly like a paper plane in a wind tunnel. "I have no idea. Coffee after?"

"You're gonna need it."

As I walk away, my phone beeps with a message.

Kennedy dear. You must come to the Christmas potluck dinner on Friday at 7 at Maude's flat. Everyone will be there! You can bring a festive pudding. Make it something decadent that we'll all regret eating immediately afterwards. Flat 4b. Sincerely, Barbara.

I smile to myself. I love the way she signed off a text message with "Sincerely, Barbara." It's so *not* my generation. Seeing the Ducks again—this time when I'm prepared for them—will be fun, and the fact I'm sure Charlie won't be there means it'll be a stress-free evening. Well, as stress-free as it can be while being interrogated by a group of nosy neighbors that is.

I tap out a quick reply.

I'd love to come. See you then with a festive pudding in tow!

I resist the urge to sign it "Sincerely, Kennedy," and instead hit send.

I take the short walk across the floor to Edina's office and knock on her closed door.

"Come in!" she calls, and I push the door open to see Jodi from the social media department dabbing at her eyes with a tissue, her face pink and blotchy.

"Oh, sorry. I'll come back later," I say, backing out of the room.

"It's fine, fine, fine," Edina replies brightly. "Jodi here is just leaving."

I shoot Jodi a sharp look. Leaving as in leaving the magazine? Surely not. She rises to her feet and offers me a watery smile as she turns to leave.

"You okay?" I ask her under my breath.

NEVER FALL FOR YOUR ENEMY

She shakes her head and rushes from the room, leaving me and a smiling Edina alone.

Worry spreads across my chest. Has Jodi just been fired?

"Close the door, will you?" Edina instructs.

"Sure." I pull the door closed behind me. "Is everything okay? It looks like Jodi is upset and I thought you'd done all your reorganizing already."

"She's fine," is her evasive response, and I instantly regret coming across as nosy.

"Now, Kennedy Bennet." She sits back down behind her large desk. "I do like that name of yours. It's very...something."

"Jane Austen?" I offer.

Her mouth forms an "O." "That's it! You sound like you're from an Austen novel. Kennedy Bennet. Kennedy Bennet. I'm going to use your full name always."

"Okay," I reply, because what else can I say? "I'm pretty sure my name was half the reason why my sister signed me up for the *Dating Mr. Darcy* reality show. I think she thought fate would intervene."

"Did it?"

"No."

Her eyebrows lift to her hairline. "So, you were on the reality TV show with that sexy aristocrat?"

"Sebastian. I was one of the final five on the show."

"Have you written about that for the magazine?"

"No. Sandra wanted me on harder-hitting stuff."

She harrumphs. "What could be harder-hitting than an exposé on reality TV by a contestant who has lived it?"

Errr, a lot of things? Off the top of my head: the Me Too *movement, what's happening in Afghanistan, the environment...*

But keeping my job is the goal here.

"I'd be happy to write something if you want."

She flicks her wrist. "Let's keep that in the back pocket.

What do you have for me today? Time is a luxury, a seven-star hotel, a Michelin-star restaurant."

"I sent you the first draft of my article last night. I've got a copy of it here if you haven't had the chance to see it?" I offer her the printed copy and she takes it from me and begins to read.

I stand on the other side of her desk, chewing nervously on my lip.

"Yup…okay….interesting…oh, no she didn't…oh, no she didn't!... uh-huh…hmmm." She pulls one of the metal balls she has hanging from a frame on her desk, and they start to ricochet off one another, making a clanking noise every few seconds.

She slaps the article down on the desk, rises to her feet and plods over to look out the window.

"Everything okay, Edina?"

She turns back to me. "I like it, Kennedy, really I do. The ballerinas are hilarious. Did they really attack one another?" she asks, but it's clearly rhetorical. "Because that is amazing. Novelty dining is so freaking interesting. Who are the performers? Who goes to these places? Why do they go there?"

"Exactly. I can do a whole thing on London novelty dining experiences if you want. There are tons of them."

She claps her hands together, her eyes bright. "Yes!" Her features drop. "But you know what? This?" she picks my article up off her desk and waves it in the air. "This I do not love."

Back up the bus. What? I thought she loved it a second ago?

"Ok*aaay*."

She taps her chin, her mouth twisted. "It's missing something. It needs an angle. Do you know what I mean? It's like a loaf of bread that's got all the ingredients, but it still tastes like sawdust."

"Sawdust?" I make a face. That cannot be good. "I'm sure I can rewrite it, maybe add in some color somewhere? If you don't like my angle, I'd be happy to revisit it, although I do think my take on subverting the traditional passive female role plays out nicely in the piece."

"I'm not feeling it. And I need to feel it in here." She slaps her chest rapidly with her palm.

"But they're ballerinas. Totally femme. Like, as femme as you can get. And they're *fighting*. Do you see? It turns the female stereotype on its head."

Personally, I think my angle is brilliant. Edina's clearly not so convinced.

She scrunches up her nose and returns to flicking those dang balls on a string. After a few clunks, she suddenly exclaims, "I've got it!"

"You have?"

"Oh, yeah." Her grin claims her face. "I'm thinking *Sex in the City*. I'm thinking *Emily in Paris*. I'm thinking *Love Island* singles looking for love."

"*Love Island*? In London?"

"Why not? It's sexy, it's now, it's hot, hot."

"But it's also winter. With all due respect, I can't spend my time flouncing about in a bikini. I'll get hypothermia." I'm joking, of course, but part of me is seriously concerned this is the direction she's going in.

"You are gonna love where I'm taking this. You're single. You like to date, right?"

"I guess," I reply uncertainly.

"Do you date guys?"

"Well, yes, but—"

"Find men! Go out with them! Write about the dates!

What's it like to be all alone and single at Christmas time, and how can you fill that void?"

Is she serious right now?

I shift my weight, uncomfortable. "It's not a *void*, exactly."

She ignores me. "I want you on the apps. I want you out there." She gestures out the window like I'm some kind of superhero who can fly out of windows fourteen stories off the ground. "I want you meeting men, meeting dates, meeting potential lovers."

I swallow. Lovers? *Ugh*.

"Go to these hip, unusual, new places, report on them, tell us what's hot right now, but go to them all on dates. Blind dates. Yes! Tell us what it's like to go to the hot new place with a guy you've never met before. *That* is an angle. A double whammy. A twofer one. We can call it Blind Dating London. Are you feeling it?"

Uh, no?

"I guess," I reply, but she's not interested in my half-hearted response.

"Blind Dating London. It's got that x-factor, you know? It's not just regular dating. Anyone can to *that*. It's blind dating with all its potential, all its expectation, all its gooey, oozy excitement."

Gooey and oozy excitement does not sound good to me, particularly when it comes to blind dates.

"We'll do regular articles online as well as one designed for print. That way you can really hit this hard." She slaps her desk to make her point. "This is the angle. This is what was missing. Aren't you just *loving* this?"

Loving this isn't quite what I'm doing right now.

"Can I ask a question?"

"Absolutely." She waves her hand as though she's being magnanimous in her generosity to allow me to ask anything.

"Are you saying you want me to write more of a relationship column now? Because I'm not sure that's in my wheelhouse. I mean, I've never written about relationships before."

"It's only an angle, a layer, a frame of reference."

"So, it's still an article about what's hot in London right now?"

"Exactly, only it's got an extra sexy sizzle to it, you know? You can start straight away. What's next on your list?"

I glance down at my list of potential places to visit that I compiled with help from my good friend, Google. "A *Game of Thrones* themed restaurant where you sit in a castle-like room and White Walkers serve you."

"B*ooo*oring," she trills. "So a few years ago, even if Jon Snow could rock my world anytime he wanted."

Dang it, that was my best one.

I move on. "How about we go festive, what with it being Christmas time. I'm thinking ice skating at Somerset House, followed by crepes from the French cart."

"That's been done." She waves her hand in a dismissive gesture. "Next?"

"Visit the Winter Wonderland in Hyde Park?"

She drums her fingers on her desk. "Next."

"A tour bus of all the Christmas lights?"

She shoots me an *are you serious?* look.

Increasingly desperate to land on something that she'll like, I move to the less Christmas and more outlandish end of the spectrum. "There's a *Rocky Horror Picture Show* night club called Rocky's where you get dressed up like the characters from the show and dance to the songs."

"Who would you dress up as?"

Heartened by the fact she's showing at least a hint of interest, I search my mind wildly for a character from the show. I've never seen the movie, so it's a near impossible task.

I take a stab in the dark. "The sexy girl?" I hold my breath.

Her face lights up and I know I've got her. "I love it. Kennedy Bennet, it's perfect. Go get sexy and go out on your first blind date to Rocky's."

"Sure, I'll—" I begin.

"Tonight!"

I open my mouth to protest, but there's no point. I know she's set on this. And having witnessed Jodi most likely being summarily fired only moments ago, the last thing I want to do is refuse Edina.

I need this job.

"When do you want the article?"

"Thursday morning good for you?"

"In two days' time? Sure."

Sleep is overrated, anyway.

She sits back down at her desk. "Do you have all the dating apps?"

"I've got some of them, but I haven't really used them."

"Well, unless you can come up with someone you meet between now and tonight, I suggest you use the rest of the day connecting with the single population of this city to arrange a date and get out there amongst it."

Any fight I had not to have to do this has well and truly deserted me. "Sure thing. I'm on it."

"That's the spirit, Kennedy Bennet," she replies, turning her attention to her screen, indicating our conversation is now over.

I skulk back to my desk and plunk myself down heavily in my chair. I've got to go on blind dates to these places now? How humiliating. Anyone who's ever been on a blind date knows what a disaster they can be. Sure, there are always those one in a million stories you hear about people meeting the love of their lives on blind dates, but personally, I suspect they're either urban myth or put out by the P.R. division of Blind Dates Incorporated.

I slip my phone off my desk and pull up a dating app I'd half-heartedly used when I arrived in the city. I'd met two guys from it, neither of whom were a fit for me—which is a polite way to say they were utter weirdo creeps, of course. I pull up my profile and with a sigh, I click the reactivate button.

Here goes nothing.

I do the same with a couple of the better-known apps, avoiding the ones everyone knows are designed purely for quick hook ups. I did not want to go on blind dates with those guys.

My phone pings with a message from Esme, telling me she walked Lady Moo already, with an ablutions count, and returned her to the flat. I tap out a quick reply to thank her and remind her not to bother with the ablutions info—because *ew*—and then flick over to Hugo's Instagram.

There's a new photo of him and Fleur, this time sipping hot chocolate by an open fire, looking loved-up and happy in their thick winter sweaters.

I chew on my lip.

I know, it's a terrible habit. I know I need to just stop looking at his IG and #moveon.

But every time, I find my finger itching to see what he's up to, who he's with, how happy he is.

It's almost like I'm punishing myself.

Who am I kidding? It's *totally* like I'm punishing myself.

Every photo I see tells me he's happy with his new wife, the one from the "right" family.

Every photo I see tells me I didn't fit into his world. Not like she does.

With a heavy heart, I close Instagram and pull up one of the dating apps to see if anyone has bitten.

They have.

A *lot* of them.

Frankly, I'm shocked. I mean, I know I'm no troll, but the sheer level of interest from London's single males is staggering.

I begin to scroll through the possible candidates, filtering them out until I get a list of the least horrendous ones. I know I'm not actually looking for Mr. Right, but I want to make this whole blind date thing as palatable as possible.

Can you tell I'm not loving this?

I select one guy who looks like he might be vaguely in my target market—young enough, male, all his own teeth, I'm not being too picky at this stage—and send him a message, asking if he'd like to go on a date tonight. With his dark brown hair and broad smile, he looks harmless enough, and he listed "adventure" as one of his interests. Let's hope his idea of adventure includes going to a *Rocky Horror Picture Show* themed nightclub in costume with a total stranger.

Part of me is judging him if he does.

"Coffee time?" Shelley asks over the partition.

"You're speaking my language. Do you think we can sneak out, or will we have to hold our noses and down the horrible coffee here to get our caffeine fix?" I glance over at Edina's office. She's got the Venetian blinds open, and I can see her with her feet up on her desk, leaning back in her black leather chair as she chats on the phone.

"I'm not sure we should risk it. I've heard of three people who have lost their jobs this morning alone."

"Jodi from social media?" I ask, aghast.

"Yup, and two assistants from fashion."

I widen my eyes. "Not Lulu and Peta."

She pulls her lips into a line and gives a grim nod of her head. "They were lovely, but I never knew what they did."

I picture the two girls with their enviably long legs and slim, willowy figures. They always wore the latest trends, looking like they spent hours dressing each day, from their huge false eyelashes down to their intricately painted toenails. They were perfect for the Fashion department, but as Shelley says, we never actually saw them *do* anything. Other than look amazing, that is.

"Let's just grab a quick coffee here," I say.

The two of us take the short walk past Edina's office into the break room.

"What are you working on?" she asks, as I press the buttons on the machine for the plastic liquid that passes for coffee around here.

"Edina's added a new layer of excitement to my Single American Girl in London column: blind dates."

"You're going on blind dates?"

"Mmm-hmm. I'm trying to set one up for tonight. I've been busy on the dating apps this morning. There seem to be a lot of options out there."

"Who have you targeted? Anyone cute?" She pours a dash of milk into each of our cups, and we both sit down at the Formica table.

"That's not the goal here. I just need a guy to go to these places with me so I can add in a whole heap of awkward to the article. Seriously, I think all she wants to do is humiliate me."

"Come on. You know you could be using this opportunity to your advantage. You're single. They're single. Well, presumably, anyway."

"Don't even go there."

"Who's to say you don't inadvertently stumble across the love of your life on one of these dates?"

"On Tinder?"

"Okay, not on Tinder. What other apps are you on? Any of the good ones?"

I flip my phone over and show her the apps. "These."

"Two? You're on two apps?" She blinks at me as though she can't quite comprehend this fact.

"Is that too many? Should I be on just one and put all my efforts into it?"

"Are you insane? You need to be on more than just two if you're going to have any chance of meeting anyone even half normal. Here." She puts her hand out, palm up.

I snap my phone up off the table and hold it against my chest. "I'm not letting you loose on my phone."

"Relax. I'm not going to do anything. I'm just going to show you the good apps."

I soften. "Okay, but don't go creating any profiles for me. I'll do those."

"Sure."

I place my phone in her outstretched hand and try not to be bothered by the look of glee on her face. She taps quickly, downloading a bunch of apps in record time.

"There you go. Those are the ones that work for me. I've had some pretty good nights out, thanks to these."

I run my eyes over them. "Good to know."

"Look, it's a numbers game. You've got to throw yourself out there to see what you get back. How many guys have you contacted about the next place you've got to visit?"

"One."

"One?" she guffaws. "That is not playing the numbers, babe. That's the opposite of playing the numbers. That's…I don't know what that is."

"I figured he was the only guy who looked reasonable enough."

"You've got to be less picky. Find at least ten more guys and send them hearts or swipe them or whatever it is on each of the apps to show them you're interested. That way you're more likely to get a bite."

"Ten is a lot."

"One is nothing."

"Good point."

She takes a sip of her coffee and makes a face. "Ugh. Maybe we should have risked our jobs to get a decent cup."

"No way. I'm doing whatever I can to keep this job. I don't want to have to go back home."

"Because warm weather, beautiful beaches, and happy people are the pits?" she asks with a laugh.

My insides twist. "Something like that."

We down the terrible coffee and I return to my desk. I spend the rest of the day making profiles for myself, sending out messages, even flirting with a couple of guys who don't turn my stomach. By late-afternoon, I've got three guys who've said they're free tonight, and I'm holding my breath having just told them I want to go to the *Rocky Horror Picture Show* club, dressed in costume.

My phone vibrates on my desk with a reply from one of the guys.

Don: *You're clearly into some stuff. You do you. I'll do someone else.*

Wow. Just wow.

Well, Don, I will do me, thank you very much.

Okay, that didn't come out quite right, but you know what I mean.

Time to move on.

The next message is much more positive.

Carl: *That sounds like a right laugh.*

Carl is a guy I've been messaging with sporadically for the last couple of hours or so. He's been fun and flirty and not nearly as intense as some of the others, one of whom asked me for a photo of my bare feet. Don may draw the line at going in costume to a *Rocky Horror Picture Show* club, but mine is definitely feet pics.

Seriously, today has been an education.

Carl's profile picture shows a guy with light brown hair, kind eyes, and a full beard. There's a big grin on his face.

I tap out a quick reply.

Me: *Perfect. Just so you know, I'm writing an article about going on a blind date at the club. Full disclosure and all that.*

Carl: *I feel so used.*

I push out a breath. So, Carl's a no…

My phone beeps with another message.

Carl: *Just kidding. Ten o'clock good for you?*

I grin at my screen. Bingo.

Me: *What will you be wearing so I recognize you?*

Carl: *A pair of gold shorts and a blond wig. Obviously.*

I snort-giggle. This guy is funny.

Me: *Seriously now.*

Carl: *I am serious. I'm going as Rocky. Haven't you seen the show?*

Me: *Can I admit to you that I haven't?*

Carl: *Looks like I'll have to educate you. What costume do you have in mind?*

Me: *I'm not sure.*

Carl: *How about you come dressed as Magenta?*

I don't have a clue who Magenta is, but that's what Mr. Google is for. As long as she's sexy, Edina will be happy.

Me: *Is Magenta sexy?*

Carl: *Definitely.*

Me: *Perfect. See you there at ten?*

Carl: *Deal.*

I grin to myself as a seed of a thought is planted in my mind. Maybe Shelley's right? Maybe this whole experience might help me find a great guy?

And maybe that guy might even be Carl?

I know, I know. I'm getting w*aaaaa*y ahead of myself. But a girl can dream about the guy she's only just "met" on a dating app and going to a themed nightclub with, dressed as someone called Magenta.

Yeah, it doesn't sound good.

I can't help that seed of a thought from sprouting a couple of leaves.

CHAPTER 10

I am seriously questioning my choice of careers right now.

Not too long ago, I was writing interesting, thought-provoking articles about topics that matter for a women's lifestyle magazine I loved and respected.

Now? Now I'm at a nightclub wearing the least revealing French maid's costume I could find—which is definitely still way too revealing for my tastes, and way *less* revealing than virtually everyone else's costumes around me—I've got on a wig that makes my head seem like an oversized lollipop, and my feet are squished into a pair of black heels that are already making my feet sore—and I just got here.

I wait for my date as I watch the roomful of people in East London, in weird and wonderful costumes, dance to a song that appears to be all about a guy named Eddy who didn't like his teddy bear.

So just your typical Friday night for me, then.

What's more, I can't find my blind date.

You'd think when he described that he was going to wear a pair of gold shorts with a blond wig it'd be easy to spot the guy. You'd be wrong. So wrong. There has to be at least twenty guys here dressed exactly like that right now, ranging from total gym body to suspected couch potato. I have no clue which one is Carl.

I glance back at his dating app profile on my phone, and then search the room once more. I'm about to give up when I feel a tap on my shoulder. I turn around to see a man in a pair of gold shorts, a blonde wig on his head—and an impressive six-pack.

"Are you Kennedy?" he asks in a voice loud enough to hear over the music.

"Carl?"

"That's me." His face breaks into the smile I recognize from dating app. He leans closer to me and says in my ear, "You make an amazing Magenta. Christina Milian's got nothing on you."

I catch a whiff of his stale beer breath, but smile at the compliment. Christina Milian is a hundred percent hotter than me, but I'm more than happy to take it.

"Thanks, you look like whoever played the guy in the gold shorts."

He shoots me a questioning look. "Rocky. I'm the scientist's creation."

"Is that how the story goes? I just Googled Magenta after you suggested her to me."

"Want to dance, Magenta?" he asks.

I look out at the sea of people. The song has changed to one about some people named Brad and Janet, and everyone is singing along to it, having a great time. "Sure. Why not?"

We hit the floor and dance, along with the rest of the outlandishly-dressed patrons. Some stay in character as they move to the music, some simply dance. One guy in particular, who's dressed as some sort of creepy older Goth guy, is doing a stiff-limbed dance that is quite frankly unsettling.

Carl and I do normal people dance moves, and after a while I loosen up and begin to enjoy myself.

This place is fun. Definitely weird, but fun.

The song changes to the only one I recognize from the show, and everyone follows the moves as they "jump to the left, and take a step to the right," as the song instructs. Before long, Carl and I are doing the actions along with everyone else, laughing and having a great time.

We dance to the next two songs, and then I suggest we take a break. We head through a set of double doors into a quieter area. Like the nightclub, it's dimly lit, with red velvet curtains lining the walls and a bar against one wall. Groups of people are sitting in comfortable chairs and beanbags scattered all over, and Carl gets us a couple of drinks as I sit in one of two beanbags in the middle of the room.

"Here's your water. Are you sure you didn't want anything stronger?" he says, as he passes me a glass.

"I'm so thirsty after all that dancing, this is just what I need." I take a grateful slug of water as he lowers himself into the opposite beanbag. "Have you been here before, Carl?" I ask.

He lets out a laugh. "You said 'Coral.'"

"No, I didn't. I said Carl."

"You said Coral."

"No, Carl."

"Exactly. How about you pretend there's no 'r' in my name?"

"Then you'd be Cal, as in California."

He grins at me. "That's a whole lot better than being called Cor-ral. You make me feel like an octogenarian who attends the Ladies' Auxiliary and volunteers at her local church fair."

"I'd like to meet Coral. She sounds like an amazing person," I reply with a smile.

He laughs as he raises his bottle of beer and I clink my water glass against it. "Just make sure everyone in your article knows I'm a guy."

"Of course."

"And that I'm a Greek god who knows his way around the dance floor, dressed in gold budgie smugglers."

"Budgie smugglers?" I question.

"My shorts. Speedos. It's an Australian expression." He shrugs. "My ex was an Aussie."

"So, some Aussie person decided that a Speedo makes it look like you're carrying a small bird in your pants?"

He laughs. "Yup."

"Good to know."

We share a smile.

We chat for a while and he tells me about his job (an accountant at a large London firm), his cat (tabby, with her own Instagram page and over a thousand followers), and the fact he's from Oxford and just moved to London a few years ago.

He bounces up from the beanbag with impressive ease and extends his hand. "Let's dance some more. I feel like flexing my Rocky muscles out there with the best of them."

I try my best to stifle a yawn. "Isn't it super late?"

He takes me by the hands and hauls me out of the beanbag and onto my feet. "I thought you had an article to write. Don't you need more material?"

My rubber arm has been twisted. I love to dance, and Carl is really growing on me.

"Let's do this."

And that's how I end up dancing until after three in the morning. I laugh and have a super fun time with Carl in his "budgie smugglers," who it turns out is a regular guy with a wicked sense of humor and depth.

It's a win, win, win, win as far as I can tell.

By the time we're done, my feet are killing me, my heavy makeup has started to run, and I probably look like a French maid who's had to clean one too many bathrooms. But, to my surprise, I've grown to enjoy the whole *Rocky Horror Picture Show* thing.

We reach the street and I check my phone. "My ride is here." I see a Prius sliding to a stop twenty feet away and I check the license plate. "Hey, this was fun. Thank you so much for educating this *Picture Show* newbie."

"Let's do it again," he replies, his winter coat covering his Rocky costume.

"I think once in this place is enough for me."

"We could, I don't know, go for a coffee or a drink sometime?"

I feel a little spike of excitement at the prospect of seeing Carl again. "I'd like that."

"Good." He takes a step closer to me and places his hands on my upper arms. Gazing at me, he says, "Is it okay if I kiss you? Because I really want to."

As I gaze into his eyes, a hopeful look on his face, the part of me that's looking for love tells me to do it. To kiss the guy. To see if we've got chemistry.

So, I lean into him, my heart rate rising at the prospect of kissing a guy for the first time in w*aaaa*y too long. He presses his warm, soft lips against mine.

Huh. This is what kissing's like. It's been so long, I'd barely remembered.

"I'll call you," he says as we pull away, his face morphing into a grin.

"Sure." I shoot him a smile before I dash up the street and climb into my ride.

As my driver pulls out from the curb, I find myself smiling over Carl.

Who knew I'd meet a great guy on a blind date at a *Rocky Horror Picture Show* themed nightclub?

Not me, that's for sure.

I lean back in my seat, the late hour—well, early really, because I check the time on my phone and notice that it's almost three-thirty. Three-thirty! I don't think I've stayed up this late since I was in college.

I feel wild and free.

Carl-slash-Rocky has been so good for me.

I'm just beginning to drift off when the car jerks me fully awake. I reach out and grab ahold of the door beside me. My driver begins to spout some colorful language as he slows the car and pulls it to the curb on a deserted street.

"Everything okay?" I ask.

His response is gruff. "Yeah, what do you think? Flat tire."

"Oh, no."

He turns to look at me. "You want to get another ride? Or you can wait for me to change it."

I glance up and down the street. We're in some suburb I don't recognize, all the buildings dark, as sensible people who didn't have to visit a themed nightclub for their column sleep. "How likely is it that I'll get another ride?"

"I dunno."

Helpful.

The thought of having to get out of the car and wait for another ride, which could be a long time, is not appealing. "I guess I'll wait."

"All right." He gets out of the car and begins to rummage around in the trunk, more expletives punctuating the night air.

"You okay?" I question, not sure I want to hear his reply. It's quite obvious he's not.

"Fine," he grumps.

Ok*aaaa*y.

I lean back in my seat and pull my phone out. I begin to take notes on my evening to put into an article when I hear a tap on the window.

Startled, I look up to see my driver on the sidewalk, a look of concern on his face. He stands back as I push the door open. "What's up?" I ask, keeping my tone light—and not as though he might have lured me here to murder me.

"I don't know quite how to ask this," he begins. "Can you change a tire?"

"Sure can. Why?"

"I, well, I've only been driving for a week, and this is my cousin's car and he told me it was a good 'un but it's not and I don't know how to do it."

"Change a tire?"

He hangs his head. "Yeah."

"Do you have a jack and a wrench?"

"Is that what these are?" He holds up exactly what I named.

I climb out of the car, push my sleeves up, and tell him, "I'm on it."

His face creases into a smile. "You're ace. I'll give you a five-star review."

All I want is a ride home, but that's not in the cards until this is fixed. "Cool."

Forty minutes later, the tire changed by yours truly, and my driver having shared the story of how his girlfriend had dumped him by text the same day his boss fired him from his shelf-stocking job at his local supermarket, all because of a misunderstanding with a ferret and a six-pack of beer—don't ask—I climb out of the car, bid him farewell, and trudge up the steps into my building. I slide my key into the lock and push my way into the lobby on painful feet, supremely thankful to finally be home.

I yawn, my exhaustion hitting me, with the realization

that the night is finally over and I can head to my bed, curl up in a ball, and slip into blissful sleep.

As I close the door behind myself, I turn around and come face to face with the one person who I can't seem to avoid these days.

Charlie Cavendish.

"Kennedy," he says by way of greeting, as he sweeps his gaze over me.

I shift my weight.

I've gone from wearing the world's most ridiculous cow-inspired robe, complete with padded udders and "Love Moo" embossed on the chest, to a worse-for-wear sexy French maid in front of the guy.

This is *so* not good.

Charlie, on the other hand, looks totally put together. He's wearing a similar outfit to the one I saw him in the morning he woke me up, only this time he's also got on a navy hooded sweatshirt and a pair of headphones slung around his neck. He's casual Ken, not his buttoned-up usual self—and it suits him.

I try my best to regain my composure. "Hey, Charlie."

"Been out for an early morning run?" he questions, the edges of his mouth twitching at his joke, as his eyes slide down to my high heels.

"Hilarious," I deadpan. "I've been out at a club, actually."

"In…that?" He gestures at my clothes, and I pull my coat even tighter around my body.

"For your information, I've been working."

"You do know you're doing nothing for your case right now, don't you?"

I pull my brows together. "What? Why?"

"Out 'working' at this hour of the morning?" He uses air quotes as he smirks at me, those ridiculously blue eyes of his dancing in mischief.

I shoot him a look. "For your information, I work for a magazine. I'm writing about novelty experiences in London while on blind dates."

"You were on a blind date dressed as a French maid?"

"It was at a *Rocky Horror Picture Show* themed club."

"I see. Which magazine do you write for?"

I cock an eyebrow. "Don't pretend you have any interest in my life, because we both know you don't."

The words come out much harsher than I anticipated. I notice his brows ping up in surprise.

"Sorry. Long night."

"I can tell. I'm just making conversation."

I offer him a smile. "Well, as my granny always says, save your breath to cool your porridge."

He lets out a sudden laugh that fills the echoey lobby. "Did your granny eat a lot of porridge?"

"It's a saying. It means stop talking. My granny is Scottish. She has a way with words."

"A Scot who eats porridge? Will wonders never cease?"

"Ha."

"I thought Americans called it 'oatmeal,' anyway."

"Not the point."

"I'll be sure to economize on my breathing around you in future. Are you going to the Christmas potluck tomorrow?"

"I'm planning on it."

"I'll see you there."

"But you don't go to their things. They're the Ladies' Committee, remember?"

His face lights up in a smile as he removes his hand from the elevator door. "I thought, why not? It seems like the neighborly thing to do."

I open my mouth and close it again.

"Have a wonderful day, Kennedy, what you're awake for."

"You, too," I reply, as I step into the elevator.

The doors swing closed, and I'm whisked up and away from him.

Great. That's all I need. Charlie Smug Cavendish at the Ducks' Christmas dinner.

It's so much easier to deny the feelings I've started having for him if I don't have to actually see the guy.

I'll just have to avoid him. I'll stick to the other side of the room. I'll chat with the Ducks and ignore him.

Easy.

CHAPTER 11

Or...not so easy.

I show up to the Christmas potluck dinner at Maude's place, hoping there's some work- or gym-related crisis that's kept Charlie away.

No such luck.

He's here, in Maude's living room, with its festive Christmas tree and holly hanging from the mantel, Christmas carols playing in the background.

It gets worse.

Not only is Charlie in the room, but he's somehow managing to completely charm the Ducks, who are currently surrounding him as he sits on the sofa, and hanging on his every word, like he's the most fascinating person in the room.

"Kennedy?" Elsey calls out to me, as I place my offering of Marks and Spencer's Christmas pudding on the table filled with delicious looking food. "You must come over here. Charlie was just telling us the most interesting story."

I flick my gaze to Charlie. He shoots me a smile, making my belly flutter, the way it insists on doing around him these days. If he was Casual Ken on his way to the gym the other morning, today he's Cool Ken in his slacks and open-neck shirt under a blue tailored blazer. Cool *Posh* Ken is probably a better label, because most men I know his age rock the jeans and hoodie look, rather than looking like an off-duty James Bond.

I eye a lone dining room chair by the Christmas tree. "I'm happy here," I tell her.

"Nonsense," Barbara declares. "Come over here. There's plenty of room and you have to hear about Charlie, our hero."

Charlie Cavendish is a hero?

Yup, that definitely was a flock of pigs I just spotted flapping their wings as they flew by the window.

With reluctance, I make my way over to the group.

"Charlie's a hero, is he?" I question, my eyes sliding to his.

His lips quirk as he lifts his brows in response.

"Oh, yes," Elsey says, her face bright. "He's ever so brave. We had no idea. Did we, ladies?"

There's a wave of agreement that ripples through the group.

What the heck is going on here? Don't they all hate the guy?

"It was nothing, really. I don't even know how you found out about it," he protests, but anyone can see his heart's not in it.

Barbara balks. "Oh, listen to him, will you? 'It was nothing.' Modest as well as heroic."

"I imagine modesty is his only flaw," Gertie says, and I swear the woman bats her eyelashes at him.

I arch an eyebrow in his direction, and he has the decency to look embarrassed. "What wonderfully heroic thing did you do?" I ask him.

I've got a string of suggestions:

1. He donated a spare million to a worthy cause, such as teaching kids from rough neighborhoods how to waltz?
2. He set up a dog shelter for the ladies of Notting Hill to entertain their pooches when they can't take them on their superyachts?

Really, the possibilities are endless.

"They're making a much bigger deal of this than they should," he replies, doing his best to look bashful.

He genuinely looks like he's blushing. Wow. The guy could have a second career on the stage.

Elsey bats his hand. "Oh, rubbish, Charlie."

"Stop being so modest," Maude scolds.

"Young men really should own their successes," Barbara says, and everyone in the room agrees.

"Without being boastful," Elsey adds.

"I can't imagine Charlie being boastful. Can you?" Gertie asks, before she returns her attention to batting her eyelashes at him.

Seriously, I think the woman is in love with him.

"Absolutely not," Barbara chimes. "And I for one am sorry that I ever misjudged you, Charlie. It was wrong. Please forgive me."

I blink at her in shock. What the heck has this guy done?

He smiles benevolently. "I hadn't put in an effort with any of you since I moved into the building. *I'm* the one who should be apologizing. If I knew these potluck dinners were this fun, I'd have told my boss to sod off and would have come the moment I moved in."

Elsey claps her hands together in glee. "That would have been splendid."

"We could have saved all that time talking about how

awful we thought you were and talked about other awful people instead," Evelyn says.

"Thank you?" he says with a laugh, and as his eyes land on mine, his face creases into a grin.

I blink at him in disbelief. What is with this new, unadulterated adulation?

It was so much easier when they all hated him.

"I still don't know what Charlie did that's so great," I say with a shrug.

"Look at you standing there. Why don't you come and sit over here, Kennedy, and Charlie can tell you all about it." Elsey pats a spot on the sofa between her and Charlie.

I stay rooted to the spot. Sitting next to Charlie, close enough to touch, will do nothing for my state of equilibrium.

"Come on, love. There's plenty of room over here," Elsey says, patting the spot once more.

Everyone is watching me in expectation, even Maude, and I'm not sure she's even heard any of this.

I know I've got no choice. Not without being rude, anyway.

I avoid making further eye contact with the newly-popular Charlie as I sit down gingerly, making sure I don't brush anything of mine against anything of his. I sit rigidly in my seat. My back is ramrod straight, my hands placed primly on my knees, like a demure 50s housewife.

"Go on then, dear. Don't be shy," Elsey says to him.

"I'm sure Kennedy doesn't want to hear the story," Charlie replies.

"Oh, I'll tell her then," Barbara exclaims in frustration. "Charlie saved a man's life!" she pronounces. "A famous man, too."

"He probably wasn't going to die," he explains.

"A man fell off a boat into rough, shark-infested waters—"

Charlie shakes his head. "Not shark-infested. Smooth as glass."

"—in the dark—"

"It was daylight."

"—and it turns out the poor man couldn't swim—"

"He could swim, but he panicked a bit."

"—so, what did our Charlie do? He dived in after him—"

"I kind of jumped, actually."

"—and he swum that nearly-dead man to safety, back on the boat."

I look at Charlie for his rebuttal.

He shrugs and replies, "That part's correct."

"Tell her the most important part," Gertie instructs.

"I think you've got it covered," he replies.

"The most important part," Gertie says for him, "is that the man who nearly died was Stephen Hislop, that billionaire chap who makes all the computers and whatnot."

"Stephen Hislop?" I ask, incredulously. "As in the founding CEO of Hislop Computing? Britain's answer to Apple?"

This sounds like a totally made-up story to me. A story made up to impress a group of elderly women. And it clearly worked.

"Who ate an apple?" Maude asks.

"No one ate an apple," Evelyn explains.

"Well, why are you talking about apples?" Maude complains.

"We're not talking about apples," Evelyn replies. "We're talking about how Charlie saved a man from drowning."

Maude scrunches up her nose. "With an apple?"

Evelyn lets out an exasperated sigh. "Put in your hearing aids next time, Maude."

Elsey leans back in her seat with a look of satisfaction on

her face. "He did save Stephen Hislop. Isn't our Charlie quite something?"

She's right about that. He *is* quite something.

But wait. *Our* Charlie?

And seriously, are they really buying this? It's so obviously a ploy to win them over. I'm a journalist. I can sniff out a fake story a hundred yards away, and this is definitely a fake story.

Problem is, it's clearly working.

Oh, how I miss the days when the Ducks outright hated him.

"You're telling me you were on a boat with Stephen Hislop, he fell into the water, and you saved him?" I narrow my eyes at him.

"Really, it was no big deal," Charlie replies. "How about we talk about something else for a while? The weather's been awfully chilly, hasn't it?"

"I love this time of year when the evenings close in early and the Christmas lights are up. It's my absolute favorite time of year," Evelyn tells us, taking the bait.

"What was that? Speak up, will you," Maude exclaims.

"Nice Christmas lights," Evelyn says loudly.

"Oh, yes. Lovely. Just lovely," Maude replies.

"The Christmas lights alleviate the winter gloom, don't they?" Barbara says.

"I like the mulled wine," Elsey says as she holds her empty glass up.

"Is that your way of asking for another glass?" Barbara replies with a laugh.

Elsey grins at her friend. "Am I being too subtle?"

"Go on, then. Let's get another glass for you. It might be about time to start eating, too."

Grasping the opportunity to get away from Charlie, I spring to my feet. "What can I do to help?"

"You can sit down and chat with the delectable Charlie," Barbara tells me. "You two are the youngest people here by a country mile. You must have lots to discuss."

"Oh, no, it's fine. I'll chat with him later," I protest, as I follow her across the room.

"No, I insist." She takes me by the elbow and leads me back to the sofa. "And don't you go getting any ideas about helping either, young man. As the newest residents, you are our guests of honor tonight, and guests of honor don't help."

"Yes, ma'am," Charlie replies with a grin.

I roll my eyes. With his fake heroics and simpering niceness, he has them eating out of the palm of his hand.

Knowing I have no choice in the matter, I plop back down next to the alleged hero of the hour. I shoot him a tight smile

"Welcome back," he says.

"Thanks," I grind out.

Barbara winks at me before she turns and walks away.

She winks at me, people!

Oh, good grief.

As the ladies go about their business of getting new drinks and heating up food, Charlie and I are left alone on the sofa.

So much for staying on the other side of the room from him.

"Did you really save a billionaire?" I ask him.

"Why would I make that up?" he replies with a laugh.

I shrug. "I dunno. For a whole host of reasons."

"It is true, but for the record, I didn't raise it. That's not my style."

I study his face. There's something in his eyes that makes me wonder if I've judged him unfairly. But who knows? Maybe he's just a good actor. I clear my throat. "How was your trip?" I ask.

"It was fine. I got a lot of work done."

"So, exciting times."

"Well, they could be, under different circumstances. I brought you back something." He leans down and collects something from beside the sofa. "It's the arancini. I hope you like it." He passes me a glass jar tied up with a ribbon, filled with strips of lemon rind covered in sugar.

I take it in my hands, touched that he actually followed through on his promise. "Thanks. That's…sweet of you. I'll think of you when I eat these."

He smiles, and the skin around his eyes crinkles. "You do that."

"You know you didn't need to get these for me. You apologized, so we're all good."

"I know. I wanted to."

I swallow. "'Kay."

"'Kay."

We sit in silence as I wrestle with my conflicting feelings. He's rude and then he's nice. He's condescending and then seems genuine. Then there's the whole hero saving a famous guy from drowning thing, that has my brain whirring.

Could the real Charlie Cavendish please step forward?

"So, what are you doing for Thanksgiving?" I ask, to fill the awkward silence between us.

"Surely you know we don't celebrate Thanksgiving in Britain, so that's not even a real question," he tells me.

"Maybe some people do?"

He shakes his head. "They don't."

"Americans here would definitely celebrate it."

"That's different."

"How's it different?"

"Because your question was how I'm celebrating Thanksgiving this year, and the answer is that I'm not."

So we're back to sparring now? Talk about whiplash.

"Aren't you thankful for anything in this country?" I ask him.

"That's not the point. It's an American tradition, not a British one. We've got our own traditions, and we're more than happy with them, thank you very much."

"You mean like Bonfire night?" I ask, remembering the fireworks display my friends and I went to at Battersea Park in November.

"Actually, it's officially Guy Fawkes, to commemorate a foiled plot by Guy Fawkes and his cronies to blow up the houses of Parliament in 1605 in what was called the Gunpowder Plot."

"Well, aren't you the history professor," I reply with a laugh.

Forget the fact that it's quite interesting.

"I take an active interest in my country."

The doorbell chimes, and the door swings open. Another older woman in glasses and, you guessed it, pearls, waltzes into the room and proceeds to greet everyone with double cheek kisses.

"Another Duck," I mutter under my breath.

"Did you just call her a duck?" Charlie questions.

"It's the name I have for the ladies of this building. I mean it in a nice way."

He cocks an eyebrow. "Because every woman of a certain age likes to be called a duck?"

I shoot him a look. "You call them the Ladies' Committee. What's wrong with the Ducks? Ducks happen to be my favorite species of bird."

"I did not have you pegged as a duck lover."

"What sort of bird did you think was at the top of my list? Actually, don't answer that. I don't think I want to know."

"I was going to say the swan."

I open my mouth to reply and close it again. Although

swans are known for their beauty and elegance, I'm not going to let what could be his attempt at a compliment thaw me. It'll take a lot more than that.

Like a personality change.

"I quite like the term: The Ducks. It has a ring to it, and they do tend to waddle around together in a group, quacking about things."

I press my lips together to stifle a smile as the image forms in my head. They'd all be wearing their mandatory strings of pearls and glasses as they waddle around the building, sticking their beaks—okay, bills—into everyone's business.

"Can it be?" he asks, watching me.

I snap my attention back to him. "Can what be?"

"Can I have made Kennedy Bennet smile?"

"I smile."

"Really?"

"Yes. All the time. I'm always smiling. I'm known for it, in fact."

Okay, that's not strictly true, but I do smile.

His lips twitch. "You're known as Kennedy the Smiler, are you?"

"Just because I don't smile around you doesn't mean I'm not a smiler, you know."

He cocks his head to the side, his eyes boring into me. "Why is that?"

"Why is what?"

"Why don't you smile around me?"

"You know why."

"Because of our conversation on that blind date a long time ago? I've moved on from that."

"Oh, I've moved on, too."

He lets out a laugh.

"What? I have moved on. I'm Zen. I'm chill."

"Oh, I'm sure you're many things, Kennedy, but I'm confident when I say Zen is not one of them."

"I—" I begin only to be cut off by a woman arriving in front of us with a beaming smile on her face. She's wearing a floral dress and pair of sensible shoes, her silver hair cut in a blunt bob, and no less than three rows of pearls around her neck. Naturally.

"You must be Charles and Kennedy," she says. "I'm Winnifred Davies from flat 1a."

The famous Winnifred, the alleged building gossip.

"Hello," I say, as Charlie rises and greets her with a kiss, telling her how nice it is to see her again.

Total suck up.

"It's so lovely to finally meet you both properly. Well, I've met you before, Charles, of course, but we didn't get the chance to chat, did we?" She sits in an empty armchair next to us. "Now, tell me all about yourselves. Kennedy, ladies first."

"I've just moved into Delphine's flat on the fifth floor. I'm housesitting for six or so months."

"Oh, I know all that," she replies, with a wave of her hand. "Let's get to the juicy stuff, shall we?"

"The juicy stuff?" I give a nervous laugh.

She leans in closer. "I'm told you're single and ready to mingle." She shoots me a meaningful look and then flicks her gaze to Charlie.

Subtle? Not so much.

"I might be single, but I don't do a lot of mingling," I reply lightly.

"Oh, but a girl who looks like you should be a wonderful mingler," she protests.

Is that even a word?

She turns to Charlie. "Wouldn't you agree?"

"Oh, absolutely. I'm sure Kennedy is a wonderful 'mingler,' as you put it, Mrs. Davies," Charlie says. He leans in conspiratorially toward her. "In fact, Kennedy was out 'mingling' just the other night. We met in the lobby. She was coming home at about the time the rest of the world was waking up."

"Did you, now?" Winnifred asks me, her eyes wide.

I resist the urge to give Charlie a quick shin kick, mainly because the Ducks would notice.

"Tell us, Kennedy, because I'm sure we all want to know: was it a date you were coming in from at that time?" he continues.

I twist my mouth, as I imagine what it would be like to lock Charlie Cavendish in the hallway closet with the Winnie the Poohs.

I allow myself a brief moment to digest the idea.

"It was, as it happens," I tell him. "With a very nice man. I got home so late because we went dancing and then my ride home got a flat tire. So, it's not much of a story, really."

"You went out dancing?" Winnifred asks. "Barbara? Elsey? You must come over and hear all about this. Kennedy went out dancing with a young man and didn't come home until the morning!"

Oh, great.

I narrow my eyes at Charlie. He's smiling at me with a level of obvious satisfaction that tells me he's loving every moment of my humiliation.

"Oooh, now that's good gossip," Elsey says.

"What's good gossip?" Maude asks, straining to hear.

"Kennedy went out with a young man," Elsey tells her in a loud voice.

"Who?" Maude asks, looking confused.

"Kennedy, the new girl," Elsey tells her.

"Well, good for her," Maude says. "I remember when I

used to step out with a young man. Awfully handsome he was, too. Always brought me flowers. That's why I married him, you know."

"Yes, we know, Maude dear, but we're trying to hear all about Kennedy's young man right now," Gertie says.

"Is it love, Kennedy?" Barbara asks and the room falls into silence, every eye trained on me.

I want to shrink into my chair and disappear.

"If you don't tell us, dear, we'll jump to our own conclusions, and who knows what we'll all come up with?" Winnifred warns with a glint in her eye.

"It was a blind date with a guy named Carl," I concede finally. "So, it was the first time I'd met him."

"Coral?" Barbara questions. "Odd name for a man."

"Coral's a color, not a name," Gertie declares.

"It's a plant, too. You know, coral reefs?" This from Elsey. "Perhaps his parents are particularly fond of coral reefs?"

"They might be divers. Or Australian," Barbara offers.

"People are called all sorts of things now," Winnifred says. "I've got a friend whose brother is Lesley, her sister is Morgan, and her cat is Mr. Twiggles."

"Mr. Twiggles is fine," Evelyn comments.

"The cat is female," Winnifred replies.

"Oh, that is very peculiar," Evelyn adds.

"Would you stop talking about names and let Kennedy answer the question?" Gertie asks. "Now, Kennedy. Tell us about this Coral."

"His name is Caaaahl," I say, in my best imitation of an English accent.

"Well, why didn't you just say that in the first place?" Winnifred complains.

I shoot her an exasperated look.

"I don't believe you've answered the question, Kennedy," Charlie says, so very helpfully. "Is it love?"

He earns another glare from me.

All pairs of bespectacled eyes and one pair of very blue, amused eyes are trained on me in expectation.

"It's 'like,'" I pronounce. "But I just barely met him."

"Well, 'like' is a start. Isn't it, Barbara? It's a start," Elsey says.

Barbara gives a sage nod. "We all have to start somewhere."

"It took me two full weeks to like my Brian," Maude tells us.

"Why? Did he smell?" Winnifred asks.

"Of course he didn't smell," Maude scoffs. "That's ridiculous."

"Well, what was it then?"

"It was his feet. Very large."

As the Ducks begin to chat among themselves, I use the opportunity to extricate myself. I make my way over to the window and look out at the garden, with its bare trees and green lawn. After a beat, I feel a presence nearby and swing around to see Charlie standing beside me.

My traitorous body flushes with pleasure.

Dang it.

"You needed an escape?" he asks quietly, his breath making the hairs on my neck stand on end.

"Something like that."

"They can be intense."

I round on him. "You didn't exactly help, dude."

He arches his brows. "Dude?"

I challenge him with my gaze. "Yes. Dude."

"It was just a bit of fun. And to be fair, you did come in late. You should be pleased I didn't mention what you were wearing."

"Again, it was for work."

"So you said."

"At least I didn't make up a story about saving a famous guy to impress the Ducks. That is so not cool."

"I wasn't me who told them about it, as I've already said."

"If you didn't tell them about it, then who did?"

"Google? I don't know. Barbara raised it. She'd clearly read about it somewhere."

Taken aback, I mutter, "So it is true?"

"I don't spend my time bragging about helping a friend out of the water when he'd had a little too much sangria. It's not my style." He narrows his gaze at me. "You know, I'm really not the ogre you think I am."

"Really? Because I think telling a group of gossipy ladies that I came in super late was fairly ogre-ish behavior. Don't you?"

"I didn't realize it would upset you. I was trying to have a little fun. I apologize. It was wrong of me."

I slide my eyes to his and am surprised to see the usual patronizing amusement gone from his face. "You're making a habit of apologizing to me."

"How about I try to behave myself in future?"

Was that flirty? It sounded flirty.

"Good idea."

Our gazes lock, and before I even know what I'm doing, I imagine what it would be like to kiss Charlie Cavendish. To have those sexy lips of his pressed against mine. To feel his strong, muscular arms wrapped around me. To breathe in his intoxicating scent.

Entirely without my permission, my insides begin to buzz.

Wait, *what?!*

I did not just think that. I don't want to kiss Charlie Cavendish! Not now, not ever.

I clear my throat and drag my gaze from his.

I'm not going back to a man like him. I've been there, and it doesn't end well for me.

So, he can be all apologetic and flirty and give me foreign candy and look the way he does at me, but there is no way I will ever kiss Charlie Cavendish. Not if he were the last man in London.

CHAPTER 12

I stamp my feet against the cold, gray day as I wait in a park in Kensington, steam clouds forming with every breath. I glance at the time. Zara's a couple of minutes late, so I do what I always do when I've got a spare minute. I open Instagram and immediately type in Hugo's profile name. There's no new photo this time, just the collection of the happy couple I've seen over the last week or so.

I close the app and pull up my browser. The page that greets me states *Stephen Hislop nearly drowned.*

Yup, I did it. I checked the story out. My journalist's sleuth brain got to work on fact finding soon after I got home from the potluck dinner last night. And there I saw it in black and white: Charlie was on a fishing expedition with Stephen Hislop and five others when the famous billionaire fell into the water. Charlie saved him.

I twist my mouth as my eyes glide over the now-familiar words.

When told he had performed a heroic act, the man, who wished only to be known as 'Charlie,' stated modestly, "I only did what anyone else would have done under the circumstances."

I admit it. I misjudged him, pure and simple. I jumped to the conclusion that he made the story up to impress the Ducks. I was wrong.

There, I said it. I was wrong about Charlie Cavendish.

Well, I was wrong about Charlie Cavendish lying about saving a famous man from drowning. He's still the smug, smarmy, rich guy he's always been.

The smug, smarmy, rich guy who has apologized to me twice.

The smug, smarmy, rich guy who bought candy for me in a foreign country because he thought I'd like to try it.

The smug, smarmy, rich guy who has ingratiated himself to the ladies of the building who now think he's the cat's pajamas.

The guy I want to kiss.

Argh!

Talk about the guy being a conundrum wrapped up in a riddle.

It's like that episode of *Friends* where Rachel messes up the holiday dessert recipe. There are layers of sweetness to him—the jam, the custard, the fruit—and then there's a whole layer of bitterness that seems out of place, that infiltrates everything, rendering the entire dessert wrong.

Charlie is that dessert.

I think on that for a while. Nope. I find out pretty quickly that imagining the guy I want to kiss as a dessert is *so* not helpful.

I tuck my hair behind my ears. Men like Charlie can be extremely charming. I know that from bitter personal experience. It doesn't change who he really is.

Does it?

I banish my unsettling thoughts from my head as I click my phone off and slide it into the pocket of my wool coat. I lean down and pick Lady M up off the grass and give her a stern look. "Now, Lady M. We are going to a pet store today with a new friend. You need to be on your best behavior. No growling at people, no trying to eat the rabbits, and most importantly, you've got to be nice to Stevie. She's a cutie-pie Jack Russell and she's a lot younger than you." I regard her liquid deep brown eyes as she gazes back at me, as though she's listening to every word. Her pointy ears are pricked. "Do we have a deal?"

Her reply is to wriggle in my arms.

I'm not full of confidence, not after the last two pet stores we visited together.

That said, the little tyke has grown on me. Yes, the whole daily, nauseating massacring of the Winnie the Pooh stuffed toys was a barrier to us growing close, but despite her aggressive tendencies, Lady M sure has a soft side. When I get home from work, she's so happy to see me that she races around in circles, her tail wagging ricocheting up her little body and making her shimmy from side to side. Sure, she makes a weird whiny sound, as though she's about to explode, but I've come to love that noise. It means she's excited to see me.

We've become a team.

"Kennedy!"

I look up to see Zara sashaying down the street toward me, her little Jack Russell puppy, the ever-adorable Stevie, bounding along next to her on a pink leash.

I look at Lady M and say sternly, "Be nice," before I put her back on the ground.

She's too busy watching Stevie and Zara, straining on her leash to get to them.

Stevie, on the other hand, is the perfect dog. As Zara approaches, she instructs her to heel, and Stevie does just that, despite the fact her eyes are trained on Lady M. They enter the park, and Lady M tugs on her leash so hard, she begins to choke, coughing and spluttering as she tries in vain to get to Stevie.

Zara regards Lady M with a concerned look on her face. "How do you think this is going to go?"

"I'm hoping she'll settle down once she gets to sniff Stevie. How about we let them give each other the once over and see what happens?"

"Let's give it a try." Zara edges closer, telling Stevie to heel, which she does until she's within licking distance of Lady M, at which point her true puppy nature bursts out, and she begins to hop and dance around, clearly thrilled to get to be with another dog.

I watch Lady M closely, her leash firmly gripped in my hand, as Stevie bounces around her face. Lady M stands and lets her do it, her stubby tail still wagging. "So far so good."

As the two dogs sniff one another, I loosen the tension in my shoulders. This is going to be okay. Just because she destroys Winnie the Pooh toys, bounces around like she's out of control, and goes crazy at men she doesn't like, doesn't make her a bad dog. She's discerning, that's all.

"Look at them!" Zara declares, as the two dogs begin to play with one another, the obligatory "get to know you" sniffs dispensed with.

"They like each other."

"We'll have to go on dog walks together. Maybe we can go to the dog park and give them some off the lead play time? Stevie loves the dog park."

I watch as Lady M's excitement level reaches fever pitch, and she begins to spin around in circles like a whirling dervish. "Let's take it one step at a time."

"Got anymore awkward blind dates set up to write about?" Zara asks me as we let the dogs play, their leashes getting twisted up more than once.

I untwist Lady M's leash from Stevie's. "I'm going out on

Sunday night with a guy named Devan to a kid-themed restaurant where we get to eat childhood favorite foods. Considering I grew up in the States, I'm not sure I'm going to recognize a whole lot on the menu."

"But you'll have an awkward date and write a hilarious article to keep your boss happy."

I giggle. "That's the plan."

"Let's go into Penelope's Pooches. I've got a client visit at eleven and I need to drop Stevie back at the shop before then."

I eye the pet store on the other side of the street. "I thought you said that store was totally insane."

"Oh, they're all complete nutjobs, but they've got the best selection of dog toys in the city. We're sure to find something to break Lady Moo's Winnie the Pooh addiction."

We head across the street.

"There are a couple of things you need to know before we head in. First, everyone is called Penelope, and yes, even the guys. They all wear the same pale blue boilersuit with pigtails."

"Why?"

"It's best not to ask those kinds of questions. Just know it's part of their dog-cept."

I raise my brows. "Dog-cept?"

"It's their ethos. Their way of looking at life, and they've got the whole canine world backwards."

"Are you sure this is the best place to get a dog toy? It sounds like some kind of cult to me."

"Just keep your eye on the prize and you'll be okay."

I eye the picture window. It has pale blue trim and clouds hanging on strings from the ceiling. "It looks harmless enough."

"Let's go in." Zara pulls the door open and we step inside,

and I immediately lose my sense of equilibrium as my feet begin to sink into the floor.

"What the—?" I take a bouncy step.

"Oh, I forgot that part. The floor's made of some kind of malleable rubber. One of the Penelopes once told me it was to create a womb-like effect for the dogs."

"Why?"

She shrugs. "Again, it's not wise to ask such questions. Believe me."

I glance down at Lady M. For once in her life, she seems totally flummoxed by the environment. Her eyes are darting around the room, her little black nose in the air, sniffing all the smells.

I spot rows of shelves filled to the brim with chew toys and beds and treats, as well as rows and rows of doggie clothes. Which totally makes sense. We *are* in Kensington.

A woman dressed exactly as Zara had described, in a boilersuit and pigtails, bounce-walks over to us. "Welcome to Penelope's Pooches," she says to Lady M and Stevie, who both wag their tails as they gaze up at her. "I see you brought your humans with you today. Who's a good doggie? Who's a good doggie? Yes, you are. Yes, you are." The Penelope looks back up at us. "How can I help those wonderful canines today?"

"We've come to take a look at your chew toys," I explain. "I have a very fussy dog who only likes one toy, and I want her to branch out into something more…appropriate."

The Penelope's features drop. "We don't sell chew toys at Penelope's Pooches."

I eye the rows of chew toys on the shelf. "Uh, I think you do."

The Penelope turns to look at the shelves. "Oh those? They're definitely not chew toys. They're Canine Primal Manducation Facilitation Devices, or CPMFDs for short."

"That's for short?" I mutter to Zara under my breath.

"Good to know, Penelope," Zara replies. "My friend here brought her dog along because she needs to find the right CFD—."

"CPMFDs," the Penelope corrects.

"Sure, one of those," Zara finishes.

"She's a little obsessed with Winnie the Pooh right now, constantly destroying one toy after the other," I add with a laugh.

Zara shakes her head at me, her eyes as round as basketballs.

"What?" I mouth at her.

"She destroys multiple Winnie the Poohs?" the Penelope questions, her face aghast.

"Some," I reply weakly.

"Soft, fluffy ones?"

"Yup."

"Wearing a T-shirt or naked?"

I've never before described a teddy bear as naked.

"Wearing a T-shirt," I reply.

"Size?"

"About this big." I gesture with my hands. "Why do you need to know all this?"

"Wait here," she instructs, before she immediately turns on her heel and bounds away.

I blink at her receding figure. "What the heck was that all about?"

Zara shakes her head at me. "You've really gone and done it now, Kennedy. It's officially a thing."

"What's a thing? Me buying a canine CF whatever it's called?"

"Yup."

"What does that mean, it's become a thing?"

"You'll see," she replies evasively, with a knowing look on

her face.

The Penelope comes back accompanied by another, older Penelope. They both have equally grim looks on their faces.

"I understand we have a childhood toy situation here," the older Penelope says, looking between us.

"Err, I guess," I reply.

Her eyes glide down the leash in my hand to Lady M, who's still straining to go investigate the store. "I think you should come with me." She lifts her eyes. "Both of you."

I shoot Zara an uncertain look.

"Do you want me to come with you?" she asks.

"Only you," the Penelope snaps, pointing at me.

This one has quickly become Scary Penelope in my head. I named the first one we met Baby Penelope on account of her relative youth. I wonder if Ginger Penelope will make an appearance in her Union Jack costume next?

Zara gives me a barely perceptible nod, as if telling me to it's okay to go with this woman.

I turn to Scary Penelope. "Sure thing."

I'm seriously wondering about my sanity right now.

Lady M and I trail behind her as the three of us bounce through the store. I gaze longingly at all the doggie chew toys as we pass by, before we walk through a door and into another area. A dog is standing on a bench having a haircut by another Penelope, and there's a room with a black leather recliner and a desk chair.

"In here," Scary Penelope instructs, and I follow her into the room before she closes the door. I look around. There's a window that looks out into the store, and I can see Zara, peering in at us.

"We call this the Canine Couch Therapy Room. We find it's extremely effective in getting to the root of the cause of persistent blockages in our clients."

"Oh, we're not clients," I protest.

"Did you enter Penelope's Pooches?" she asks, and I nod, because I did. But I thought it was a regular store with some quirky aspects, not whatever *this* is turning out to be. "Then we consider you a client." She smiles a crooked teeth smile at me as she gives an expansive gesture with her arms.

I force a smile, my fear that coming here was a big mistake growing inside. "Awesome."

"Take a seat," Scary Penelope instructs, as she herself sits down on the office chair.

"Sure." I lower myself onto the recliner.

"Not you," she snaps. "The Boston Terrier."

Is this woman serious right now?

"Lady Moo?" I question. "You want the dog on the couch?"

The name Canine Couch Therapy Room instantly makes sense.

"Are you the one destroying the childhood toy?" she asks.

"No." I press my lips together as I glance through the window at Zara. She's now engrossed in looking at one of the chew toys—sorry, CFDPM or whatever the acronym is—and doesn't look up at me.

I scoop Lady Moo up in my arms and set her on the couch, images of Freud psychoanalyzing a dog flashing before my eyes.

"Sit. Stay," I instruct her, and she does as I say, looking up at me with expectation.

"Sit!" Scary Penelope barks, and I snap my attention to her.

"She's already sitting."

"No, you. Sit next to Lady Moo."

"Okay." I plunk myself down.

How did I get myself into this situation? That's right, I followed this crazy woman to a secondary location of my own free will.

Scary Penelope crosses her legs and fixes me with her stare, a clipboard and pen appear in her hands that seemingly materialized out of thin air. "Now, tell me about this Winnie the Pooh situation."

"Well, Lady Moo has a thing for the toy. She likes to rip them to pieces."

"Them?"

"There's a whole closet of them. I need to add that she's not my—"

Scary Penelope holds her hand up to silence me. "I don't want explanations. Stick to the facts, please. What exactly does she do with these Winnie the Poohs? From start to finish."

"Well, she starts by gnawing off the ears, then she rips off the nose. After that—"

"What does she do with the nose?"

"She spits it out."

She scribbles something on her notepad. "Go on."

"Then, I think she eats the eyes, but I can't be one hundred per cent sure."

"What does she do with the eyes?"

"Oh, she swallows them."

There's a shocked intake of breath from behind me and I turn to see two more Penelopes standing in the now-open doorway.

"Don't worry," I say hurriedly. "She used to swallow them, and we'd have to fish them out of her…you know what, but I've started removing the eyes from the toy first to avoid having to do that. They are a choking hazard, after all."

There's another sharp intake of breath from all three Penelopes.

"What? I thought that was a good thing."

The three Penelopes share a look, and I squirm in my seat.

"We'll have to talk about this before we can help you further," Scary Penelope tells me. "We take the defacement of treasured childhood toys very seriously at Penelope's Pooches."

They do?

I rise slowly to my feet. Whatever's going on here is now over, as far as I'm concerned. "It's not a big deal, really. I just wanted to find a toy that can replace the Winnie the Poohs for her. But it looks like maybe I should try another…approach."

"Actually, if you could please give us the room, that'd be great," Scary Penelope replies.

I take a step toward the door. "Good idea. I think I'll get going. Come on, Lady Moo," I call, and as she jumps down from the couch, one of the newly-arrived Penelopes dashes forward and grabs the leash.

"You'll need to leave Lady Moo with us," she tells me.

"But why?" I question.

"It's part of our dog-cept to give dogs the ability to communicate with us without the hindrance of human input," the other one says. "It's the Penelope Pooches way."

I glance between all three of them. If this isn't a cult, I don't know what is.

There's no way I'm leaving Lady Moo with these looney tunes.

"You know what? I think I'll go get a toy from another store. But thank you so much for your help today. It's been," —*weird? unsettling? completely certifiable?*—"so great. So, so great. Now, if you would all please excuse us?" I tug forcefully on the leash, and it pops out of the Penelope's hand. The resulting jolt gives Lady M a shock, and she bolts from the room, dragging me along with her.

Exerting more strength than I'd ever expect from a small

dog, she careens around the corner, banging my arm against the doorframe, causing the leash to jolt from my grasp.

Lady M immediately scampers into the grooming area, where a startled Penelope can only stand and stare, as she climbs the set of dog steps up onto the grooming table and proceeds to launch herself at the white West Highland Terrier, mid-groom.

As she lands heavily on top of the poor unsuspecting dog, she lets out a whine like she's Braveheart going into battle, and the groomer is knocked away by the sheer force of this Boston Terrier on a mission. The buzzing clippers in her hand cut a long path in the dog's fur, from its tail to its head.

"Lady M! No!" I shout, lunging for her as she attempts to clamp her teeth into the Highland Terrier, who quite rightfully begins to growl and bark and bare its teeth at her.

I manage to get a hold of Lady M around her middle, and lift her off the dog, tucking her hot, squirming body under my arm as she barks and barks at the other dog.

"I cannot believe you did that," I scold.

Her behavior with Stevie had clearly lulled me into a false sense of security.

"My dog! My beautiful dog!" A middle-aged woman in a thick wool floral dress and sensible lace up shoes dashes over to grooming table, where her dog now sports an inverse mohawk.

She rounds on me. "You've ruined her! You and your unruly, ill-disciplined dog have ruined my Trixabella-Sophia."

I throw my eyes over her dog, who she now has cradled in her arms. "I'm so, so sorry."

Lady M growls at her. It's clear she's definitely *not* sorry.

"I will happily pay for another groom," I offer.

"And make her look even worse?" the woman sniffs. "I

think you and your dog have done more than enough for one day."

"Mrs. Dunlop. Allow us to help you," Groomer Penelope says.

"How can you help? You can't make it grow back." She collects a wad of fur from the floor and brandishes it at her. "Look at it! Her beautiful fur."

"Actually, Mrs. Dunlop, we have a supplier who has an incredible line of toupees."

"You do?" Mrs. Dunlop questions, clearly softened by the idea of sticking a wig on her dog.

Dog toupees? That's a thing now?

"Oh, yes. Why don't you and Trixabella-Sophia come with me, and we can have a look at the catalog?" Groomer Penelope offers.

"Who's going to pay for *that*?" Mrs. Dunlop looks at me in expectation. Surely, she doesn't think I'm going to pay for a dog wig?

I open my mouth to reply when Senior Penelope steps in and saves me. "Penelope's Pooches would be happy to cover the cost of the toupee, Mrs. Dunlop."

I heave a sigh of relief. "That's awesome," I say with a smile to Senior Penelope. She doesn't return it. Instead, she says something to Junior Penelope out of earshot, before she gestures for Mrs. Dunlop to leave the room with her. They disappear through a door.

I glance warily at Junior Penelope. After an unexpected dog therapy session and grooming disaster, my appetite for any more dog-related drama has well and truly vanished.

She produces a fluffy green turtle dog toy and holds it out for me. "We decided this CPMFD would work for Lady Moo."

I blink at her in disbelief. In all the commotion, the

Penelopes found the time to agree what toy Lady Moo might like and then went and got it from the shelf?

I reach out and take it and offer it to Lady Moo. "Err, thanks."

She begins to sniff it, and I place both her and the toy on the floor—her leash firmly in my grasp. She pounces on it, and immediately begins to chew on one of its legs.

I look up at Junior Penelope. "How did you do that? She's never even gone near a toy that wasn't Winnie the Pooh."

"It's what we do," she says simply.

"Thank you."

"You will find this turtle is virtually indestructible, and she won't be able to disembowel it the way she was doing with your Winne the Poohs."

I watch as Lady M makes contented gnawing noises as she lies on the ground, the toy held between her front paws. "I'll take two," I tell her.

We return to the main part of the store, where I purchase two turtles for an outlandishly high price—which is still a whole lot cheaper than having to buy a dog wig for a disgruntled Mrs. Dunlop—and Zara, Stevie, and Lady M, who refuses to give up her new toy for anyone, happily made our retreat from the insanity that is Penelope's Pooches.

CHAPTER 13

As I knock on her open door, Edina looks up at me from her computer, her wild, auburn hair curling in all directions, a pair of tortoiseshell reading glasses perched at the end of her nose. "Kennedy Bennet has arrived. I was considering sending out a pack of wild dogs to track you down."

A gory image from *Game of Thrones* flashes before my eyes.

"I was on another blind date for the column last night. I stayed up to write a first draft while it was still fresh."

"Where was it this time? That *Rocky Horror* place will be hard to beat."

"It was a kid-themed restaurant where you get to eat your childhood favorites. It was fun, but I didn't know a lot of the food."

"See? That's where the American perspective comes in. You can be so much more objective than your British blind date. Did you have a lot of awkwardness with the guy?"

I think of Devan, the tall, slim guy with pale blond hair and Roman nose I met at the restaurant last night. He was super shy and blushed virtually every time I spoke to him, spending most of his time looking down at his plate.

"Oh, yeah. Super awkward."

Edina's face lifts into a smile. "Perfect. Have it on my desk by the end of the day."

The end of the day?

"But it'll take some time to write and finesse," I protest.

"What you might not realize is that we need content at this magazine, Kennedy Bennet. Content, content, content. Online is a hungry environment to operate in."

"I get that, but—"

"What have you got next for me? Give me unusual. Give me out of the ordinary. Give me unexpected. And it needs to be Christmas themed, considering the big day is almost here. People are obsessed with Christmas, aren't they?"

I run through the mental list I've been building up for conversations like these. "I told you about the bus tour that shows you all the best Christmas lights," I offer, knowing she's already rejected it once before.

She cocks an eyebrow. "What's the angle?"

"The blind date angle on a bus might be different?"

She waves my suggestion away. "Next."

"*Hogwarts in the Snow* at the Warner Bros. Studio? I could meet a blind date dressed as my favorite *Harry Potter* character?"

"If I see another Hufflepuff scarf and pair of round glasses I think I might die."

I don't point out that Harry, the owner of the pair of round glasses, is in fact in Gryffindor. Not overly helpful right now.

"I guess that rules out visiting Santa's grotto, the sing-along Christmas carols at Shakespeare's Globe Theatre, and all the ice skating rinks around town."

"Can you ice skate?" she asks, and I shake my head.

"Now *that's* an angle." Her face brightens at the thought of me making a fool of myself on the ice—or possibly injuring myself. I'm not sure which. "Go meet your blind date at an ice skating rink. Do they still have one at Hampton Court Palace?"

"I don't know, but I can find out."

"Yeah, do that. Nothing says Christmas like ice skating on a blind date at the misogynistic polygamist Henry VIII's palace."

Really?

"Okay. I'll go line it up." I turn to leave.

"Have it on my desk by the end of the week."

I paste on a smile. "Sure thing."

That means I've got to arrange a date, meet the guy, attempt to ice skate, and then write the whole thing up in just three days. Lucky, lucky me.

Edina returns her attention to her computer, signaling our conversation is now done, and I trudge back to my desk.

I slump down in my chair and stifle a yawn. Blind dating and writing articles into the night has me beat. Benjamin Franklin might have been happy with just five hours of sleep a night, but I'm finding out today that just isn't nearly enough for this gal.

I open my phone, flick over to Instagram, and open Hugo's page. There's a new photo this time. It's of him at a Christmas party with his parents and his wife, Fleur. The four of them are standing arm in arm, smiling at the camera as they stand in front of a beautiful Christmas tree. I peer closer at the image. I recognize it as the country club I used to work at, only these four are members, not staff.

I let out a breath and pull up one of the dating apps. I begin to scroll through the options when a message appears on my screen.

How's my favourite Magenta?

I smile to myself. Carl, otherwise known as Caaaahl. I type a reply.

Me: *Good. How about Rocky?*

Carl: *You free for coffee today?*

Although I'm working on a deadline and am in a serious sleep-deficit, I figure I can slip in a quick coffee. Having a little romance at Christmas in London has to be good for a girl—particularly a girl who's had less than zero romance for w*aaaa*y too long now.

Because you know what being in a city filled with whimsical Christmas lights, the smell of gingerbread wafting out of coffee houses, and pretty snowfall has done to me? It's made me lonely. It's made me miss that feeling you get when you share something special with someone. Someone who can marvel at how gorgeous it looks when it snows instead of rains endlessly. Someone who can walk hand in hand with you down the busy city streets and look in wonder at all the spectacular Christmas lights.

Someone to kiss under the mistletoe.

And who knows? Maybe Carl could be that someone?

And I won't know until I give it a try.

I type out a reply.

Me: *Sounds great. I can meet later today, if that works?*

We message each other, finding out where we both work and realizing we're only a few Tube stops apart, and within the hour I tell Shelley that I'm going on an actual date with a real person. She high fives me and wishes me luck, then I slink out of the office, ride the elevator down to the street.

I sashay across the lobby floor with a fresh spring in my step, and push my way through the revolving glass doors when something—or rather some*one*—catches my attention. A man, walking into the building, so close to me we could reach out and touch if it weren't for the glass between us.

Charlie Cavendish.

Here.

At my office.

What the...?

Our eyes meet for a fraction of a second through the glass. It makes me take a wrong step and I almost faceplant, right up against the glass.

So smooth.

Thankfully I right myself in time, to avoid making a total fool of myself. I flick my attention back to him and note his lips curving into a smile—at my expense—while the doors continue to revolve.

A second later, I burst out onto the sidewalk, dazed and confused.

This whole thing happens within the space of about two seconds, but it's sent my mind reeling.

What is he doing here?

Isn't it enough that I have to see him in the building I live in? Now he has to torment me at my office, too?

Sure, the magazine is only one of several businesses in the office tower, so he must be on his way to one of those. But still. This is *my* place. How dare he think he can just waltz on in here looking all sexy and—

"Well, this is a coincidence," a deep voice says behind me.

I whisk around to see him standing on the sidewalk. Wearing a navy coat over a tailored suit and tie, he looks like Clark Kent, all buttoned-up and simmering sex appeal in that *I want to rip his glasses off and kiss him silly* kind of way. Do I try not to notice how good he looks? How blue his eyes look in the winter gloom? How his coat outlines his tall, athletic physique?

How his face lights up as his eyes land on me?

Of course I do. But I fail. Horribly.

I gawk at him, trying to regain my equilibrium, my belly

fluttering and my heart thudding at the unexpected sight of him. "I…err, yes, it is a coincidence."

That told him.

He gestures at the building looming over us. "This is where you work."

It's a statement, not a question.

"Yup."

"You write for a magazine."

"Yup."

He lets out a laugh. "Well, aren't you the Chatty Kathy today."

"I'm plenty chatty," I reply lightly. "In fact, I'm on my way to meet a guy for a date, and I plan on being very chatty with him. So, if you'll excuse me, I have to go or else I'll be late."

"I wouldn't want to make you late for your date," he consults his wristwatch, "at one forty-three in the afternoon." He pauses before he adds, "On a workday."

His point?

I'm about to open my mouth to reply that what I do with my work time is totally up to me—well, me and my boss that is, but what Edina doesn't know in this instance won't hurt her—when I clamp it shut. It's none of his business what I do with my time.

So, instead, I simply muster the sweetest smile I can manage, and say, "So nice to see you, Charlie. Bye for now," and turn on my heel.

"Did you like the arancini?" he calls out after me.

I stop and turn back. I should have thanked him without the need for prompting. Where are my manners? "It was good. Thank you again."

"My pleasure." His smile renders his face irresistibly handsome, and I find myself staring at him, my belly fluttering. "Well, I won't hold you up."

"No. Right."

"Bye then."

"Bye."

He turns and makes his way back through the revolving doors.

I make my way toward the Tube, trying my best to shake myself out of my Charlie-induced miasma.

A short train ride later, I enter a cute little Italian coffee house that's playing Christmas carols with a brightly-lit and festive Christmas tree in the corner, the aroma of gingerbread and cinnamon enough to make my mouth water. I spot Carl at a table, and he stands and greets me before we order our coffee.

"So, this is what you look like in your 'normy' clothes," I say to him, as we take our piping hot coffees to a table by the window. He's wearing a V-neck sweater over a plain white collared shirt and a pair of olive pants, a winter jacket folded over one arm. Without his blond bowl-cut Rocky wig from the club, I barely recognized him with his short brown hair. Luckily, he recognized me.

"Can I let you in on a secret?" he asks.

"Always."

"I found that whole dressing up as Rocky thing really freeing. Like I could be someone else for a few hours, you know?"

"Don't you like being Carl Newton?" I ask with a smile.

"Oh, he's fine. But being Rocky is a whole other level."

"So, I should expect you to turn up in your gold shorts and blond wig again sometime soon?"

He laughs. "If I want to catch hypothermia. But you know, perhaps he's here with me now?"

My smile drops a fraction. "What do you mean exactly?"

"I mean I can carry his essence with me. Inside." He taps his chest.

His essence. Right.

I'm suddenly having some second thoughts about this guy. "Good for you."

He scrunches up his face. "You think I'm weird. Don't you?"

I wave my hand in the air as I blow on my hot coffee. If I can cool it down quickly, I can drink it fast and then get out of here. "No, it's all good."

"It's nothing weird. Just a self-esteem boost. Does that sound mad?"

I've lived here long enough to know "mad" means crazy in British English, not angry.

"Nope. It sounds sane enough, I guess."

His features relax. "Good, because when I said it, it sounded pretty freaking mad to me," he replies with a laugh.

I relax. "I can totally get on board with carrying a little alter ego around with you."

He grins at me, the skin around his hazel eyes crinkling. "There is one thing."

"What's that?"

"You mentioned seeing me again. Are you already arranging our next date before we've even taken a sip of our coffee?" His eyes are teasing me.

"You noticed that, huh?" I reply, as I pull my foot out of my gaping mouth. "I'm one smooth operator."

His laugh is low and warming. "Actually, I've got to admit something to you. I was nervous about seeing you again. You know, after we got on so well the other night."

"Getting along with a girl on a date is a bad thing?" I ask, as I take a sip of my coffee. It's warm and sweet and creamy and delicious.

"Weird, I know. I've been in the situation with online dating where if you get past the initial meeting in real life and you're not running a mile, then it can seem too good to be true. You know?"

"I hear you."

"And you're even cuter not dressed as Magenta."

"You're not into that whole French maid thing?" I tease.

"Oh, I'm into it," he replies with a suggestive laugh. "But it's good to see the real you." He grins at me, and I return it.

This is easy. Nice.

"Have you written your article?"

"Yes, and my boss even liked it. Don't worry, I referred to you as my cute date and didn't name you."

"I like that: cute date."

I take a sip of my coffee. "So, you work a couple of stops from here?"

"Yeah, I'm a statistician at Dumbflowers Research. I collect and analyze information for the bigwigs to make decisions."

"You're a numbers guy, huh?"

"Absolutely. Numbers have always been my thing. Designing studies and getting all that raw data to play with? That's my idea of fun. I know, I'm strange."

"That's not strange at all."

A phone chimes and we both reach for our respective devices. It's Carl's.

He reads the screen, and his features harden. "Unbelievable. She's having a laugh."

"Everything okay?"

He pulls his attention from the screen. "It's nothing." His jaw is locked, and his nostrils are actually flaring, like an angry bull.

"It looks like something to me."

"It's my ex. She just texted me." He waggles his phone from side to side in the air. "She's stolen my cat."

"That's terrible," I exclaim.

"My cat. *Mine*. Not hers. I chose him. She can't just waltz into my home, my *home*, and take him. She can't do that."

"I think that's breaking and entering, as well as theft."

"Exactly," he replies, sitting back in his seat. "Breaking and entering and theft. Huh."

We fall into silence, me awkward, him fuming. Eventually, he looks back at me and tells me, "I'm sorry this has interrupted our coffee date, but it's hard to hear when someone's stolen your cat."

"I'm so sorry she did that."

"I'll get him back. Mark my words."

"Sure."

"This isn't the first time she's pulled something like this."

I don't reply. I don't want to know what else this woman has done, especially on a second date with the guy.

Boundaries, people.

"What am I thinking? I'm here with a beautiful woman and I'm complaining about someone I'm no longer with. I'm sorry."

I offer him a smile. "Don't be. It's all good."

"I hope you still want that third date?" he asks, and he looks so cute and vulnerable, I nod my head.

"Of course I do."

He returns my smile, his eyes soft. "Great."

Just as we're getting things back on track, his phone beeps again. He picks it up and then looks back up at me. "Not her, don't worry. But I've got to cut this short. They need me back at the office."

"But you haven't even finished your coffee."

"I'll have to get it in a takeaway cup. I'm really sorry about this. I thought I had the afternoon clear."

"No worries. These things happen. You're a statistician in demand."

"You have no idea. Want to get yours to takeaway, too?"

"Sure."

We get our coffee transferred to paper cups and together we head out the door and into the cold.

"You know what, Kennedy? I'm going to ask you out again."

I laugh. "Are you warning me?"

"No, I'm asking you. Will you go out with me again?"

I smile at him as a warm feeling claims my stomach—despite the slightly unnerving ex-slash-cat-slash-criminal-activity situation. "I'd like that."

"Friday night?"

"Oh, I can't. I have a thing."

His face falls. "Okay. Another time, maybe."

"I really do have a thing. It's my birthday party. Just a small get-together with friends at my local pub."

He gives a short-lived smile. "Happy birthday. I'd better get going. Thanks for… this. I suppose I'll see you around." He looks dejected, and I instantly feel bad.

As he turns to leave, I make a rash decision. One I hope I won't regret. "Carl? Would you like to come? It's at The Black Cat in Notting Hill this Friday at seven."

"Are you sure? You're not just saying that because I'm a sad loser with a thieving ex?"

"Of course not. I'd love for you to come. See you then?"

His face creases into a broad grin. "See you then."

As I turn to leave, I push the awkwardness of the date aside. He can't help it that he got a badly-timed unpleasant text from his ex. He seems like a nice guy, and I'm sure he'll fit in just fine with my friends at my birthday party.

CHAPTER 14

I zip up my calf-length dress, slip on my shoes, and turn to look at myself in Delphine's full-length mirror. Even though tonight's thirtieth birthday party is a relaxed celebration with just my closest friends at my local pub, that doesn't mean I haven't gone all out with my dress. No way. A girl only turns thirty once, you know, and considering I woke up today with a sinking feeling that told me my youth was gone and never to be found again—okay, I was in an overly dramatic mood—I could sure do with feeling pretty tonight. This dress is the bomb.

"Kennedy, you look *stunning*," Lottie breathes behind me, her long hair falling in soft curls over her shoulders, her full lips painted red. "What's that material?" She collects a handful of the skirt of the dress in her hand.

"It's tulle. You don't think the yellow is too much?"

"Babe, with your dark eyes and hair and that gorgeous skin tone, you look like a tall Salma Hayek in that dress. Seriously. I've got major dress envy right now."

I regard my less than buxom-movie-star cleavage critically in the low-cut, strappy dress that I paid a cripplingly high price for at a boutique specifically for tonight. Even with the clever cut there's no way I could be considered buxom. "Yeah, if Salma Hayek had B-cups and next to no hips."

"You're beautiful, babe. Trust me. Inside and out."

I grin at my friend in the reflection. "Keep those compliments coming. I sure need 'em tonight."

She scrunches up her face. "Is thirty all that bad?"

Satisfied with my party-ready appearance, I turn to face her. "It's a weird feeling to know I'll never be in my twenties again. Like that part of my life is suddenly gone, over, and instead I'm hurtling toward middle age."

She leans closer to peer in the mirror and flicks an eyelash from her cheek. "But it's just a number, babe. It's not like you've got to walk around with the number thirty sewn onto your top or something. Like in that Emma Stone movie."

"Wasn't than an 'A' for adulteress?" I ask with a laugh.

"You get what I mean. You still look like you did yesterday. As far as the world knows, you're still in your twenties."

I let out a sigh. "It's not just about how I look to everyone. It's where I am in life, you know?"

She makes a face. "You mean single?"

I nod.

"Try being me, with a mother who's matchmaking you with every straight guy under the age of sixty in the greater London area. It's not fun, believe me."

"Single, no kids, career taking a weird turn for the *I don't know what* right now. All that stuff. I should be settled, in control, know where I'm going and how I'm gonna get there. You know?"

"Babe, that sounds so freaking boring to me. What about adventure? What about spontaneity? Excitement? Where's all that in your *I know where I'm going and how I'm gonna get there* plan?"

"Excitement is overrated," I reply, as I pick Lady M's Penelope's Pooches chew toy off the floor. "I want certainty. Stability."

She arches her eyebrow at me. "Do you really?"

"Yes!" I insist. "It's fine for you. You're not thirty until next year. I'm old now. More mature." I offer her a grin.

"Okay, Ms. Mature, you've got a party to get to. I hope you're not too mature to have some fun tonight."

I flick the closet light off and collect my coat and purse from the bed before I take the well-chewed toy to the living room and offer it to Lady M. She wags her tail fiercely at the sight of it, before clamping her jaw onto it and scuttling off to her bed.

"You must be so happy she's taken to that. What have you done with all the Winnie the Poohs?"

"Still in the hallway closet," I say, as I pull the door open for her to see.

"It's like a shelf at Hamleys, but completely dedicated to one toy," she says in wonderment.

I inspect the rows of toys. "I've saved you all," I tell them.

Lottie lets out a laugh.

We make our way to the front door, and with my hand on the doorknob, I turn to her and give her a quick hug.

"Thanks for getting ready with me tonight, Lottie. I was feeling a little down in the dumps, and you really pulled me out of it."

"Are you kidding me? There was no way I was giving up the chance to use a three-headed shower in a marble bathroom." She winks at me. "Oh, I almost forgot. I got you a birthday gift." She reaches into her purse, produces a pink envelope, and hands it to me. "Does it suck to have a birthday this close to Christmas?"

"It did when I was a kid, but now I'm quite happy to fly under the radar." I rip the envelope open and pull out a card and hand-written voucher. "'This voucher entitles you to a Lottie-guided tour of a London museum of your choice, followed by a special afternoon tea at The Ritz.' The Ritz is so fancy. Lottie, that's so sweet of you."

"I know you don't always appreciate my weird and wonderful museum choices, so I thought I'd let you decide."

"It takes a certain type of person to enjoy seeing an operating room in a church where people had surgery without anesthetics."

"It's historically—"

"Important," I finish for her. "I know. You've told us." I give her a quick hug. "Thanks for this. You know I'm choosing Madame Tussauds, right?"

She rolls her eyes at me. "So mainstream."

A short walk later, we can hear the music and chatter from The Black Cat out on the street, the windows lined with Christmas lights, welcoming us inside. We push through the door, and I'm immediately hit by the aroma of freshly cooked pub meals and my friends' smiling faces.

"Happy birthday!" everyone chimes, and the entire pub breaks into applause as the birthday song is played on the stereo. People sing along, those patrons who don't know me fudging my name, and I grin at everyone, happiness radiating across my chest.

"You guys are the best."

"Pass me your coat, babe," Lottie instructs, and as I slip my long wool coat off, I'm thankful the pub is super warm. Someone whistles, and I do a little twirl to show off my dress.

"You look like a beauty queen," Zara gushes as she pulls me in for a hug.

I laugh. "Do they have thirty-year-old beauty queens?"

"Welcome to the thirty club. It's a great place to be. Right, Asher?"

"Totally. No more of that twenties angst," he replies, as he plants a kiss on my cheek. "Happy birthday, fellow American in a sea of Britishness."

"Hey! I'm here too, you know," Emma, my friend from the *Dating Mr. Darcy* reality show and all-around Texas gal complains.

"Ash, I bet you never had a moment of 'twenties angst' in your life," Zara says.

"It was too long ago to remember," he replies.

Zara rolls her eyes good-humoredly.

"I need to hug the beautiful birthday girl," Emma says, as she does just that. "How do you smell so good? New perfume?"

"A birthday treat I bought myself. I figured I deserved it," I reply.

"Oh, you so do. Our gift is with the others over on the table. You can open them all after we get some champagne into you."

Emma's husband, Sebastian, kisses me on the cheek. "Happy birthday, Kennedy. I've been advised I'm on champagne duty, and here's your glass." He passes me a flute, filled to the brim.

Tabitha's the next to say hello, wrapping her long, slim arms around me and pulling me into a tight hug. "Oh, girl, I just love you so darn much! The happiest of birthdays to you, babe."

Shelley, the only person I invited from the magazine, introduces me to her boyfriend, Brendon, a fellow New Zealander who she met at a "SANZA" pub in London a few months ago. She tells me SANZA stands for South Africa New Zealand Australia, and apparently the pubs are super popular with our antipodean friends, full to the brim with them every night. When I asked her why she would travel 12,500 miles from home only to socialize with people from her country, she told me it was a good point and she'd get back to me on it.

I have yet to hear her reply, but by the looks of her and Brendon, stealing looks at one another and sharing kisses when they think no one's looking, it's worked out perfectly for them both.

Shelley and her boyfriend complete my little party, except for Carl, who has yet to arrive. If I'm being totally honest, I'm not even sure I want him to come. It's a fun, cozy group of my closest London friends, and the conversation flows easily as we sip our drinks and nibble on the trays of snacks I'd arranged. But then looking at Zara with Asher, Emma with Sebastian, and Shelley with Brendon, I can't help but feel a pang of loneliness. When is it going to happen for me? When am I going to find my Big Love, the love that feels so right? When am I going to be swept off my feet by my prince?

The night presses on and the champagne starts going to my head. Pretty soon, I have Tabitha gushing about how amazing I am as she props herself up on the bar, Lottie and Zara insisting I ask a cute guy to dance who's sitting in the corner with his buddies and looks about eighteen—my response is a firm no because I'm not interested in that level of cougar-ness, or any level, for that matter—and my friends bringing out the cutest birthday cake. It's shaped like Lady Moo, with #BirthdayMama and #NoWinnieThePooh written in icing on the base. What's more, its rich chocolate, and tastes like heaven on a plate.

I'm chatting to Emma as we hold our empty plates in our hands.

"You see, that's the thing. There isn't enough quality activewear for toddlers in this country, so Penny—" Emma trails off as her eyes grow wide.

NEVER FALL FOR YOUR ENEMY

"What is it, Em?" I ask.

She's focusing on something behind me, and by the looks of her, it's something unexpected. She nudges me with her elbow, her eyes wide.

"Hello, Kennedy," a deep voice says, and I turn to see Carl standing there, grinning at me. Only it's Carl the way he looked the first night I met him. Yup, you got it. He's in his Rocky outfit, from his blonde bowl-cut wig to his gold shorts. And not a lot else.

"Carl, hi. You're…here," I manage, as my brain scrambles to compute.

Why has he come to my party dressed as Rocky?

Everyone around me has stopped their conversations and are now gaping with a mixture of shock and amusement at the *Rocky Horror Picture Show* vision that has stepped into the pub. The music may still be playing, but it's the only sound in the room.

Carl grins at me as though he's wearing more than just a Speedo over fifteen percent of his body. "Happy birthday," he says.

"*This* is Carl?" Emma asks, her face lighting up in a grin.

"Wow. That's quite an outfit." Tabitha looks him up and down. Which, to be fair, everyone is doing right now, because did I mention he's wearing nothing but gold shorts in my local pub? In winter.

Wow. Just wow.

He presses a gift into my hands. "I'm sorry I'm late. I had to get Rocky-ed. You know?"

"Yeah, I can see that," I say through my forced smile.

Mt friends are still gawping.

"Aren't you gonna introduce us to your date?" Asher asks with a glint in his eye, and I shoot him a look.

Carl takes a step to the left and lifts his hand in a wave. "All right, everyone? I'm Carl."

There's a chorus of "Hello Carl" and he beams at them all.

"Someone get this man a drink," Tabitha exclaims, and Sebastian asks him what he wants.

"Something warming, I think. It's cold tonight," Carl declares.

"Whiskey? Brandy?" Sebastian offers.

"I'll come with you," Carl tells him, and the two men make their way through the still-gaping patrons to the bar.

"What the heck, Kennedy?" Zara says to me, once they're out of earshot.

"That's a wig, right? It looks like a wig," Lottie says.

"That's what you're focused on?" Tabitha replies, her eyes wide.

"I think the guy is in serious need of a psych evaluation," Emma tells us.

I put my hands up. "I just need to put this out there: I did not ask him to wear that outfit tonight."

Zara shakes her head. "Why would you? What guy wears that kind of thing to a girl's birthday party where her *friends* will see him?"

Lottie scrunches up her nose. "It's an odd choice."

"It's his *Rocky Horror Picture Show* outfit. He's Rocky," I explain, trying to make this all feel a little less bizarre. "It's from the club I went to with him, remember?"

Tabitha regards him through narrowed eyes. "Well, he's got nice abs, I'll give him that. Even if he looks like a hen's night entertainer."

"OMG, he so does!" Lottie exclaims, wide-eyed. "He's not, though. Is he?" she asks me.

"He's a statistician," I explain.

"How do you know?" Lottie asks.

"Because he told me."

"Maybe he's a statistician by day and a ladies' entertainer by night?" Tabitha suggests.

"Totally plausible," Zara agrees. "Do statisticians need to supplement their income?"

"Maybe it's his thing? You know, like Asher likes to surf," Lottie offers.

"I'd hardly say surfing and stripping are the same sorts of hobbies," Zara replies.

Lottie shrugs. "They could be. They're both athletic."

Tabitha laughs. "Well, it wouldn't take him long to strip if he did. He's hardly wearing anything. In *December*. Didn't it snow earlier?"

"Maybe his abs are your birthday gift," Emma suggests.

I let out a puff of air as I glance at Carl. He and Sebastian have their drinks, and are walking over toward us.

"Quick! Act natural," Lottie tells us.

I turn and smile at Carl when he and Sebastian join our group. "Hey, Carl? Want to go have a chat?" I ask.

"Okay," he replies pleasantly.

I lead him past my friends' prying eyes and find an empty spot by the bar where we perch on a couple of bar stools.

"Cheers," he says, as he clinks his tumbler against my flute. He takes a sip and declares, "That's better. I can see why St. Bernards carry brandy. Keeps you nice and warm."

I take a sip and then place my glass carefully down on the bar. "You're dressed as Rocky, I see," I lead.

"Yeah. Obviously," he replies with a laugh.

"Can I ask why? Are you on your way to the club?"

He shakes his head. "It's strange, I know, but I think being Rocky is me. Do you know what I mean?"

Uh, no.

"How, exactly?"

"It's like by being him I can be the best version of myself. Uninhibited. New. Free. Does that make sense?"

"Oh, I totally get it. It's just—" How do I put it? It's weird?

You're freaking me out? It's completely inappropriate for my thirtieth birthday party at a pub?

He saves me from having to finish my sentence by pushing out a breath, his shoulders slumping as he hangs his head, muttering, "It's no use. It's no use."

"Carl? Are you okay? I didn't mean to upset you or anything."

He looks up, his eyes filled with sorrow, the grin he was sporting only moments ago now vanished from his sunken face. "It's my ex."

"The one who stole your cat?"

He nods, his lips in a thin line. "Yup."

"Could you not get it back or something?"

To my surprise, his eyes well with tears, and he tries in vain to blink them away. Instead, they run down his cheeks, his bottom lip trembling.

I blink at him, not sure what to do. I have a guy I barely know, who showed up late to my birthday party dressed in gold shorts and is now literally crying over another woman.

I'd say this third date hasn't gotten off to the best of starts.

"She... she," he starts, but he's unable to carry on as he dissolves in tears, his shoulders heaving, choking sounds emitting from his throat.

I place my hand tentatively on his bare back and give him a couple of pats. "There there, Carl. It can't be all that bad."

Maybe the cat is dead?

"It is, though. It's terrible," he splutters, as he wipes his running nose with the back of his hand. He rests his head on my shoulder and continues to heave.

I look over at my friends, not sure what to do, when a familiar form catches my eye.

It's Charlie Cavendish, and he's looking at Carl and me with a smirk on his face.

How fan-freaking-tastic.

"Everything okay here?" Charlie asks, as he leans his elbows on the bar. His *clothed* elbows, unlike my date's.

I paste on a smile, as if I don't have a 6'1" barely dressed man in a wig sobbing on my shoulder. "Fine, thank you."

Charlie's gaze flicks from me to Carl and back again. "I'll have to take your word for that."

"Carl here was just telling me about his cat," I explain.

"Ah, this is Carl."

"Yup."

The edges of his mouth curve upwards as his eyes flick to Carl's heaving form. "Good to know."

What the heck is he doing here? I certainly didn't invite him, and even though some of my friends are friendly with him, they know better than to invite him behind my back.

"You know, Charlie, this is my *private* party tonight? As in, invitation only."

He raises his finger at the server. "I'm very happy for you."

Annoying much?

Carl lifts his head from my shoulder long enough to wipe his eyes before he sniffs boisterously, and nuzzles my shoulder once more.

"Your date sure is having a good time."

"He's just a little upset about his cat," I reply through my teeth, as I pat Carl on the back. "Really, I don't know why you think you can just waltz in here and crash my party like you—"

I'm interrupted by the server pushing a brown paper bag across the bar at him. "Here you go, Charlie. One cottage pie with extra mash and gravy to takeaway."

"Thanks, Brian. Add it to my tab?"

"No worries, Charlie. See you next week."

"You know I can't get through the week without one of Cheryl's cottage pies." Charlie turns to me with a smile on his face and says, "I'm sorry, Kennedy. What were you saying?"

"Nothing," I mutter, as heat springs into my cheeks.

Sure, I just made a rather large leap, but he doesn't need to be all smarmy about it.

Carl chooses this moment to raise his head once more, tears streaming down his face, and declare, "I want her back. I do. I want her back so bad."

I flick my eyes to Carl's damp, wet face. His wig has shifted, and his nose is all pink and splotchy. "I thought your cat was a male?"

"I don't mean Sir Purrs-a-lot. I mean my ex. I love her and I want her back." His face crumples as a sob escapes his lips.

Oh, good grief.

With a pint glass of trepidation, I lift my gaze to Charlie, expecting his eyes to be full of hilarity.

He's gone, the door to the pub closing softly behind him.

CHAPTER 15

"Okay, Lady M. You be a super, super good girl for Esme and her family while I'm away. Eat your dinner, chew your new toy, and most of all, behave."

Lady M's eyes are trained on me, and as the last word leaves my mouth, she cocks her head to the side as though the word *behave* is a foreign concept to her.

Figures.

I pick her up off the floor and plant a kiss on her forehead. "I'm gonna miss you, little girl."

Her response is to lick my face, her little stub of a tail brushing side to side against my arm.

Esme smiles as she stands in the doorway, holding Lady M's bed filled with her food and new favorite chew toy in her arms, watching us say goodbye. "She'll be fine with us, Kennedy. Don't worry about her. Mum said she'll give Lady Moo turkey for her Christmas dinner, and there's already a gift for her under the tree."

"You're so sweet, Esme. I don't know what I'd do without you. Thank you for everything." I hold Lady M close, her warm little body soft against my chest. The thought of not seeing her face each day while I'm home for Christmas makes me sadder than I thought I would be, considering we've only been together for a matter of six or seven weeks. But the little scamp has really grown on me.

"I've got the keys in case I need anything else. Have a safe trip and I'll see you on New Year's Eve." She holds her hands out to take Lady M, and I reluctantly hand the dog over to her.

"Merry Christmas for tomorrow, Esme," I say.

"Merry Christmas. Come on, girl, let's go." She flashes me a smile and carries Lady M down the hall.

I close the door and allow myself one moment to think of her before I snap into organization mode.

In the bedroom, my packed suitcase lying open on the bed, I run through my checklist.

Passport? *Check.*

Kids' Christmas presents, including a red London double decker toy bus, a teddy bear with *I heart London* on its T-shirt, an old-fashioned red telephone box, and a couple of Union Jack backpacks? *Check.*

Quintessentially London Christmas treats, such as a selection of handmade chocolates from Harrods that I in no way sampled (okay, yes, I did, but it was purely for quality control reasons), the prettiest tin of Fortnum and Mason cookies with a merry go round illustration that actually revolves as it plays music, and a box of the world's most expensive Christmas crackers, filled with classy British trinkets and probably jokes none of us will get? *Check.*

Totally cute holiday outfit that says *I'm a strong, independent woman in charge of my own life despite the fact you all think I ran away from home to nurse my broken heart?*

I mean seriously, can one outfit really say all that?

I zip my suitcase up and pull it off the end of the bed. I wheel it to the front door. Doing one last check that everything in the flat is switched off, I slip on my coat, collect my purse from the hallway table, and lock the door behind me.

I wheel my suitcase down the hallway to the elevator and press the "down" button. The creaking sound of metal machinery tells me the elevator is coming down from above, which can only mean one thing: it was at Charlie's floor.

As it glides down the elevator shaft, I say a little prayer that it was dropping him off—and not picking him up.

When the doors swoosh open, I learn immediately that my prayers have definitely *not* been answered.

Standing in front of me, leaning against the back of the elevator as though he owns it, is the man himself.

He's wearing the same suit and tie combo and winter coat he had on when I bumped into him at work, and he has his head down as he reads something on his phone.

Thoughts flood my mind.

Why didn't I take the stairs?

He really did save someone from drowning.

Why does he have to look so darn good all the time?

He gave me candy.

What must he think of me after the Carl-sobbing-on-my-shoulder-in-a-gold-Speedo incident last night?

And finally, the most unsettling thought of all:

He looks so darn kissable.

What can I say? There's a lot going on in there.

He lifts his eyes to mine, and his lips do that characteristic twitch. "Miss Kennedy Bennet. What a wonderful surprise," he says, his tone droll.

"Well, it's a surprise, at least. I'm not sure how wonderful it is," I say tersely, as I do my best to ignore the way things flutter inside my belly.

I step inside the elevator and turn my back to him. Although the "G" button for the ground floor—which should logically be called the first floor but isn't in this country, for reasons unknown to me—is already lit, I press it again for good measure.

"Merry Christmas Eve to you, too," he says with a light laugh.

The doors swoosh closed, and as the elevator begins its descent, I glance up at the mistletoe tied with a festive ribbon over my head.

That's all I need.

I keep my gaze trained on the door, as though it's the most interesting set of doors I've ever seen, willing this ride to be swift.

Why do I have to feel things for this man? Sure, from the moment I laid eyes on him, I've been fully aware of how attractive he is. I'm only human. And then he opened his mouth with his smug privilege and any interest I might have in him was well and truly squashed.

Or I thought it was, at least.

The problem is, now that I'm getting to know the real Charlie, my resolve to hate him is slipping.

And I can't let it slip.

Not if I'm going to protect my heart.

His voice punctuates my inner wrestling match. "Is Carl okay?"

"He's fine. Thank you for asking."

"Good to know. Are you going somewhere?"

"No, I'm just taking my suitcase for a walk," I reply, pleased with my retort.

"You're taking your suitcase for a walk in the *snow?*" he questions.

With my lips drawn into a line, I flick my eyes briefly to his. As expected, his face is lit up in a smile, rendering it ridiculously, and more importantly, irritatingly handsome. "It's snowing?" I ask.

"Just started a few moments ago. Perfect for Christmas Eve, don't you think?"

He's right. Snow makes Christmas Eve even more magical. I'm not going to agree with him, though. So, instead, I return my attention to the door. "Great. That'll make my trip so much faster."

"Your trip to the airport, I presume?"

"Yup."

"Because you're going to Paris to spend Christmas with your scantily-clad boyfriend and his cat?"

I stare straight ahead and press my lips together to keep from smiling. That was actually quite funny.

"He's not my boyfriend," I reply, as the elevator suddenly gives a giant lurch and I lose my balance. I grasp for something to hold on to but find only thin air. I stumble and fall face first into something firm and warm and... *oh, no.*

His strong, muscular arms wrap around my body to steady me, and I try my best not to breathe in his intoxicating scent.

The elevator bounces up and down, up and down, and I hold on to him to keep from falling as the lights flicker around us and then go out altogether. Plunged into sudden darkness, we both stagger a couple of steps, and then he rights himself, standing strong and firm as I hang off him like a monkey on a tree. A warm, strong, impossibly sexy tree.

And then, mercifully, the bouncing comes to a grinding halt, the lights flick back on, and the bottom of the elevator no longer feels like the springy floor at Penelope's Pooches.

My heart is banging out of my chest from the shock, and I work hard at steadying my breathing.

I look up at Charlie's square, stubble-lined jaw, noticing for the first time that he has a small mole by his ear, and I have the strangest need to reach out and touch it. I lift my hand and—

Wait, *what?!*

What the heck am I doing?

I snatch my hand back, utterly discomfited.

I cannot allow his good looks and general sexiness to get under my skin, even if he does smell amazing. I definitely cannot allow contact, like having his arms wrapped protectively around me just now.

He's Charlie Cavendish for goodness' sake! I should not be standing in a confined space with him, alone, locked in an embrace, as I have unsettling thoughts about his facial moles and my irrational and frankly weird desire to touch one of them.

"Are you okay?" he asks as he looks down at me, our bodies still smooshed up against each other, his arms firmly wrapped around me.

I snap to attention, leaping back from him as though he's scalding me with his heat—which, let's face it, he kinda is—I try to regain my aloof composure from before, all while knowing that ship has sailed so far, it's halfway across the Atlantic by now. "Yes. Fine, thanks." I adjust my clothes and smooth out my hair. "You?"

"All in one piece." He lifts the ancient-looking phone receiver from the wall and presses the button. "The lift must have broken down."

"Well, color you Sherlock Holmes," I scoff, and then immediately regret it. I might have conflicting feelings about the guy, but he did just save me from hitting the elevator wall.

"Sorry," I mutter. "Habit."

"I'm nothing if not observant," he replies absently, as he holds the receiver to his ear. "Hello, yes. The lift appears to be stuck between floors," he says into the receiver. "Right…

yes…myself and one other…yes, we're both unharmed…I'm not sure but I'll find out." He looks at me. "Do you know which floors we're between?"

I look up and see a five-inch gap that shows the edge of a hallway carpet above us. "I can't tell, but maybe close to the first or second floor?"

"We're not sure, sorry. Perhaps the first and second," he says into the receiver. "All right…Yes, I understand, although it would be helpful if you were to prioritize us…Yes, I am aware it's Christmas Eve… Ah, yes, the snow. Thank you. We'll hold tight until then." He hangs up the phone and turns to me. "We're stuck for now."

"Really, with detective skills like that, you should join the police force." Despite wanting to sound dismissive, my lips curve into a smile.

He returns it, his eyes soft. "Not a career I've ever considered, but thank you for the compliment."

"Not a compliment."

"I got that."

"How long did they say it would be before we can get out of here?"

"Apparently, coupled with the fact that it's Christmas Eve and it's snowing, it may be some time."

"What does 'some time' mean, exactly?"

"She didn't say."

I twist my mouth as I begin to pace up and down the small space. "They need to get here fast because I've got a plane to catch, and I can't miss it."

Add to the fact that being stuck in here with a man I have definite feelings for, who I don't want to have definite feelings for, this is not an ideal situation for me.

"Because then you'll miss your romantic getaway with the guy in the gold shorts who's not your boyfriend?" he asks.

"How can you joke at a time like this?"

He shrugs. "What else is there to do? We're stuck in here for now."

With my hands on my hips, I declare, "Well, I for one am not going to put up with this."

"What do you propose doing about it? Shimmying up the wall and condensing yourself to fit through that tiny gap up there?"

"I'm going call them again. Demand better service."

He steps away from the wall phone. "Be my guest."

"I will. Not that I'm being your guest by using this phone. It's public property," I sniff, not even sure why I'm making such a petty point.

All he does is smile at me.

I lift the receiver and listen to it ring. A moment later, it's answered by a woman with a low, gruff smoker's voice. "Hey, there. My…neighbor called a few moments ago about the elevator on Hewitt Street."

"Has it started working again?" she asks.

"No. It hasn't. We need you to get it fixed pronto. You see, I've got a flight to catch and—"

"It's in the queue."

"Which means what exactly?"

"Which means it's in the queue."

Helpful.

"How long is this queue?"

"Long."

Also helpful.

"Can you bump it up the queue?"

"If I did that for you, I'd have to do it for everyone, wouldn't I? And then the queue would still be the queue."

"Sure, I get it. The thing is, I really need to not be in here." I flick my eyes to Charlie. He's tapping something on his phone, not paying me any attention. "Is there anything you can do to speed it up?"

"Look, there are only so many service technicians in West London, and what with it snowing and being Christmas Eve an' all, you might be in for wait."

"But—"

"We'll let you know when we're working on it."

"I can't—"

"Hold tight until then. Bye for now."

I let out a resigned sigh as I hang up the phone.

The reality of the situation well and truly sinks in.

Charlie Cavendish and I are stuck.

Together.

Alone.

CHAPTER 16

*T*en long minutes later and we're still here.

I push out a breath as I glance over at Charlie. He's leaning up against the wall, one leg crossed over the other, as he concentrates on tapping on his phone. His eyebrows are pulled together into an eleven.

I return my attention to my own screen, typing out a message to the London Babes WhatsApp group to complain about my current predicament.

Thank goodness we've got coverage in here, that's all I can say.

I flick over to Instagram. This time, Hugo's got a new photo. It's of him and his wife at the beach, wrapped up in sweaters, the wind in their hair. Hugo's holding a sprig of mistletoe above their heads as they kiss.

Ugh.

I glance up at the mistletoe above my own head and chew on my lip.

I check the time. It's been eleven minutes since my conversation with the elevator lady, but it feels like a *lifetime*.

Charlie and I have not uttered another word to each other since.

Once again, I check the airline app. It's still saying my flight is on time, which means I have less than three and a half hours to get out of this elevator, get to Heathrow, check in, drop my luggage, clear customs, get to the gate, and board my plane.

It's doable, but only if I can get out of here in the next fifteen minutes, max.

My phone vibrates in my hand as a new message arrives in the London Babes WhatsApp group.

Lottie: *You're stuck in your building's lift? Poor you!*

Me: *My sentiments exactly.*

Lottie: *Wait. Aren't you meant to be on your way to the airport?*

Me: *Yup. Not happy about it. I'm worried I'll miss my flight.*

Lottie: *Are you on your own? Because that would be the worst. #claustrophobia*

I flick my eyes to Charlie once more. He's still focusing on his phone, but as he lifts his eyes and our gazes lock for a moment, it makes my body flood with warmth as the memory of the way it felt to be held in his arms hits me in the chest.

Geez! Where's an ice bath when you need one?

I offer him a terse smile and return my attention to my phone.

Me: *Nope. I'm lucky enough to be stuck in here with my enemy.*

Lottie: *Wait, what?!! Do you mean that right this very second, you're stuck in a lift with Charlie Cavendish?*

Me: *I've only got one enemy. ;)*

Lottie: *What are the chances?*

Me: *High if you consider how often I accidentally bump into the guy.*

Lottie: *I've got to process this...*
Me: *What about me? I'm living it right now.*
Tabitha: *Kennedy, I've just read that you're stuck in a lift with Charlie Cavendish. Can this really be happening? I'm glad I'm sitting down for this. We need to discuss this. Now.*

Tabitha has clearly entered the conversation.

Me: *It's happening.*
Tabitha: *Oh, babe. I SO want to be a fly on the wall for this. You, stuck with Charlie Cavendish. OMG!*
Lottie: *I want to be a fly on the wall, too. One hundred percent.*
Me: *It's fine, really it is. We're both on our phones and I'm sitting on my suitcase that's filled with Christmas treats.*

Not that I have any intention of being stuck in here long enough to need them.

Zara: *Am I really reading what I think I'm reading? Kennedy's stuck in a lift with Charlie?*

Aaaaaand Zara's joined the chat.

Lottie: *Isn't it exciting?*
Zara: *Yes! So exciting!*
Me: *No, it's not exciting in the least. It's a pain in the butt and I might miss my flight home.*
Lottie: *Tabitha and I want to be a fly on the wall.*
Tabitha: *Totally.*
Zara: *Count me in!*
Me: *You know I've got a fly swatter in my suitcase?*
Zara: *No, you don't.*

She's got me, but still. I don't want my friends spying on me. This is an endurance activity I hope will be short-lived. It's not entertainment.

Lottie: *The excitement of being stuck with your enemy aside (and can I just say, OMG, Charlie Cavendish is one sexy customer!), I hope you make your flight.*

A sexy customer? Oh, good grief.

Tabitha: *It's unlikely she will.*

Lottie: *Don't be a negative nelly, Tabitha.*

Tabitha: *I'm being realistic. She's stuck in a lift, it's Christmas Eve, it's snowing, and we live in London. It's stacked against her.*

Lottie: *Miracles can happen, you know.*

Tabitha: *At Christmas? Pull the other one.*

Lottie: *Yes, at Christmas. Haven't you heard of a Christmas Miracle?*

Tabitha: *This isn't a Hallmark movie, Lottie. This is real life.*

Lottie: *You're so cynical.*

Tabitha: *No, I'm realistic, that's all.*

With my WhatsApp group highjacked by two of my friends squabbling, I gaze wistfully up at the edge of the carpet in the crack at the top of the doors. If only I were just five inches wide, I could squeeze my way through that gap… Who am I kidding? Not even Lady M is only five inches wide.

I push out another breath and slump my back against the wall. I chance another look at Charlie. He's still standing, his head bent as he taps away on his phone, concern etched on his face.

I break the silence.

"You gonna be late for something?" I ask.

He presses the button on the side of his phone and slips it into his inner coat pocket. "A meeting."

"You're working on Christmas Eve?"

"Of course." He looks at me as if I've asked him if he breathes oxygen. "You were flying home for Christmas, were you?"

"Not 'were.' I *am* flying home for Christmas. I'm gonna make my flight. I've got to."

"What time's it due to leave?"

"Two twenty from Heathrow."

He glances at his wristwatch. You know, the *Rolex*. "Catching the Heathrow Express?" he asks.

"I plan to."

"It's the fastest way."

"Yup."

"By my calculation, you'll need to be out of here in fifteen minutes."

"Fifteen minutes," I say at the exact same time.

We share a tentative smile.

I cut it short, because sharing an elevator is more sharing than I want to do with him. Particularly after how good it felt to be held protectively in his arms only moments ago.

We fall into silence once more, and I flick my phone back on. My London Babes WhatsApp chat has morphed into my friends' Christmas plans, so I flick it back off again. I stare at the phone on the wall, willing it to ring with news that a technician has fixed the problem and we'll be free to go in less than a minute.

Its silence taunts me.

Charlie unbuttons his coat to reveal a well-cut navy suit jacket, dress shirt, and monogramed tie, then slides his back down the wall until he's sitting on the floor facing me. He unbuttons his jacket and loosens his tie.

He looks incredible.

I study my hands.

He stretches his long legs out, and they come within inches of touching mine, before he pulls them back in, hooking his elbows over each knee. "We should probably talk about something," he says, his deep voice punctuating the silence. "You know, to pass the time."

"That's not necessary. We've got these." I wave my phone in the air.

"I don't know about you, but I've rearranged my meetings for the day, caught up on the news, and ordered next week's groceries already."

"You could check your IG," I suggest, knowing full well the guy isn't on social media. Which is so weird.

"You come up with the first topic." He's clearly ignoring my suggestion.

I shrug. What do you talk about with a guy you hate, who you've recently developed some unsettling and completely inappropriate feelings for?

I turn it back on him. "What do *you* want to talk about?"

"How about we start with why you hate me?"

His directness catches me off guard. "I-I don't hate you."

Smooooooth.

He scoff-laughs.

"I don't. I don't *anything* you," I protest.

"That's good English."

"You know what I mean."

"So, you're telling me I've had it wrong all this time, and you don't hate me?"

"Hate is such a strong word, Charles," I say, putting on my best school teacher voice. It masks my discomfort at his candor. "I might not find that I ever want to be in your company, but that doesn't mean that I hate you."

"Okay, so 'hate' is too strong a word. Why don't you like me? Is that better?"

"Why don't I like you?" I let out a laugh. "That question's a little desperate, isn't it?"

He shakes his head at me, pushing out a breath. "You're infuriating. But I imagine you know that already."

"I'm not infuriating."

"Frustrating?"

"No."

"Exasperating?" That smile of his teases the edges of his mouth.

"No!"

"Irksome?"

"Is this your chance to show off your command of the English language?"

"Is it working?" He looks at me with a full-blown cheeky grin on his face, and I can't help but melt a little. But not much.

He's still Charlie Cavendish, and I still have inappropriate feelings for him.

"If you're not going to tell me why you 'prefer not to be in my company,' as you put it, I'll take a stab at it, shall I?"

I give a wave of my hand. "Be my guest."

"On that fateful blind date of ours, you took offense at me thinking you didn't know anything about polo," he begins. He clearly has a list, as he starts counting off on his fingers. "Then, you took umbrage at me running my family business because I was supposedly given it without having to interview for it. And then you told me I like to deliberately pollute the world's oceans by pouring petrol directly into them. For fun." He pauses, then adds, "Tell me if I've got any of that wrong."

I cross my arms over my chest and glare at him. "Do we really need to go over all this?"

Because when he puts it like that, I seem like a totally irrational woman who jumped to conclusions about the guy.

And I'm not. Really, I'm not.

"I think we do, yes."

I throw my hands in the air. "Why?"

"Because I'm not who you think I am."

I arch my brows at him. "You did assume I didn't know anything about polo."

"That was wrong of me and I'm sorry."

His apology takes the wind from my sails. "Thank you," I murmur, nonplussed.

Apologies from Charlie Cavendish: three.

"I wrongly assumed it wasn't something a California girl would be interested in."

"Well, you know what they say about assuming," I reply, and immediately regret my flippant tone. "Sorry. Force of habit."

His features soften. "As for your other point, I don't pour petrol into the world's oceans. I like boats, but I sail, too."

"Sure. It's gas, though."

His lips curve into a smile, his bright blue eyes shining. "I'll give you that one. As for the fact that I run my family's business? My father is in charge, and I answer to him."

"Potato po-tah-to, dude."

"Although you're right, I didn't need to interview for the job, I paid my dues, I've worked very hard to get where I am, and I'm not some spoiled idiot who doesn't appreciate what he's got. I studied hard to get my degree, I gave up the things I wanted to work for my father. I know I'm lucky. I know many others don't have the opportunities I've had, and I am deeply grateful for the life my family has afforded me. But I also know I could make a wrong move and hurt everyone. It's a lot of pressure, and choosing to take the job was not something I did lightly. In fact, it wasn't really a choice at all."

"It wasn't?"

He shakes his head. "It wasn't."

I sense there's a lot more to the story. I chew on my lip as I consider my options. Sure, he's defending himself over accusations I lobbed at him when we first met, but he's also opening up to me in the process. Do I go with my Charlie Cavendish modus operandi and verbally slap him back down, tell him to get over himself, the poor little rich boy that he so obviously is? Or do I act graciously and allow the guy to apologize?

I take the high road.

"I get it. You've got your crap to deal with, just as much as the rest of us."

"Thank you."

"I'm, err, sorry, too. I jumped to conclusions about you."

He cocks his head to the side. "You did, didn't you?"

"Don't go making a big deal about it. I can take my apology back, you know." I shoot him a cheeky smile, feeling a little lighter.

His laugh is low and warm. "Let's keep this truce going, shall we? We don't know how long we'll be in here."

"True."

We fall into silence once more, although this time the atmosphere is less loaded. Easier. Convivial, almost.

We've made a kind of peace.

Wait. Are we...*getting along?*

"Tell me something. Why did you jump to those conclusions?" he asks.

"Excuse me?"

"We'd only been talking for a short while on that date, and I don't know about you, but I thought it was going pretty well up to that point."

I recall the way he made me feel the moment I clapped eyes on him. All those blind date feelings, filled with hope, and instant attraction. I mean you can't blame me, the guy looks like Bradley Cooper, Theo James, and Chris Hemsworth, rolled into one. Plus, he's got that sexy English accent of his.

Really, I didn't stand a chance.

"We were getting along pretty well," I concede.

"And then suddenly we were at each other's throats over...nothing. Why was that?"

I shrug. "I dunno."

"Really?"

I chew on my lip, memories of our date rolling around in

my mind. "I guess you...reminded me of something I would've preferred to have not been reminded of."

"That's a little cryptic."

"It is what it is, dude," I quip.

"Don't do that, Kennedy. Please."

I lift my gaze and see a fleeting dash of hurt in his eyes. "Old habits die hard, I guess."

He studies me for a beat before he nods and pulls his lips into a line. "What was the thing I reminded you of?"

"A situation I was in a while back where things didn't work out well for me."

"A man."

I give a reluctant nod.

His features soften. "I reminded you of a man who hurt you. Didn't I?" His eyes are trained on me, his gaze intense, like he can see the real me. Not the snarky, cutting version who puts on her armor around him. That's the version that's so much easier to be. Full of bravado and sass, the confident version that takes no prisoners.

The version that keeps me safe.

His words hit their target as my heart twists.

Sure, he doesn't know the specifics, and how could he? It's not like I walk around with a big sign slapped on my forehead that reads *My heart was broken when I was dumped for a more "appropriate" girl*. Yet somehow, he's seen my hurt, he's seen my pain, he's seen my feelings of inadequacy.

I hang my head, flicking my nails in my lap.

Strange as it may seem, part of me is glad he can see behind my mask. Because hating Charlie Cavendish takes a lot of energy.

If I'm honest with myself—truly, truly honest—I know he's right.

This has not been about him. It's been about the way Hugo treated me, about the way it made me feel to be dumped for a country club girl with "good breeding," who knew which fork to use at the dining table, and why Jackson Pollock was an important part of the Abstract Expressionist movement. When Hugo did that to me, he confirmed everything I'd feared in my relationship with him.

That I wasn't right for his world.

That I didn't belong.

That I was an imposter.

"Kennedy?" Charlie asks. "I'm sorry if I've upset you."

I steel myself before I raise my eyes to his. The look on his face tells me he's genuine.

"There was this guy," I begin hesitantly. "Hugo Carter. We dated for almost three years. He was from a different background than me, your kind of background, and I always felt a little out of my depth around him. His family was super wealthy. You know the type: country club, multiple homes dotted around the country, skiing in Aspen every winter. The whole gambit."

"I reminded you of him?"

"I guess. Not consciously, I don't think. But the things you said brought up some feelings. Feelings I thought I'd overcome." I scoff-laugh. "I clearly haven't."

"What kinds of feelings?"

"He dumped me for a girl who came from his world. I'd waited her table many times at the country club. They're married now."

He makes a face. "Ouch."

"Right? I mean, it's been a while. But meeting you brought it all back in a way I wasn't expecting."

"You're still in love with him?"

I shake my head. "No."

"He made you feel inferior."

I study my hands. "I guess."

"No one can make you feel inferior without your consent, Kennedy."

I arch my brows at him. "That's very deep of you."

"It's a famous quote from Eleanor Roosevelt, actually. One of yours."

"Good old Eleanor Roosevelt."

"I'm serious though. You've got nothing to feel inferior about. That guy was a plonker."

I let out a giggle. "A plonker?"

"A plonker. You know, knob head. A pillock."

I shake my head at him, a giggle bubbling up inside of me.

"An idiot," he adds.

"I like that. Plonker. I'll be sure to use it next time I see him."

He grins at me. "You do that."

I smile back at him. Something has shifted between us. I'm letting go of my anger, my hatred. It feels…nice.

"So, does this mean we're all good?" he asks, as he shifts himself so that he's sitting beside me. He extends his hand.

I take it in mine, enjoying its warmth, his sudden proximity heightening the tension between us. "We're good," I reply, my voice breathy. I try my best to ignore the way his touch makes my whole body tingle, my heart beating like heavy footsteps in my chest.

"Thank the Lord for that." His deep, gentle laugh rolls through me.

We sit side by side, leaning up against the wall, our bodies almost close enough to touch. As he looks at me with warm, tender eyes, I notice his gaze drop to my lips for a fraction of a second, before he lifts it once more.

Is he about to…*kiss me?*

My breath catches in my throat. I glance up quickly at the mistletoe above our heads. Suddenly, kissing Charlie under that festive green plant is the only thing I want to do.

The.
Only.
Thing.

To feel his lips against mine, breathe in his delicious scent, feel his large, strong body close to me as he wraps those arms around me once more.

All this time I've hated him, I can finally admit that I've wanted him, too.

And now, maybe, it's time to act on those feelings.

I lean a fraction of an inch closer to him, hoping to signal that yes, I want it too. I want to kiss him.

His eyes are still locked with mine, and I know. I just *know*.

It's about to happen.

And then, the elevator phone's shrill ring sounds, slashing the silence and tearing into our moment. Charlie breaks our gaze, and in one swift movement, leaps to his feet and removes the phone from its socket.

"Hello?...Yes, I see...Well, that's good news...Thank you." He hangs the phone up and turns back to me. "The technician is downstairs and it looks as though we're about to be saved."

Saved. *Right.*

I paste on a smile, my body still flushed with the anticipation of what was almost about to happen. "That's great news," I reply, my voice unnaturally high.

"You won't make it to the airport in time to catch your flight, I'm afraid."

"I figured."

The lights flick off and then back on again, and the elevator springs into life. It lurches and then glides downward. Within a few seconds, it comes to a stop, and the doors fly open to reveal a graying man in a grubby dark blue boilersuit and a thick mustache.

"Sorry about that, folks," he says. "Technical issue. All sorted out now."

"We're very pleased to see you," Charlie replies. He turns to me and offers me his hand, his face impassive. Unreadable. I slide my hand into his and he pulls me to my feet.

As I take my first step onto solid ground, he drops my hand to talk to the technician, and I'm left standing awkwardly in the lobby, my mind reeling.

Did I imagine it all? The lingering look? The almost-kiss? The moment, now lost?

As I watch Charlie walk with the technician to the front door, chatting with him about the snow and his Christmas plans, humiliation creeps down my limbs.

It was all in my mind.

CHAPTER 17

The building front door swings open, obscuring the retreating technician's back as Charlie calls out a thank-you to him.

I wasn't listening to their exchange. I was too busy scrunching my eyes shut and working hard at not feeling like a total and utter fool.

It's futile.

Humiliation quickens my pace in an effort to get away from Charlie as quickly as humanly possible.

What was I thinking?

Charlie didn't want to kiss me! All he wanted to do was clear the air because I live in the same building as he does now, and he has to see me in the common areas and at the Ducks' events.

And anyway, what the heck am I doing? I admit I misjudged him. I melded him and Hugo in my mind, and fully expected Charlie to be just like him. I can see that now. It was wrong of me.

But to take the sizeable leap and think that he might feel something more for me is a whole other ball game.

A ball game I had no right to try to play.

Reeling from my embarrassment, I snap myself out of it, turn on my heel, and begin to wheel my suitcase through the lobby toward the stairs. There's no way I'll make my flight now, so I might as well try to reschedule it from the comfort of my flat.

And being far away from Charlie right now is pretty high on my list, too.

I lift my suitcase by its handle and begin the climb. A five-story climb is a lot when carrying groceries, let alone a forty-pound suitcase. But such is my need to get the heck out of dodge, I put one heavy foot in front of the other as I steadily climb.

By the time I've managed one flight, Charlie dashes up the stairs two at a time with his long, athletic legs. "Here. I'll take that for you."

"It's fine. I got this," I reply, as my heart pounds from the exertion and my forehead begins to sweat. I wheel the bag along the landing and then begin the slow climb to the next floor.

I'm not going to lie. It's hard work. Super hard work. But I'm determined. I've had enough humiliation in front of this guy for one day. I'm not going to be some damsel in distress who can't lug her own belongings up a few measly flights of stairs.

"Are you sure? Because you really do look like you could do with some help," he replies, as he trails behind me.

"I'm...fine," I manage between heavy puffs, as I take another step on burning legs, my humiliation driving me on.

Why did I pack so many shoes?

Panting like I just ran up a steep hill, I reach the top of the second flight and drop my suitcase on the floor with a *thud*.

Right now, it's like we're two different species. He's a gazelle on his long, lithe legs, bounding easily up the stairs.

I'm an un-caffeinated sloth, lugging what feels like a house—and looking just as sexy.

I unbutton my coat and wipe my damp forehead with my sleeve, and then lean on the banister as I catch my breath.

Should I leave the case and make a run for it?

"I admire your determination, Kennedy, but really, I'd be more than happy to help you carry it."

I slide my eyes to his. I'm sure he's finding this whole thing quite hilarious, the girl who readied herself for a kiss he never intended to deliver, who's now panting from the exertion of carrying her bag.

My heart rate begins to return to normal—well, as normal as it's been since what I mistakenly thought was a moment between us in the elevator. I open my mouth to reply when a door to my left suddenly swings open, practically making me jump with surprise.

"Oh, it's you two. I wondered what that noise was," Winnifred says, as she eyes us both through her thick-rimmed glasses. She takes in my suitcase and my frenzied state. "What are you doing, Kennedy? Why didn't you get the lift? It's so much easier with a suitcase."

"The lift broke down with us in it, I'm afraid," Charlie explains. "Kennedy seems to want to carry her suitcase unassisted back up the stairs."

"To the fifth floor?" she questions, a look of disbelief on her face.

"It's not that heavy," I protest, even though it is.

She eyes my case. "Well, it doesn't look light. But what a nuisance you got stuck in the lift. Was it just you two?"

"It was," Charlie replies.

"I see. The two of you stuck in the elevator, hmm?" Her face morphs into a smile, and I know exactly what she's thinking. "Were you in there long?"

"Long enough," I murmur under my breath, and Charlie shoots me a quizzical look.

"It was quite some time, actually, Winnifred. It was good we had one another for company," Charlie replies smoothly.

Winnifred's eyes flick from him to me, and back again. "Well, that sounds like quite the adventure for the two of you. I imagine you…got to know one another better while you were in there. Hmmm?" She widens her eyes as she shoots us both a meaningful look.

What did she think we were doing? Making out on the elevator floor?

Prickly heat rises in my cheeks.

"Weren't you meant to be going home to see your family, Kennedy? You were flying to America, weren't you?"

"Well, that was the plan. I missed my flight."

"Oh, shame," she exclaims. "You'll have to spend Christmas here, now." She grins at us as though this is the best idea ever.

I need to get out of here.

"I'm gonna go rebook. So, I'll see you later." I begin to move away. "Merry Christmas."

"I was just telling Kennedy that she really should allow me to carry her case for her," Charlie says.

"Oh, absolutely. Look at the man," she instructs me. "He's big and strong and awfully muscular. Don't you think?"

I stop, press my lips together, and work hard at *not* thinking how big and strong and "awfully muscular" Charlie is.

Fail.

"Carrying your suitcase would be nothing to the likes of him, Kennedy," Winnifred insists. "There are few things in this life that men can do better than women, but carrying suitcases up flights of stairs is certainly one of them."

"I'm going to take that as a compliment," Charlie says with a laugh.

Winnifred simply smiles at him.

I force out a breath and admit defeat. "Sure, thanks."

He reaches for my suitcase, looks up at me in question, and begrudgingly, I allow him to take it.

That's a nail in the coffin of women's rights—and for my ability to get away from the guy.

With my suitcase in his hand, he says, "Have a wonderful Christmas with your sister, Winnifred, and please send my best to Henry. I hope his hip in on the mend."

"Better day by day. Merry Christmas, Charlie." She beams at him. "Oh, and you, too, Kennedy," she adds as an afterthought.

What the heck? Not long ago Winnifred and the Ducks couldn't stand the sight of him, and now he's asking about someone named Henry's hip?

Who is this guy?

Charlie carries my suitcase up to the next floor with ease as I trail behind him. "We were too busy talking, we didn't get to eat any of your Christmas treats."

"Well, they were supposed to be for my family, but I'm not sure I'm gonna make it home in time to see them for Christmas."

"By the weight of your bag, I'd say you've got a few in here," he says, as he steps up onto the next stair.

"That's mainly shoes. Oh, and Harrods's chocolates."

"I bet," he replies with an easy laugh, as he glides up the stairs to the next floor.

We reach my floor, and he places the suitcase outside my door. "There you are, mademoiselle. We trust you enjoy your stay."

I offer him a weak smile. "I'll try my best. Thanks for your help."

"My pleasure." His gaze lingers on mine before he adds, "Sorry you missed your flight."

"Yeah, me too."

"I'll…I'll see you around?"

"Sure. Thanks."

"Merry Christmas."

"Merry Christmas," I echo.

I stand and watch his receding figure vanish up the stairs, the sound of his footsteps echoing in the empty stairwell.

Well, if I needed any further evidence, that confirms it. It wasn't an almost-kiss situation.

It was all in my head.

My heart sinks to my belly like a brick in water.

With humiliation still coursing through my veins, I push my way through the door and into the cool, darkened flat I wasn't expecting to see until New Year's Eve. I slide my suitcase against the wall and let out a sigh.

I slip off my boots and pad on sock-covered feet over to the living room. I slump heavily down on the sofa. Pushing Charlie from my mind as best I can, I pull out my phone and open the airline app to search for a new flight. As I'm blinking at the cost to fly out tomorrow, there's a knock on my door.

Weird. No one knows I'm here.

No one except Charlie and Winnifred, that is.

I'm sure that's who it is. Winnifred must have alerted the Ducks and they'll show up in droves wanting to know what happened in the elevator. Well, I can tell you now, Ducks. It was a whole lot of nothing.

I reach the door and swing it open, only to find out it's not Winnifred or any of the Ducks.

It's the last person I expected to see right now.

Charlie.

My belly does a flip at the sight of him, heat flashing like wildfire through my body, reminding me of my humiliation—and something more.

Desire.

"You're not the Ducks," I mutter dumbly, my voice breathless.

He doesn't reply.

Not with words, anyway.

With fire burning in his eyes, he takes a step closer to me so that we're mere inches apart and his intoxicating scent fills my nose. Right on cue, my heart begins to thud as heavy as the baseline at a club while my belly tightens in anticipation. With our gazes locked, he reaches out and slips his hands around the back of my head, tangling his fingers in my hair and sending a sharp jolt of electricity down my spine.

"But I thought—" I begin, confused.

"Don't think," he replies, his voice low and thick.

He moves closer, and I barely have a split second to notice how firm his body feels against me before his lips collide urgently with mine.

There is nothing gentle and tentative about this kiss.

Oh, no.

The kiss is full of urgency and need. Of pent-up feelings, finally being released.

He pulls me against him in a passionate, insistent kiss, and I melt into it as his hands trail down my back, pulling me more tightly against him.

And oh my, what a kiss.

His lips are soft but demanding, as though he's hungry for me and is too impatient to take this slow.

All the anger I once felt for him, the hatred and disdain, has built into an explosive connection that leaves me breathless and dazed.

"Kennedy," he murmurs against my mouth as he pushes my back up against the door, before his delicious lips find mine once more. I slide my arms around him, feeling his firm bulk against me, and I kiss him back. All my feelings for him pour out of me, brought to life by his exquisite touch.

Finally, after what I can only describe as the best first kiss of my life, he pulls away, his breath jagged as his chest rises and falls.

His face morphs into a smile.

"Where did that come from?" I ask him, my own voice thick and breathless.

He shakes his head. "From far too long ago. Far too long." He leans in and kisses me on the lips once more. This time it's a softer kiss, gentler, less urgent. It lingers, making me want more.

"What do you mean?" I ask, returning his smile.

"I met this stunning, feisty girl in a Soho pub a while ago and I can tell you now, she captivated me."

I blink at him in shock. "You've wanted to kiss me like *that* since we met?"

He shrugs. "It was either that or never speak to you again. It was a fine line."

I swat him lightly on the arm as I let out an ecstatic giggle. It ends in a snort, and he laughs in surprise, making me giggle some more.

"You can't tell me you didn't feel it, too," he says as he toys with my hair, making it virtually impossible for me to concentrate on forming a coherent sentence.

"I decided to hate you instead," I manage.

He leans down and brushes his lips tantalizingly against mine once more. "I'd say that was the wrong call. Wouldn't you?"

"Uh-huh," I reply, my knees actually turning to jelly.

"So, neighbor, do you think you might invite me in? I'd say we've had enough time together in this building's public spaces for one day. Wouldn't you?"

I offer him a wobbly smile.

Talk about having your mind blown by a kiss.

I never knew it was possible until this moment.

Best first kiss? Forget that. Best kiss *ever*.

I nod. "Sure thing. Come on in."

He takes my hand in his and leads me into the living room, my front door slamming behind us, making me jump. I flick my gaze to his and we share a smile.

"Nice place, although it's a little cold."

"I switched the central heating off. As you know, I'm supposed to be on a plane flying to California right now. I'll go turn it on. Make yourself at home." I gesture at the sofa. "Actually, I don't have any food in the house to offer you, sorry."

"I heard a rumor you had some Harrods's chocolates."

"You know they're for my family."

"I'll take you shopping and get you some more."

I can't help the smile that bursts out across my face. "I guess you can twist my arm." I drop his hand from mine and leave to switch the heat back on. Instantly, the radiators click and groan, their familiar starting-up sound. I lay my suitcase on the floor, unzip it, and pull out the Harrods's chocolates.

Returning to the living room, I find Charlie with his back to me, looking out the window. He's taken off his wool coat, revealing his suit jacket and pants. His broad shoulders taper into a slim waist, and I can't help but notice he's got a pretty dang cute butt.

"I can offer you chocolates and black coffee," I say, holding up the Harrods' chocolate package.

He looks back over his shoulder at me, just like Keanu Reeves in *Point Break*, and I swear my heart skips a beat.

Geez. One kiss and I go all gooey over the guy.

"Come over here," he says, and I place the chocolates on the coffee table and walk over to his side.

"It's still snowing," he tells me, as he returns his attention outside.

I take in the snowflakes, dancing and floating in their downward motion, settling on the trees, the cars, and the road. With the gray afternoon light fading, the Christmas lights in people's windows glow brightly, rendering the scene holiday picture perfect.

"It's just gorgeous," I whisper. "I'm a total sucker for a winter wonderland, especially at Christmastime."

"It's magical, isn't it?"

I sweep my eyes to his and find him already looking at me, a hint of a smile on his face.

I offer him a shy smile. "That's exactly the right word. Magical."

He slides his hand into mine. "You know, as bad as it is that you missed your flight, I'm glad we got stuck in that lift."

"Me, too."

We stand together, hand in hand, as we watch the gentle snow fall, the Christmas lights twinkling.

This morning when I woke up, I hated the man currently standing at my living room window with his hand pressed into mine. The man I've just shared a ridiculously passionate kiss with.

And now, here we find ourselves, alone together in my flat, a new and wonderful sense of closeness between us as the snow falls on a magical Christmas Eve.

CHAPTER 18

As far as Christmas Eves are concerned, I have to say this one ain't half bad.

Charlie and I are sitting together on my sofa in front of a glowing fire, soft Christmas music playing, glasses of wine in our hands as we digest our meal. I was totally on the money that Winnifred and the Ducks would spring into action and turn up on my doorstep. They came bearing food and between the ham, roast potatoes, and surprisingly delicious Christmas cake, Charlie and I have eaten like royalty.

Of course we had to answer all their probing questions about our time in the elevator, but it was worth it to get to be alone with Charlie again once they were gone.

After we'd watched the snow fall, he told me he was going up to his flat to change into more comfortable clothes. I found out soon enough that by "comfortable," he clearly meant "hotter." He made me want to repeat our passionate kiss from earlier when he walked into my flat in a V-neck sweater over a white T-shirt that showcased his wide shoulders and firm, shapely pecs, and a pair of jeans that told me what his suit pants had hinted at earlier in the day: he is in possession of a really spectacular butt.

Since then, we've been talking. Wow, have we been talking.

We've covered a huge array of topics so far, from our favorite childhood cereal—*Froot Loops* for me, and something called *Sugar Puffs* for him, both of which are clearly top of the healthy choices list—to the music we liked as teenagers—Kelly Clarkson and Maroon Five for me, and Green Day and Gorillaz for him—to why he thinks butter chicken is an abomination. Something to do with it being inauthentic or too delicious, from what I can tell.

You know, the important topics.

Relaxed against the sofa cushions, our fingers tangled together, my phone lights up on the coffee table. I can see it's a message from Lottie with a row of exclamation points.

Charlie noticed me looking over at it. "Would you like to check that?" he asks.

"Do you mind? Lottie was going out with a guy for coffee today and…" I trail off as he shakes his head and smiles.

"I get it. This is empty, anyway." He grabs the bottle of wine from the coffee table. "I'll go upstairs and get us another bottle."

"Sounds great."

With Charlie temporarily gone, I scan the messages.

Lottie: *Did you make your flight, Kennedy?*

Lottie: *Where are you?*

Lottie: *Heeeeellllllooooo? I need a distraction and I NEED to know what happened with Charlie Cavendish!!!!!*

Lottie: *Mum has really gone and done it this time.*

Being Christmas Eve and the fact they're both with their families, neither Zara nor Tabitha have replied. I dash out a reply.

Me: *What's happening, girl?*

Lottie: *Kennedy! Did you make your flight? Are you messaging from the plane?*

Me: *I'm still in London. Fly out tomorrow. What has your mom done this time?*

We all know Lottie's mom is a major meddler. She can't see why her only daughter isn't married with kids by now, and takes every opportunity to tell her what a disappointment she has become. Poor Lottie. It can't be easy for her to love her mom and hate being around her half the time.

Lottie: *She's managed to get Nana and Pops and my Auntie Doreen in on the "why aren't you married with kids by now" bandwagon and it's a NIGHTMARE! They're setting me up with some son of Auntie Doreen's friend next month. I just know he's going to be an idiot.*

Me: *Blind dates suck.*

I smile to myself. Except with Charlie, that is.

Lottie: *I had to promise I'd go on the stupid blind date to shut them all up, and then Mum said she'll choose my outfit for me. Can you believe that?*

Me: *Does she have good taste?*

Lottie: *She wears lilac pant suits.*

Me: *Enough said.*

Lottie: *This suuuuuuucks.*

Me: *My sister likes to meddle in my love life, but the rest of my family stays out of it.*

Lottie: *Where are you right now?*

I press my lips together as a smile threatens my face.

Me: *I'm at my flat.*

I pause, my thumb hovering over the keyboard. I add another line.

Me: *I'm not alone.*

Lottie: *Because you've got Lady Moo there with you?*

Me: *Uh, nope.*

Lottie: *Who's there then?*

Lottie must connect the dots because my phone rings within three seconds. I pick up.

"You cannot tell me you're with Charlie Cavendish," she blurts out before I even say hello.

"Technically he's gone back to his flat to get another bottle of wine."

"*Another* bottle of wine?" she questions, her voice high. "That would suggest you've already drunk a bottle. Together. You and Charlie Cavendish."

I grin, my body warm and tingly at the thought of him. "We have."

"Tell me *every*thing."

"Well, you know how we were stuck in the elevator? We got to talking and it turns out I misjudged him. He's actually a really great guy."

"A really hot and gorgeous great guy, you mean."

My grin reaches my ears. "Yeah, that too."

"And?" she leads.

"And…well, we kissed." I hold my breath, bliss hitting my every pore.

"*What?!*" she shrieks, and I'm forced to remove the phone from my ear to save my eardrum from spontaneously bursting. "What was it like? How did it happen? Did you kiss him back?"

I giggle. "So many questions."

"Well? Tell me. I need to live vicariously through you because I'm getting no action on the guy front whatsoever."

"No coffee with Matt today?"

"No. He has yet to notice me as a woman, although I'm still working on it."

The door to my flat opens and Charlie walks in holding a bottle of wine.

"Hey, Lottie? He's back so I've gotta go."

"Call me after, okay?"

"I will."

"Promise me. I need details. It'll help me get through Christmas with my meddling family."

"I promise."

"Good. Kiss Charlie for me. No, wait, That's weird. Don't do that."

I laugh as Charlie sits down next to me once more. "Bye, Lottie." I hang up and place my phone back on the coffee table.

"Catching up with one of your BFFs?" he asks.

"Do grown men actually use that term?"

"Oh, sure. I'm always talking about my BFFs."

I giggle. "I bet you do."

"Okay, we've covered a bunch of stuff, how about something a little more serious? Like, where you see yourself in five years' time?"

I cock an eyebrow. "Is this a job interview, Mr. Cavendish?"

He lets out a laugh and it makes my tummy tingle. "I'm interested."

"Okay. You asked for it. I'm gonna put it out there: I want to be married with at least two kids by then. I'll be thirty-five."

"Well, unless you're going to start immediately, you might find that's a tall order," he replies, and I blush.

"I can be a little flexible on the exact timing. What about you?"

"Oh, I'd like to be onto my second wife and fourth child by then. Clearly."

A laugh escapes my lips. "Do you already have a wife and kids?"

"No."

"You're gonna be busy."

"You're right. I clearly don't have the time to lounge

around on sofas with beautiful Californians on Christmas Eve. Do I?"

More blushing.

Yup, I'm that girl. The blush around the guy I'm crushing on type.

Thank goodness it's dimly lit in here.

"Top up?" he asks.

"Sure. But only a small glass. I don't want to be on my flight with a hangover tomorrow."

"It's great you could reschedule it."

"Mom would have had kittens if I hadn't."

He fills my glass halfway. "Here's to a Christmas miracle," he says, raising his glass.

"What's the miracle?"

He flashes me his sexy grin. "The Great Thaw of Kennedy Bennet. I never thought I'd see the day."

"Well, in that case, I'm going to drink to The Unmasking of Charles Cavendish as a Decent Human Being and Not the Jerk I Thought He Was."

"Snappy title you've got there. I can tell you're a writer."

"Thanks. It's among my best work."

He clinks his glass against mine and we both take a sip.

"I'm glad we got here, even if it took us some time," he says.

"Yeah. Me too. I've got a question for you, now."

"I've already told you about my multiple wives and children goal."

"Not where you see yourself in five years. I want to know what your idea of the perfect date is."

"You know, sitting in front of a fire, talking over a delicious meal made by a group of Ducks is pretty high on my list," he tells me.

I grin at him. "It's high on my list, too."

"What's your idea of the perfect date?"

"That's easy. I think the best dates are the simple ones. You shouldn't need anything flashy or complicated. If you do, you're trying too hard."

"Agreed."

A thought occurs to me. "Hey, aren't you supposed to be somewhere tonight? I bet you're supposed to be going to the country to see your family for Christmas."

"I'll drive down early tomorrow."

"Are you sure? Don't stay on my account. The last thing I want to do is keep you from your family at Christmas."

"You're not. I've already informed them I'll be driving down tomorrow, and besides, the traffic will be intense by now, particularly thanks to the snow."

"Are you sure?"

"I'm sure. I'm happy here. With you."

"Me too."

I sit and watch the fire crackling, feeling so very comfortable in Charlie's presence.

Remembering how he alluded to once being a party boy and learning his lesson, I say, "You know how we're being open with each other in this brave new thing we have going on?"

"A brave new thing?" he asks with a laugh. "Is that the label we're using?"

"Sure. Why not?"

"Ask away."

"You know how on that terrible blind date of ours I asked if you liked to party, and you said you thought you were invincible but you found out you weren't?"

"I remember. You wanted me to expand on it, but I had begun to sense you weren't exactly enjoying my company."

"It made me wonder if something had happened to you."

He tilts his head and fixes me with his stare. "You *have* been thinking about me all this time. Haven't you?"

"Just occasionally."

"And here I was thinking you hated me, when you were really fantasizing about me all along."

"It was mostly hate," I reply with a grin.

"Thank goodness for that."

"So?" I lead. "The invincible thing. What happened?"

He takes his time, swirling his red wine in his glass as he looks at the fire. "A couple of things happened the year I graduated from university. Things that changed the way I looked at life, I suppose. The first was my cousin, he and I had gone out and drunk far too much, he decided to drive home, and he never made it."

"Car crash?"

He gives a grim nod.

"Oh, that's horrible. Were you in the car with him?"

"I was. I got away with a couple of fractured ribs and a few cuts and bruises. James wasn't so lucky. He was in a bad way. Ended up in a coma and lasted for a week before he passed away. It was a tough time."

I place my hand on his arm, my heart breaking for Charlie as a young man, losing his cousin in such a horrific way. "I'm so sorry. That must have been so hard."

"I saw that life can be snatched from you in the blink of an eye. That you can make one dumb decision and it can all be over. It was at that time I decided to get away from it all. I booked a trip to South America with a mate. We were going to take a gap year and travel through the Americas. I'd always wanted to see Machu Picchu and the Amazon, tour the Incan ruins and hit the beach in Rio."

"I know all about running away," I reply with a wry smile. "What was your trip like?"

"I didn't get to go. My father told me I needed to start working in the business, learning the trade. You see, my cousin James was older than me and had been working for our dads at the business for a few years. He was always meant to be the successor, and I was happy with that. I love and respect my dad and I wanted to please him, so I did exactly that, putting my dreams of travelling the world on ice."

"You got serious."

"I suppose so. Someone needed to step into James's shoes. But look, I'm not complaining. I know I'm incredibly lucky to do what I do, but I thought I had more time before I had to do it, if that makes sense."

"You didn't get the time to grieve your cousin."

He shakes his head. "I threw myself into the business. It was therapeutic, in a strange way. Now that my uncle has stepped back from the business, I'm Dad's right-hand man."

"Maybe you need to hand the reins over to one of your sisters for a while and take that trip?" I suggest.

His smile is tinged with sadness. "That's what you would do. Like the way you decided you wanted a new life and then moved to London."

"All it takes is making the decision to do it. And why not do it? As long as you have someone you trust doing your job for you, why not get out there and do what you want for a while? I'm not saying abandon the whole thing, just take a vacation and go see Rio and all the things you want to see."

"Rio would be amazing."

"Book it."

His jaw locks. "Cavendishes don't go gallivanting around the world. They work. Always have."

My heart squeezes for him. No wonder he's such a workaholic. Rising before the birds to get a gym workout in before he's needed in the office. Working late. Always so buttoned-up.

"Maybe it's time to try on a different you?" I suggest.

"Maybe." He smiles at me as he holds my gaze, but I can tell he's pulling back from the conversation.

"You know what? I don't even know what your family business is," I tell him, to move the subject along from his suppressed travel desires.

"Boring."

"Not to me it, isn't."

"Next topic."

"If you don't tell me what you do, I'll assume that you're a horrible boss who insists on having a red carpet rolled out when you arrive each morning and has weird demands, like having a peacock in your office and only hiring people named Samuel to work for you."

"It's a swan, actually, and I like people called José."

I give him a quizzical look. "Not seriously."

"Oh, yes. The swans are called Bill and Bob and they wear suits and top hats and sing *God Save the Queen* at ten sharp each morning."

"Now I know you're joking." The memory of him at my office building comes into my mind. "What were you doing at the building where I work last week?"

"Well, now, that's a secret."

"Is it, now? What do I have to do to get it out of you?"

"I've got a few ideas," he replies suggestively.

"How about this for starters?" I bunch his sweater in my fist and kiss him softly on the lips.

"Tempting, but not quite enough to divulge such top-secret information."

"I clearly need to up my game," I reply before I kiss him once more, this time like I really mean it.

Because oh, my, do I really mean it.

Being with him, here in my flat, sharing a meal and talking for hours has been incredible. I have so misjudged this man. He's kind and funny and sweet and super smart. He graduated top of his class at Oxford and worked his way up in his family company, starting as a junior analyst. Sure, his family clearly has money and he's not exactly led a life of hardship, but that's where the comparison with Hugo well and truly ends.

He's nothing like him.

I pull back from my kiss and am deeply satisfied to see that it left him breathless, his hooded eyes focused on me. "Okay, mister. Spill the tea."

"Can I demand more of those kisses?"

"Not until you tell me."

"Okay. You've got me. The Cavendish Group is the company name."

"So, not a secretive name, then."

He laughs. "Ah, no. We own a bunch of different businesses, including a property company, a food manufacturer, and a group of magazines. I am the Chief Operating Officer, reporting into my dad, the C.E.O. One of my sisters runs the property company."

"You own a group of magazines? Which group?"

He gives me an odd look. "Ackerman," he replies carefully.

"Ackerman? As in the Ackerman that owns *Claudette* magazine?"

He nods his head carefully.

I sit up straighter as I study his face to tell if he's joking. "Are you serious right now?"

"That's why I was at your building the other day. I had a meeting with Pilar Shan."

"Pilar's the big boss," I say, my mind reeling. "Sh-she works upstairs," I stutter.

Charlie's family owns *Claudette* magazine? *My* magazine? Well, they own the company that owns *Claudette* magazine, but that's semantics right now.

I swear my heart just stopped.

If Charlie owns my magazine, that means…he's my boss.

I need to repeat that.

He's. My. Boss.

I try to swallow, but my mouth is as dry as my mom's roast chicken (she always overcooks it, "just to be sure.").

So that means, the day I bumped into him outside my office, I told my boss I was going on a date *in the middle of the afternoon*?

I bury my face in my hands.

Shoot me now.

Go on. Just do it. Death would be far preferable to the depth of awkwardness I'm currently swimming in over here.

"Kennedy? Are you okay?"

I pull myself from my thoughts and refocus on him. "It's a shock, that's all. I didn't expect it."

"I get it. Why would the guy you went on a disastrous blind date with, the guy who lives in your building, own your magazine? It's a crazy coincidence."

"You're telling me."

"It changes nothing, though."

"Yeah, it kinda does."

"It doesn't have to."

"Well, I don't know about you, buddy, but I've never kissed my boss, especially not like that."

He laughs, low and rumbling. "I'm glad to hear it. And I'm not your boss. I've got nothing to do with the day-to-day running of the magazine. I leave that up to Pilar and her team."

I blink at him in wonderment. This is weird. Beyond weird. From the elevator, to The Great Thawing of Kennedy Bennet, to our newfound friendship, to that kiss, and to the discovery that I work for the guy I used to hate.

And it all happened because of an elevator malfunction. And on Christmas Eve, too.

"I can't believe I've been so rude to my boss's boss's boss."

"Actually, it's my father who's your boss's boss's boss," he replies with a laugh, "but I'm splitting hairs."

I widen my eyes at him. "Will I ever see you in the office? Because, you know." I gesture between us. "We're now *familiar*."

"Is that what the kids are calling it these days?" he jokes. "Look, as much as I am enjoying getting to know the real you, and as much as I've wanted to do this for a long time now, if you're uncomfortable in any way, we can remain friends. Nothing more. Even though I quite like the 'more' component." He smiles at me, and it lights up his whole face.

How can I resist this man? He's ridiculously hot, but more than that, he's easy to get along with and I feel a connection to him that I didn't expect.

"I guess I'm okay with it, but I definitely won't tell anyone I work with that I've been making out with the big kahuna."

He laces his fingers through mine. "Deal. I'd like to take you out on a date. You know, when you're back from visiting your family."

Heat radiates through my body, from my head to my toes. "I'd like that."

"When are you back?"

"New Year's Eve."

"In that case, would you like to go out to dinner with me on New Year's Eve?"

"I'll have to check my calendar," I joke, and he reaches out and tickles me on my sides. I laugh, pushing him off me, and we end up kissing some more, right there on the sofa in front of the fire, our mouths tasting like wine and Christmas cake.

And it is bliss, total and utter bliss.

It turns out, spending Christmas Eve with the guy you once thought was your enemy is really quite spectacular.

CHAPTER 19

The next day, I repack my suitcase—minus the Harrods chocolates we ate last night, that Charlie assures me I can repurchase at Heathrow Airport—and lock up the flat. I slip a note under Winnifred's door, thanking her and the Ducks for supplying Charlie and I with our delicious Christmas Eve meal last night, and then lug my suitcase down the stairs. There's no way I'm going to chance getting stuck in that elevator again and miss this flight, particularly as Charlie left to drive to his family home early this morning.

As I sit on the San Diego-bound plane, waiting to take off, my head is filled with him.

The things he said.

The way he looks at me.

The way he makes me feel.

The way we kissed.

Today, it seems incredible to me that I could have ever hated him. He's nothing like Hugo. He doesn't care one bit about the fact I'm not all hoity toity and highbrow or from the same background as him.

I know now I did him a terrible disservice assuming that he was.

And the fact his family owns the company that I work for? Sure, that's not ideal, but we've agreed not to talk shop, and anyway, I'm just a lowly writer, one of the many, many minions in his family's empire.

My phone beeps with a message, and I look down to see it's from the man himself.

Charlie: *I miss you already. Is that weird?*

I grin at my screen like a Looney Tune, my tummy doing all kinds of flips at the thought of him.

Me: *You're a total goofball.*

Charlie: *If by goofball you mean dashingly handsome and irresistibly sexy, then yes, you're right.*

Me: *Of course, that's what I mean.*

Charlie: *I'm glad we see eye to eye on this. BTW, you're a total goofball, too.*

Me: *Thank you?*

Charlie: *I've stopped at a service station on the M4 to message you. I wanted to check you made your flight.*

Me: *In my seat right now.*

Charlie: *Good. I should hit the road.*

Me: *Drive safe.*

Charlie: *I really do already miss you, you know.*

Me: *Weird, because I miss you already, too.*

Charlie: *Can't wait for our date when you're back. I am totally going to schmooze you.*

Me: *You're going to schmooze me? That sounds painful.*

Charlie: *It won't be, I promise. When do you take off?*

I glance up and watch as a flight attendant closes the door.

Me: *Any second.*

Charlie: *Safe flight xoxo*

Me: *Safe drive xoxo*

I flick my phone off and hold it against my chest, grinning like the lovestruck idiot I've become since that life-altering kiss in my doorway.

One evening together and we're already messaging each other with *xoxo* and flirting up a storm. It's like the stupid dating rules don't apply to us. No need to hold back, no guess work in wondering whether he's into me or not. It feels…right.

It feels good.

No, scratch that. It feels *amazing*.

I look up to see a smiling flight attendant looking at me, with a nametag that reads *Crystaaaal.* Seriously, who needs that many "a's"?

"I'm gonna need you to switch that off now, please. We're about to take off," she tells me.

"You got it." Still smiling to myself, I flick my phone into flight mode and slip it into the seat pocket.

I settle into my seat, and soon enough we're in the air and on our way to my hometown. I'd like to tell you I spend the long flight reading thought-provoking biographies and watching educational documentaries, but that would be a bald-faced lie. I spend a fair amount of it daydreaming about one Charles James Cavendish, and when I drift off to sleep, he's in my dreams.

Yup, I've got it bad. And we've only spent one evening together.

After a long flight I land in San Diego, and as bright sunlight hits my eyes for the first time in months, I greet my family, all of whom have come to the airport to pick me up.

"Sweetie, you're so pale!" Mom exclaims, as she pulls me in for one of her famously wonderful bear hugs.

"It's hard to get a tan when the sunshine is liquid," I reply, my voice muffled.

"All I can say is it's good to have you home," she replies.

They drive me through the familiar San Diego streets. As we pass the tree-lined entrance to the Aldridge Country Club, memories of Hugo inevitably flood my mind. The way he left me for Fleur, the way his family treated me, the way I never felt like I fit in.

But this time, at the thought of Hugo and his wife at the club, standing in front of that huge Christmas tree, the sting has been dulled.

No one can make you feel inferior without your consent.

Words I think I can begin to live by.

When I walk through the door, I'm immediately struck by the smell of roasting turkey and the scent of the oversized pine tree reaching all the way to the ceiling, a Bennet family tradition. No fake tree for this family.

The presents are a hit with everyone, including the Harrods chocolates I bought at Heathrow. We sit down together to a wonderful dinner and catch up on everyone's news. By the time we've finished eating, I'm full and happy and ready for my bed, the jetlag beginning to make me a little dazed.

"Good night, sweetie," Mom says from my old bedroom door, the Maroon Five posters still adorning the walls. "It's so good to have you home."

"It's good to be home, Mom."

The next few days are spent doing all the things I used to enjoy when I lived here: hanging out with my family, catching up with friends, walking along the beach and breathing the wonderful fresh sea air, and even getting out on my old surfboard a couple of times, fully-clad in a wetsuit. Although this is SoCal, the winter water temperature is still cool.

Charlie and I message every day. Heck, who am I kidding, it's more like every *hour*. He tells me about how he and his family spent Christmas day doing much the same as we did: eating until they all had to take a nap—although their meal was cooked by some Michelin-starred chef, not Mom, and I very much doubt their turkey was dry and chewy. Love my mom as I do.

We move onto other topics, like what it was like growing up in our families, what our hopes and dreams were, how I'm a little obsessed with Christmas lights—okay, a lot—and who our celebrity crushes are—I'm not judging, but Dame Judy Dench may be an amazing and accomplished actor, but seriously?

So, yeah, we've begun to cover the hard-hitting questions that need answering in any burgeoning relationship.

By the time I'm due to leave to head back to London, I've had lots of quality time with the people I care about most in the world, enjoyed the mild SoCal weather, and had enough dry leftover turkey sandwiches to last me all year. And then some.

Saying goodbye to my family is bittersweet, but Mom and Dad are planning to come visit me in the spring, and I'll admit, the prospect of returning to Charlie isn't exactly a tough one. Although I do suspect the butterflies, who flutter like crazy in my belly every time I think of him, could probably do with a well-earned break about now.

The sight of him standing on the Heathrow concourse, wearing his formal workwear of a suit, tie, and overcoat, his lips curved into that heart-stopping, sexy smile of his, has those butterflies slamming into overdrive.

I wheel my suitcase behind me across the polished floor, unable to stop the broad grin from claiming my face.

Playing it cool is so not an option right now.

He envelops me in his big, strong arms, and I breathe in the scent I've missed, the unique Charlie Cavendish scent that makes me want to stay in his arms and never leave his side.

Although it's only been a week since I've seen him, and we only spent that one day together, it feels so natural to be with him.

"Welcome back, California Girl," he says softly into my ear, his warm breath sending tingles down my spine.

"Can I call you London Boy?"

His eyes are dancing as he replies, "You can call me anything you like." He goes all gentleman on me and takes my luggage as we begin to walk through the terminal. "I hope you don't mind, but I was at the office and pressed for time and I didn't want to be late for you, so I caught the Heathrow Express here."

I roll my eyes good humoredly. "*Of course* you're working on New Year's."

He gestures at himself with his thumb. "The big kahuna, remember?"

"I thought you reported to the big kahuna?" I tease.

"Semantics."

We make our way down to the underground railway station. We sit side by side on the train, our shoulders and thighs touching, as we chat quietly amongst ourselves, our hands entwined as we bask in the joy of being together once again. The trip flies by in what seems like minutes, and before long we've reached our building and are standing outside my door, having been brave enough to chance the elevator with my luggage—neither of us wanting to carry my suitcase up the five flights, even if the last time we did that ended with our first kiss.

"I'll be back to collect you at seven for our date," he tells me, after kissing me tenderly on the lips.

I beam at him. "I hear you're gonna schmooze me."

"Who did you hear that from?"

"I believe it was you."

"Well, in that case, I'd better pull out all the stops."

"You'd better."

"Christmas Eve and now New Year's Eve. Does that mean we'll be covering all the major holidays from now on?"

I grin at him. "That sounds like fun to me."

He brushes his lips against my cheek. "See you shortly."

I tingle from his touch. "Sure."

He turns to leave, and I call out, "What should I wear?"

"Surprise me."

I shake my head at him. "Uh-uh. No way. A girl needs to prepare."

"All this girl needs to know is that it's an inside event."

"Considering it's about forty degrees out, that's a good thing." I shoot him a smile before I slot my key in the keyhole and push the door open to my flat. The next thing I know, I'm being attacked by one very excited dog, who leaps and bounces and makes that weird, whiny sound I've grown to love.

"Woah, Lady M," I declare to her as I squat down and pat her wriggly body. "I didn't know you would be here already. I missed you so much. How are you, girl?"

Her response is to leap into my lap and proceed to lick my face as though I were doggie ice cream. Whatever that would be like. Gross, I'm sure.

After a serious amount of love, Lady M races off to collect her new favorite chew toy from the floor and flops down on her bed to gnaw on it.

I slip off my boots and notice for the first time that the flat is warm and there's a handwritten note on the kitchen counter.

Kennedy

Dropped Lady Moo here at four-thirty. Thought you'd like to see her when you got home.

She was her usual self while you were away, but she kept on wanting to come up to your flat, so I brought her here each day. I hope that's okay? She ran around each time looking for you.

See you soon,

Esme

My heart squeezes for her as I think of Lady M hunting me down. I sit down on the floor beside her and pet her soft fur. "You and me are good buds, aren't we, Lady M?"

Soon after, I unpack and take a much-needed shower, style my hair, and put on my makeup. I know I can't stop moving, because with the jetlag and the fact it's already dark out, I'll be asleep in record time. The last thing I want is to be disheveled and dopey for my first-ever official date with Charlie.

Standing in the huge walk-in closet, I run my fingers over my evening dresses on their hangers until I land on a metallic silver dress with long sleeves, a skirt that highlights my legs, and a cut-out back. Perfect. I slip it on and check myself out in the mirror. With its slim fit and sexy sheen, I look totally ready for a New Year's party, and the long sleeves keep it classy.

"What do you think, Lady M?" I ask as she lies on the floor, gazing up at me. She wags her little stub of a tail, but probably more because I'm showing her attention than telling me she likes the dress. Because you know, she's a dog and all.

Just as I'm sliding my feet into a pair of heels, the doorbell chimes.

My nerves instantly kick in.

"Game time," I tell her, before I top up her food and head to the door.

I swing it open to see Charlie looking spectacularly handsome in a white open-neck shirt under a dark brown velvet jacket and pair of charcoal pants. He's got his coat and scarf draped over his arm, and of course that devastating smile of his dances on his kissable lips.

"Hey," I say to him as I take it all in, my nerves converting into excitement.

"Kennedy. You look so beautiful," he says, and I instantly feel shy.

"Me? You're the one who looks like you just stepped off the cover of *GQ*."

"Funny you should say that, because that's exactly what I just did," he replies, his eyes twinkling. "Are you ready to be schmoozed to within an inch of your life?"

I collect my coat and scarf from the nearby hook and sling my evening purse over my shoulder. "Heck yes."

"Let's catch the lift. For old time's sake."

"What if we get stuck again? I'm not sure I could handle that amount of time with you again."

"I'm sure we'd find something to do." He waggles his brows at me, and my tummy flips and flops.

Inside the elevator, we stand side by side as we swoosh downward without incident. As the doors swing open, I go to leave when I feel his hand on my arm. "What?"

He glances up. "There's something we ought to do, you know."

I follow his line of sight to see the mistletoe tied with a festive ribbon, still hanging from the ceiling. "Do we have to?" I tease.

He grins at me as he cups my face in his hands. "Oh, yes. We have to." He presses his warm, soft lips against mine, and as I breathe in his intoxicating scent, I kiss him right back.

This man has such an effect on me. All he has to do is touch me and I'm a quivering, melted mass of goo on the floor.

We pull apart and I smile up at him. "That wasn't so bad."

"I'd rate it an eight out of ten."

"Room for improvement, then?"

"With a lot of practice."

"I'd be willing to put in the time if you would, too."

"I'll check my schedule."

I let out a contented giggle. "You do that."

He leans down to kiss me once more, and as his lips meet mine there's the sound of someone clearing their throat. We stop and turn to see Barbara and the Ducks, standing together in the lobby, watching us closely through their spectacles.

Talk about being totally busted.

"Happy New Year," I say weakly as six pairs of eyes gaze questioningly back at us.

It's the whole gang: Barbara, Winnifred, Gertie, Evelyn, Elsey, and Maude.

"Well, well, well," Barbara says, her arms crossed as she taps her fingers against her sleeve. "It looks like things have changed between you two."

"I knew it!" Winnifred says, as she brandishes her finger at us. "I told you all, didn't I? All it took was getting stuck in the lift together. Look at them. They're kissing!" She turns her wide eyes on the other Ducks and adds, "In the lift!" as though that part is the most scandalous of all.

"Yes, Winnifred, we all know what you think. You tell us enough," Barbara moans and wins a glare from Winnifred.

"Only because I'm right," she huffs.

"But it was Barbara who put the mistletoe in there," Evelyn says.

"That's true," some of the others agree.

"She had to change it three times as well," Elsey adds. "Maude, dear, the mistletoe worked on these two," she explains in a loud voice.

"You don't need to explain. I know kissing when I see it," Maude huffs.

"I'd say it was the mistletoe that did the trick," Barbara adds. "Wouldn't you two?" She looks at the two of us and raises her eyebrows in expectation.

"Well, we—" I begin as I flick my eyes to Charlie, not sure quite what to say.

"Yes, as Kennedy was saying, we…are very grateful that you put the mistletoe in the lift, Barbara, or we might not have, you know, kissed."

I press my lips together to stifle a smile. I've never known Charlie to stumble over his words. The sudden appearance of the Ducks has clearly rattled him.

Barbara beams at us. "I'm very glad to have been of help. I imagine now I can add 'cupid' to my list of achievements."

An image of Barbara wearing an adult diaper and brandishing a bow and arrow flashes into my mind.

I discard it quickly.

"Well done, Barbara," Elsey says.

"Hear, hear," Gertie agrees, to general agreement from the other Ducks. Not Winnifred. She tightens her mouth, looking utterly displeased with the whole situation.

"Now, tell me you two. Was this your first kiss?" Barbara asks.

"Well, no," Charlie replies, and she pulls her brows together.

"But we did get stuck in the lift while the mistletoe hung above us and ended up becoming friends on Christmas Eve," I offer.

It seems to satisfy her. "Well, that is good to hear. Isn't that good to hear, ladies?"

"It is," everyone agrees, and even Winnifred responds with a tight smile.

"A new couple in the building calls for a celebratory sherry!" Elsey declares. "Come on you two. Your place, Barbara?"

"Sounds wonderful," Barbara says, and they all begin to crowd into the elevator around us, packing in like bespectacled, pearl-wearing sardines.

Charlie and I share a look. As nice as the Ducks are—nice and total busybodies who seem to think they've masterminded our new relationship—spending New Year's sipping sherry, surrounded by a group of seventy- and eighty-year-old women in Barbara's flat isn't exactly official first date material.

Charlie springs into action. "We'd love to celebrate with a sherry, but you see we've got to be somewhere," Charlie says as he glances at his wristwatch. You know, the Rolex. "In fact, we're late. Some other time, perhaps?"

"I'm going to hold you to that, young man," Barbara says with a wink.

"Well, if you'll excuse us. Happy New Year to you all," Charlie says as he takes me by the hand, and we execute our escape.

The Ducks call out after us.

"Happy New Year!"

"Sherry on Friday!"

"Tell us everything!"

"Keep up the kissing!"

Safely out on the street, we both begin to laugh.

"Those Ducks are awesome," I declare. "Kinda crazy, but awesome."

"If by awesome you mean manipulative, then I've got to agree."

"I can't believe Barbara put the mistletoe up just for us. It's actually kinda sweet."

"I can believe it. Now, come this way." He gestures down the street at a shiny black Mercedes, with a man in a suit and hat holding the back door open. "We've got a date to get to and your chariot awaits."

"Fancy," I say.

We climb in and I slide across the black leather seat. We travel through the streets of London until we reach a part of Westminster near the River Thames that I'm unfamiliar with. I look up at the bland glass office building as we climb out of the car. "Where are we?"

"I've got to get something from the office first. I need some papers to work on tomorrow. Is that okay with you?"

"Sure thing." I already know the guy's a workaholic. I shouldn't be surprised.

He uses a security pass to swipe us into the darkened building, and as the sensor lights flick on, I notice a bronze plaque on the wall. *The Cavendish Group*.

We whizz up through the building in the elevator to the top floor. The doors open to reveal a darkened office, and Charlie takes me by the hand, leading me past desks and a kitchenette to a large window overlooking the river and the lights of the city beyond. I can see the Houses of Parliament, Big Ben, and the London Eye, all lit up and glowing against the dark sky.

It's beautiful, and it takes my breath away.

"Charlie, this is your view each day?"

"It is."

"No wonder you spend so much time here."

"I spend so much time here because I've got to, not because of the view."

"All I get to look at is a partition wall, so count yourself lucky, dude."

"Wait here for me, okay?" he asks.

I look around uncertainly. "I could come with you."

"Just wait, okay? I won't be long. Look out at the view."

I press my lips together and nod, and I'm left alone with

nothing but darkness behind me and the most incredible view of London at my feet.

Two minutes later, Charlie returns with a couple of people who are carrying a picnic basket, a blanket, a silver ice tub encasing a bottle of champagne, and some oversized cushions. They proceed to set everything up on the floor in front of the large picture window.

"Are we having a picnic?" I ask, as the two men disappear through the back door.

"I was once told by this rather beautiful and enchanting woman that the best dates are the simple ones."

A smile grows on my face. "She sounds very smart."

"Oh, she is. Smart and sexy, and a little feisty, too."

"I'm not feisty."

He cocks an eyebrow.

"Okay. Maybe a little," I concede.

"Take a seat."

We slip off our coats and sit down on the picnic blanket. I lean back against one of the oversized cushions as Charlie opens a cane picnic basket and begins to pull out champagne glasses and snacks, including three different boxes of Harrods chocolates.

"Wow, you must really like chocolate."

"As the first food we ever shared together, I thought it only right."

"Good call."

He pops the champagne cork and pours out our drinks before he leans back next to me.

Handing me a glass, he tells me, "The New Year's Eve fireworks will start shortly."

"I love fireworks!"

He leans toward me and brushes his lips against mine. "Considering you told me you were obsessed with Christmas lights, I thought as much."

I grin at him as we clink glasses.

I never want this date to end.

"To no longer being enemies," I say.

He smiles. "You were never *my* enemy."

As I look into his eyes, my heart gives a little squeeze and I know for certain he's wrong about something.

The fireworks have already begun.

CHAPTER 20

The next two weeks are nothing short of wonderful. Although Charlie sticks to his insane schedule of rising while the birds are still asleep to visit the gym before getting to his desk by seven in the morning, the evenings are ours.

Well, other than when I'm working, of course.

Yes, the blind dates in London's weird and wonderful nightlife continue, and although Charlie has told me he would prefer that he had me all to himself, he understands I have to do it for my job.

I regale him with stories when we're snuggled up together on the sofa afterwards, and I always manage to put a smile on his face.

On the evenings I don't have to work, we go out to The Black Cat for dinner, we hang out at each other's flats, and we walk Lady M through the cool evening air. Charlie even cooks for me sometimes, and it turns out he's not a bad chef, surprising me with a delicious marmalade-baked salmon steak one night and beef Wellington the next.

And I'll let you in on a secret. It's a big secret, and it's been sneaking up on me over the last few weeks.

I've got the feels for him. *Big* time.

As in, I think about him when I'm not near him. When I read something interesting, he's the first person I want to tell. I've got a selfie of us that we took when I made him watch the changing of the guard at Buckingham Palace—he was a good sport about it, although he did accuse me of being a stereotypical American tourist—and I gaze at it w*aaa*y too often.

He's the first thing I think of when I wake up each morning.

He's definitely the last thing I think of before I fall asleep.

And you know what? I haven't checked Hugo's IG, not even once. I haven't even thought about checking it. In fact, the last time I looked at his feed was in the elevator on Christmas Eve.

Charlie's words echo in my mind. *No one can make you feel inferior without your consent.* Okay, they're Eleanor Roosevelt's words, but he's the one who said them to me. I know now that even though I blamed Hugo and his family for making me feel less than, it was *me* who allowed them to make me feel that way. *Me* who felt inferior. I've got to take some responsibility for this.

So what if he chose to marry a girl from a wealthy family? I'm worth just as much as she is.

And it feels pretty dang amazing to really know that.

But I have one thing she doesn't: Charlie Cavendish, the very best man I know.

That's right. I can safely say that I have moved on from Hugo Carter, and I could not be happier. I've finally closed a chapter in my life I should have closed a long, long time ago.

And being with Charlie these past few weeks? Well, it's been nothing short of incredible.

Sometimes, though, when I'm on my own and my thoughts begin to pile up like a freeway accident, I find myself wondering if it's *too* incredible. If he's *too* perfect. If I'm too smitten.

I mean, he's a loaded, thoroughly decent, good-looking guy, with a great sense of humor, who cooks and plans great dates.

Sometimes I feel like I've discovered hot guy Yeti.

Is he too good to be true?

No. *Stop*. I refuse to let my overactive brain ruin this for me.

I deserve this happiness.

And I am worthy of it, one hundred percent.

Which brings us to tonight, in which I'm taking that big step in a new relationship known as *Meeting the Family*.

I know, right? I'm nervous as all get out, I'll admit. Nervous and excited. Charlie has told me his mom might live a fancy lifestyle with a superyacht in the Mediterranean and houses dotted around the world, but she's easy going and fun, and already predisposed to like me.

So far so good.

His dad, on the other hand, is a different story.

Everything Charlie's told me about him makes me quiver in my boots. Not only is he his dad, but he's his boss, too. He's a hard taskmaster, expecting that his son will take on whatever work he throws his way, and smile while he's doing it. Even when he hates it.

But I'm determined to win him over, and when I have a goal in mind, I usually achieve it. So, tonight's charity dinner at the swanky Savoy hotel, catered by none other than famous chef Gordon Ramsay himself, is the first step in achieving that goal.

Watch out Henry Aloysius William Cavendish, you're about to be seriously charmed.

The car pulls up in front of Charlie's parents' place, and I look out the window at a building that looks more like a palace for minor royalty than someone's house. With its three levels, tall windows, and columns, overlooking Regent's Park, it's the kind of place you see in posh home magazines.

My belly ties in a knot and I shoot Charlie a quick look.

"Don't worry. My parents will love you," he tells me with a reassuring squeeze of my hand.

The knot loosens a fraction. "How do you know?"

With his gaze still on me he reaches up, slides a hand to cup my face, and places a soft kiss upon my lips. "I know they'll love you, because, well, because *I'm* falling in love with you."

My heart thuds as a grin claims my face. "You are?" My belly knots have re-tightened, not out of nerves this time but out of sheer exhilaration.

He's falling for me? Charlie Cavendish, the man I once hated, is falling in *love* with me?

I blink at him a few times, my body going all kinds of crazy.

"It's true. I'm falling for you," he states simply, his face bright and his eyes soft.

I grab pull him into me, my lips crashing against his in a kiss so full of emotion, it sucks the air from my lungs. "I'm falling in love with you, too," I tell him.

Because I am. I know I am. And I've not felt like this since…well, since ever.

His glowing face beams back at me. "A beneficial coincidence."

I let out a light laugh, feeling as though I could float out of the car on a cloud of happiness. "If you say so."

He kisses me once more before he pulls away with obvious reluctance. "As much as I'd like to kiss you all night, we have a dinner to get to and parents for you to meet."

I rub my fingers against his face. "I guess I should help wipe off this lipstick mess then, huh?"

"That would be a good idea."

I check my appearance in my compact and quickly apply a fresh layer of lipstick.

"Ready?" he asks me, his hand on the doorknob.

"Only because you're falling for me," I tease.

He laughs as he pushes the door open, and we make our way up the steps to the shiny black front door, flanked by topiaries in Roman pots.

His mom greets us at the door. Dressed in a stunning off-the-shoulder green floor-length silk dress, and the largest emerald and diamond pendant necklace I've seen outside of costume jewelry stores, she smells of Chanel No. 5 and gives us a welcoming smile. I can see where Charlie gets his coloring. Her eyes are equally as blue, and her dark blond hair is styled into an elegant French twist.

"Charles, darling, how marvellous to see you," she says, as she pulls him in for a hug. Her eyes glide to me. "And you must be the girl my son won't stop talking about," she says, as she greets me with a kiss to the cheek.

Her son won't stop talking about me? I slide my eyes to Charlie's. He offers me a shrug, his face aglow.

"Hello, Mrs. Cavendish. Thank you so much for inviting me to your beautiful home," I coo, remembering every manners lesson Mom ever taught me.

"You are very welcome here, Kennedy. Come in. Jason will take your coat." She waves at her butler—her *butler*—who takes our coats and scarves in his white-gloved hands and disappears somewhere into the cavernous home.

"How are you, Mum? You look wonderful, as always," Charlie says, as we walk across the black and white checked marble floor. I do my best not to gawk at everything. From the sweeping staircase and double-height ceiling to the oversized floral arrangement on a round table in the middle of the lobby, this place is intimidatingly expensive.

I glance down at my white, slim-fitting dress, the one I wore on the first night of filming *Dating Mr. Darcy*. I got it on the sale rack at *Nordstrom*, and I've always felt sexy and classy in it. But tonight, in these plush surroundings, I can't help but feel like the maid playing dress up.

"Oh, you're so sweet, darling. One must try to look one's best at these charity dinners," she replies, as she breezes through open double doors and into the living room.

It's a huge room, dotted with navy sofas and chairs, with a gilded mirror over the lit fireplace, Persian carpets under foot, and long navy silk curtains that sweep the floor, held back by thick gold rope.

A man is standing beside the fireplace, his back to us, a phone at his ear. Like Charlie, he's wearing a black tux, his tall figure telling me he's his dad.

"Yes, I know, but you need to listen to me. I will not countenance such dissent. He's gone. Make it happen," he says into his phone, and I flick my gaze to Charlie. He smiles back at me as though there's nothing to be concerned about.

"Oh, darling, do get off the phone. No more work tonight. Charlie's here with Kennedy," Mrs. Cavendish says to him.

Charlie's father lowers his phone and turns to greet us, and I'm immediately struck by how much he resembles his son. From his height and build to the shape of his chin and the curve of his nose, the only thing that's different is that when he smiles it doesn't reach his eyes.

"Charlie, there you are," he says, as he shakes his son's hand.

"Hello, Dad," Charlie replies. "This is Kennedy Bennet. Kennedy, this is my father, Henry Cavendish."

I offer him my hand and smile through my nerves. "Hello, Mr. Cavendish, it's so great to meet you."

"You're American," he states.

"I've been accused of worse," I reply with a laugh.

"You knew she was American," Mrs. Cavendish says, as she takes a seat in a high-backed leather chair. "From California, isn't that right, Kennedy?"

"That's right. San Diego, California," I reply.

"See, Henry? One of us has been paying attention to our only son," she tells him. "Take a seat, you two. What will you have to drink? Henry will get it for you. Won't you, darling?"

"Of course. What's your poison?" Mr. Cavendish asks me.

Charlie and I sit on one of the navy sofas and I tell him what I want to drink.

"Charles? I need to speak with you about the Palmer deal. Things have progressed significantly from the meeting this afternoon," Mr. Cavendish says, and no sooner has Charlie sat down next to me than he immediately hops up from his seat. He flashes me a quick look to make sure I'm okay, and then leaves me to talk with his father at the bar.

"Don't mind them," Mrs. Cavendish says to me. "They're always talking shop. Really, if Charlie didn't work for Henry, I'm not sure what they'd have to talk about."

"Charlie sure works hard."

"Of course he does," she replies, as though I've pointed out the obvious. "Now, Kennedy. Tell me about yourself. What are you doing here in London?"

"I got a job writing for a magazine. *Claudette*. I'm assuming you know it, what with your company owning it and all."

Her eyebrows ping up to meet her perfectly styled hairline. "Of course, I know *Claudette*. It's been on the shelves since I was a little girl," she replies smoothly.

"I've always loved it. Even though it's a British magazine,

my mom used to get it for me when I was a tween. She'd cut out the racier articles, but I loved all the fashion and beauty, and I learned a lot from the interesting articles. I kinda grew up on it, I guess. When I saw they were looking for a writer, I jumped at the chance to work for it."

"A childhood dream come true."

"Exactly."

I broach the subject I know must be on her mind. "You know, Charlie and I have agreed not to ever talk shop, so me working for *Claudette* isn't a big deal for us."

"Oh, I'm sure," she replies pleasantly. "I find it's best to stay out of the family business myself. So much simpler."

Charlie hands me a glass of wine. "I'm sorry, but Dad and I need to talk in his office. There are a couple of things that need ironing out. Have a drink with Mum and then we'll go to dinner. Okay?"

Feeling at ease with his mom—well, as much at ease as I can be with the immaculately dressed mother of the man I'm falling in love with and want desperately to impress—I tell him to take as long as he needs, and Mrs. Cavendish and I settle into a getting to know you conversation.

The more we talk, the more I realize how disparate our lives are. She's from what was clearly a very privileged background herself, having only worked as an executive assistant at one of Mr. Cavendish's companies for a couple of years before she married him and promptly gave up working to, and I quote, "focus on mothering and charity work." Which is what she's done for the past thirty-five years, fitting in multiple five-star trips around the world and dinners with royalty in between.

As you do.

She's like Hugo's mom on steroids, leaving the Carter's wealth and social standing in the dust. But unlike Hugo's mom, there's no tone of superiority, and she calls me by my name, not the patronizing "sweetheart" Mrs. Carter perfected.

Thirty minutes and two drinks later, she rises from her seat and tells me it's time to leave.

"What about the men?" I ask, as Jason arrives with my coat and helps me into it—because clearly that's too hard for me to do on my own.

"Jason, will you go and tell the menfolk that we're leaving?" she asks.

He bows his head. "Of course, madam."

I smile at her as if sending the butler off on an errand is a daily occurrence for me.

A few moments later, Charlie and his dad arrive in the lobby.

"All work and no play make Cavendish men very dull indeed," Mrs. Cavendish scolds, and I allow myself a little smile.

My sentiments exactly.

"We have a rather large deal going on right now, dear," Mr. Cavendish replies brusquely.

"Enough shop talk for the night. The car is waiting," Mrs. Cavendish replies, before she turns on her heel and sashays down the steps and into a shiny black chauffeur-driven Rolls Royce.

It whisks us through the streets to the Savoy Hotel on The Strand.

I sit beside Charlie and give his hand a little squeeze. I want him to know that I'm doing okay, and his mom and I have bonded. He shoots me a tense smile.

As we climb out of the car outside the hotel, lined with Rolls Royces and other equally expensive cars, I whisper, "Are you okay?"

"I'm fine," he replies.

It's totally unconvincing.

"I know it's hard when your dad wants to talk about work all the time, but why don't you forget about it for the night?"

"Of course. You're right. I'm sorry."

"There's nothing to be sorry about. Your mom said there's gonna be dancing, and with you looking like a movie star on the red carpet tonight, I need to take advantage of that."

He smiles at me, his eyes crinkling. "Dancing with you sounds wonderful."

We enter the glittering reception room, and Mrs. Cavendish says, "Come and meet some of our friends, Kennedy."

Before I know it, I'm swept away from Charlie to make the rounds and meet women with names like Prunella and Bunny. They look me up and down when she tells them I'm Charlie's *beau*, but I smile sweetly at them all—and firmly push away memories of meeting too many women like them when I was with Hugo.

Sitting at the table later, I'm finally able to get some time with Charlie. He leans in and says, "I've got a question for you."

"As long as it's not what school I went to or who my 'people' are, you're good."

"You've been asked that tonight?"

"Oh, yeah."

"I'm sorry. I hope you've been all right. I've been a little distracted tonight."

I think of the way he's been huddled up with his dad for half the evening. "Is everything okay?"

His features are etched in worry. "I—" he begins, and then clamps his mouth shut.

"Charlie? What is it?"

"I can't say," he replies mysteriously, and immediately my stomach tenses.

My anxieties get the better of me. "Is it us? Have I said something wrong? Do your parents dislike me?"

He places his warm palm against my back. "It's nothing like that. Believe me. You're wonderful, and my mother has already told me how much she likes you."

The tension morphs into spreading warmth. "She said that?"

"Why should that come as a surprise to you?"

I shrug, knowing exactly why. Hugo's mom made it abundantly clear she didn't like "that server," as she referred to me. To hear that Charlie's mom not only approves of me, but actually likes me, is poetic music to my ears.

"That makes me so happy to hear," I tell him. "If we weren't surrounded by two hundred of your parents' friends, I'd kiss you right now."

The tension from his face melts away as his mouth curves into a smile. "I like the sound of that."

"Play your cards right, mister, and I'll schedule you for a make out sesh later."

He laughs as he slips his arm around my waist. "I'm going to hold you to that."

But we don't get the chance.

Straight after the meal, even before the dancing has begun, Charlie's dad tells him he needs him to leave to work on the deal, and although it's clear to me that he doesn't want to do it, he does as his dad asks.

"I'm so sorry to have to abandon you. I'll make it up to you, I promise," he says, as he holds the back door of a car open for me.

I push my deflation aside. Charlie works for his dad, and he works hard. I of all people know that. The least I can do is be supportive of him.

I slide my hands around his neck and pull him into a kiss.

"You go wheel and deal. I'll catch up with you after work tomorrow night."

He shoots me a tense look, and my heart goes out to him.

"Night," I say.

"Night," he echoes.

I slip into the car, and he closes the door. I look out the window at him, standing outside the shiny silver Savoy sign as the car pulls away, a lone figure in his tux. His features are tense, and his broad shoulders look like he's carrying the weight of the world.

CHAPTER 21

The following morning, I find myself smiling on the Tube as I make my way to work. I get a few odd looks from the glum London commuters, but I don't care. I'm happy. *Truly* happy. And the world can know it.

Sure, seeing Charlie stressed out with work last night wasn't ideal, and I don't imagine I'll ever like the way his dad says 'jump' and he does it without question. But it's part of who he is, and I have to accept it.

As I exit the Tube stop, my phone pings with a message.

Charlie: *Can we get together for coffee? The Starbucks near you at nine? Xoxo*

Me: *I've got a job to do, you know. I can't go swanning off to meet sexy men in cafés.*

Charlie: *Promise me you'll be there. No matter what.*

I pull my brows. That's a weird thing to say.

Me: *Is something wrong?*

Then it clicks. It's his dad. That deal must not have gone well last night. The poor guy probably needs me to be there for him, to offer him some assurance as they work through the deal.

Me: *I'll be there.*

Charlie: *Promise me. No matter what.*

A smile spreads across my face. Is it terrible that I love the way he needs me?

Me: *I promise. xoxo*

I arrive to an office abuzz with hushed chatter. People are standing in groups, talking in low voices, glancing around nervously. I say hello to a couple as I pass by, and they shoot me tense looks.

What is going on?

At my desk, I drop my purse and coat on my chair and walk around the partition to Shelley's desk. It's empty, but I know she's here when I spot her jacket draped over the back of her chair.

I wander over to the kitchenette, where I find her by the water cooler with Sandra, the executive assistant upstairs. They too look stiff, their heads bent down as they talk in hushed tones.

"Hey, girls," I say as I approach them. "What's going on here today? Everyone seems super weird."

Shelley and Sandra share a tight look.

My eyes travel between the two. "Girls? You're worrying me."

Shelley's the one to speak. "We've heard a rumor, and it's not a good one."

"It's more than a rumor, babe," Sandra corrects.

Shelley looks aghast. "So, it's really happening?"

Sandra gives a grim nod. "I'd say it's ninety-nine percent true."

I watch their exchange, until my need to know what they're talking about bursts out of me. "Tell me!" I insist.

Shelley huffs out a breath and says, "They're shutting the magazine down. *Claudette* is over. Kaput. Done."

I pull my brows together, not believing a word of it. "No, they're not. That's crazy."

Shelley tells me, "It's crazy, but it's true."

"But *Claudette* has been around forever," I protest. "You don't just kick a magazine to the curb because of a few months of poor sales. We're rebuilding."

Sandra shrugs. "All we know is we all have to go to the boardroom soon, and I bet it's for an announcement."

The sound of my heartbeat thrashes in my ears. "But... how can that be?"

Losing my job means I lose my work permit sponsorship, which means...No, I don't even want to think about what that means.

"We all know readership was down when the magazine was bought out a few months ago," Sandra says, "which the new management was trying to fix. Apparently, it's not been enough."

"Yeah, I knew that." Because of course I knew readership had been down, but I didn't think the magazine was doing that badly. Even if it was, Edina never mentioned it at our meetings.

Nor did Charlie.

Charlie.

My breath catches in my throat as the thrashing of my heart becomes almost deafening.

Why didn't he tell me about this? Sure, we made the call not to discuss work to keep things from getting complicated, but this? This is big. *Huge.* Something like the magazine being shut down and me losing my job should be a topic of conversation at the very least.

If what the girls are telling me is true, shouldn't he have given me a heads up in the very least?

And then it all clicks into place. *The Palmer Deal.* Palmer must be a code. That's what Charlie and his dad were talking about last night. They were talking about *Claudette*'s demise while I chatted with his parents' hoity toity friends about what's on at the theater and where everyone intended to spend their summers.

I swallow down a rising lump in my throat.

Why didn't he tell me about this?

"Look, it's Edina," Shelley says, her words slicing through my thoughts like a knife through butter.

I turn to see my boss signaling for us to follow her. "Boardroom, ladies. Now," she says, her voice flat, her features pulled.

"This is it, girls," Shelley tells us, as we make our way across the carpeted floor.

We file into the room in grim silence, like we're walking the line. The seats are already filled, so Shelley, Sandra, and I stand at the back of the room, awaiting our fate.

"Close the door, will you, Phil?" Edina says from her position at the front of the room.

"What's the point? Everyone from this floor is already in here," he replies.

"All right," she says, her lips pulled into a line. She looks out at us all, a sea of faces awaiting their doom. "By now I imagine everyone in the room has heard the rumor that *Claudette* is being shut down."

I hold my breath, hoping this has all been a terrible mistake. Hoping she'll tell us it's not the case at all. That the rumor is just that: a rumor, based on thin air.

Because if it's true it means I lose my job.

It means I'll lose my visa.

It means I won't be able to stay in England.

But most of all, what really hurts is that it means I'm not important enough to Charlie for him to share this news with me. That he kept a huge secret from me, something that will change my life forever.

Edina tucks her hair behind her ears and pulls her lips into a grim line. "I'll make no bones about it, people. I'll give it to you straight. The undiluted truth. What you've heard is true,"

I gawk at her, my jaw slack.

It's true?

"*Claudette* is being shut down."

As the words leave her mouth, my heart breaks.

Just like that.

Broken in two.

How could he do this to me? How could he let me find out like this?

"The owners instructed Pilar last night that the magazine had not performed as hoped, despite the changes we've brought in, and consequently it's being shut down. Next month's issue will be our last."

Waves of shocked murmurs roll through the room.

"Why? Why us? Are they keeping the other magazines?" someone asks.

"They are, I'm afraid. *Claudette* is the only one that won't survive."

There's an outcry from the room, and Edina raises her hands to silence us. "They borrowed to fund the purchase of the magazine group, and the profits of the business are not measuring up. The bank is calling in the loans, and they've got to do something or risk losing the whole magazine portfolio. *Claudette* is the sacrificial lamb."

"But *Claudette* is an institution!" someone calls out.

As another insists, "We're important!" to murmurs of agreement.

"But why us?" someone asks, and there's a general murmur of agreement in the room.

"We've not been performing. Simple as that," Edina replies with a shrug.

"What's going to happen to our jobs?"

"I'm not going to lie. I'm not going to sugar coat this. I'm not going to beat about the bush. Most of us will lose our jobs, but not all. There will be a few who will have the option to be integrated into another magazine, but they'll be admin staff only."

I stare dumbly ahead, the cogs of my brain whirring at a million miles per hour.

Charlie allowed me to be thrown to the wolves with the rest of the team.

Edina fields everyone's concerns, but really, when your job is gone in a flash, what else is there to discuss?

The meeting over, I file dumbly from the room, barely able to focus on what lies before me.

"Can you believe this?" Shelley says as we reach our desks. "Nine o'clock on a Friday morning and we get this sucky news. What the heck am I going to do now?"

"It's nine o'clock?" I ask.

She shoots me a sideways glance. "The time isn't the point. It's the fact that we're about to lose our jobs, Kennedy. One month and then gone."

"Right."

Nine at Starbucks. That's what Charlie said. He made me promise I'd be there.

I'm overwhelmed by a sudden, urgent need to see him.

I rise from my desk and slowly pull on my coat.

"Where are you going?" Shelley asks.

"Out," is my one-word reply, as I make my way toward the elevator.

On the street, I suck in the cold morning air, my heart heavy as my brain races to make sense of what's just happened. Only thirty minutes ago I was a happily employed *Claudette* magazine writer, falling in love with the man of my dreams.

Now?

Now I don't know what I am anymore.

I push through the doors into Starbucks and there he is, waiting by the coffee pickup counter, wearing his suit and tie. He's watching me with trepidation written across his face, his features taut.

In a flash he's at my side. He pulls me into an awkward hug. "You came."

I remain stiff, and he releases me from his grasp. I pull my lips into a line and nod.

"I've got us a place to sit."

My eyes follow as he gestures at a table and chairs with two takeout cups of coffee.

"I got you the coffee you like, with extra cream."

I flick my gaze back to his. "Why didn't you tell me, Charlie? Why?" My voice is soft, small. Full of feelings I don't want to name.

"I couldn't."

"Why not?"

"It was a confidential deal. Please believe me that I went to bat for the magazine. I tried to save it, but Dad had his mind set. He understands business so well, and I have to take his lead. He's been doing this since before I was born." He reaches for my hand, but I snap it away. "Kennedy. Please."

"Please?" I spit at him, my plethora of feelings coalescing into one feeling and one feeling only: anger.

Anger that he didn't tell me.

Anger that I'm losing my job.

"I've lost my job, Charlie. My. Job." I lock my jaw and give him a long, cold stare. "And you know what hurts? You know what the real kicker is here? You knew it was going to happen, and you didn't warn me."

"I didn't know. Not until last night. Dad had made up his mind and there was nothing I could do to stop him. Please understand it from my perspective. I work for him. I have to do what he tells me. He has to have my unflinching loyalty."

His words hit me like a fist to the face.

My unflinching loyalty.

"Even if that means you can't tell me about something that changes my *life*?" I try to keep the hurt from my voice, but it catches as tears sting my eyes.

He places his hands on my arms. "Let me help you. We have many companies. I can find you another job. Any job. All you have to do is name it."

I scoff in disbelief. "Do you honestly think you can just offer me something else and it'll all be okay?"

He has the good grace to hang his head. "I suppose not."

"You could have told me last night, Charlie. When you walked me to the car and said goodnight, you could have given me a heads up in the very least."

"Dad was adamant that this remain confidential until the announcement. If I had told anyone, it could have compromised the deal. Not only that, I would be going directly against his wishes. Please understand I was in an impossible predicament. It needed to remain confidential."

"Confidential from me?" I ask, my voice small, my stomach in knots.

"He's given me so much and I owe him my loyalty. Please be reasonable."

I let out a bitter laugh. I'm vaguely aware that people around us are watching this argument unfold, but I don't care. My world is imploding. "You want me to be reasonable about you not telling me that my life is about to change for the worse forever?"

"Kennedy, it's a job. You can get another one. I can help you."

I blink at him, my eyes wide with disbelief. "It's not just a job to me, Charlie. It's my dream job. Without it I have to go home."

His forehead crinkles. "Why?"

He didn't see that coming.

My victory is fleeting.

I tighten my lips, my glare boring into him. "*Claudette* sponsors my work permit. No *Claudette* means no permit, which means no London for me."

"I-I didn't know. But it's all the more reason to let me find you another job."

I shake my head as the tears that had been threatening my eyes slide slowly down my cheeks. I brush them away furiously. "You don't get it, do you, Charlie? This isn't about whether you can get me a job."

"It's about me not telling you. I know."

Suddenly, it's all become crystal clear. Once again, I'm the little person who can be stepped on. The little person who doesn't matter. Charlie has put his family first, and that's the way it will always be.

Just like Hugo, who I was never good enough for.

When it comes to Charlie, *I will never be enough*.

"Kennedy, please. We can get through this. Let me help you."

I shake my head slowly from side to side, tears tumbling freely down my face. "No. This isn't even about me. I'm just collateral damage in this little game of yours. This game where you don't have the guts to stand up to your dad for something that matters to *me*."

He grips my arms. "We can get through this."

My broken heart is on the floor. "We're too different. I've been here before, and I know how this ends. And let me tell you, I'm not the one who comes out on top."

"That's not fair. You know I'm not your ex."

"No. You're right. You're not. He chose another woman

over me. You chose loyalty to your dad, even when you knew it would hurt me."

The look in his eye is wary, pain etched across his face. "What are you saying?"

I wipe the tears from my cheeks with the back of my hand. I raise my chin and look him directly in the eye. "I'm saying goodbye."

And I turn on my heel and walk out of the café on shaking legs, out into the unknown.

CHAPTER 22

I pick up the stick covered in dog slobber in my gloved hand and hurl it across the park, watching as Lady M sprints after it over the damp grass as fast as her little legs will take her. She's trailed by Zara's dog, Stevie, who's joyously bouncing up and down as though this were the best game in the world.

Oh, to be a carefree dog.

"Would you look at Lady M," Lottie says. "She's like a caffeinated mini-cow this morning."

Tabitha laughs. "A caffeinated mini-cow. Love it."

I pull my lips into as much of a smile as I can manage these days, which is a poor approximation of one at best. "Delphine will be glad to hear you say that when she's back next week. She's crazy for cows."

"Why does she have to come back early? Doesn't she know how much we need you here?" Lottie asks.

"Delphine is what you might call 'changeable,'" Tabitha explains.

"She was meant to be gone for six months, now she's back after less than three," Zara complains. Stevie arrives back at her feet and drops an equally slobbery tennis ball and gazes up at Zara in expectation. "Let me guess, Stevie. You want me to throw that for you?"

Stevie bounces up and down on the spot. Zara scoops the ball up in her ball thrower and fires it across the grass. Stevie promptly chases after it.

"It is what it is, girls, and really, it's not like I can stick around for much longer," I tell them. "Remember? No job. No visa. And now, nowhere to live. It's the trifecta of reasons why I have to move back home."

"I can't believe you're leaving us," Tabitha says glumly, her hands thrust into the pockets of her black puffer jacket against the cold.

"It's just wrong," Lottie harrumphs.

"You're part of the London Babes. What will we do without you?" Zara asks.

"Say you'll stay," Lottie begins. "`Say you'll forgive Charlie for being a total plonker about the whole magazine thing and that you'll live happily ever after here in London with us."

Warmed by my friends' love, I shake my head. "Wish I could, girls."

"You could stay illegally, and we could hide you away in the attic, Anne Frank style?" Tabitha offers.

I shoot her a look.

She scrunches up her nose. "I didn't think so."

"What about Charlie?" Lottie asks.

Tabitha reacts immediately. "Don't mention that name, Lottie. He is dead to us. Dead! Isn't that right, Kennedy?"

"Right," I say with a firm nod, a horrible, all-too-familiar sunken feeling claiming my chest.

Over the last week since that horrible moment in Starbucks when my world imploded, I've tried my best not to think about him.

Tried and failed.

He keeps on creeping into my consciousness day and night. No matter how hard I try, I can't shift the terrible sense of loss that pervades every part of me. It's a heaviness so deep that it's sucked the energy out of me, leaving me like a deflated balloon, sad and empty, forgotten on the cold, hard ground.

That fateful day I walked away from him, I managed somehow, through my blinding tears, to put one foot in front of the other and stumble back to the office. I got myself together enough to tell Edina and Shelley that I was going to work from home for the rest of the day, and then I packed up my things and got out of there as quickly as I could.

I called Lottie on my way to the Tube, sobbing incoherently into the phone at her until she told me to stop where I was and wait for her to come get me, which she did thirty minutes later, a coffee and chocolate brownie in hand.

I burst into tears the moment my eyes landed on her, of course, because that's how together I am these days. A blubbering, incoherent, snotty mess.

Lady M and I have been staying with Lottie, Zara, and her dog, Stevie, ever since—and Tabitha has been camped out with us virtually the whole time in support of me and my broken heart.

We've eaten enough sugar to put us in permanent diabetic comas and watched every rom com Netflix has to offer, in an attempt to brighten my mood, and talked and talked and talked the way girls do when faced with a problem.

Did I mention my friends are the absolute *best*?

Seriously, without them I don't know how I would have gotten through this.

"Has he been in touch again?" Zara asks.

I think of the messages and calls I've received from him over the last week, none of which I've returned. "I send his messages straight to the trash."

"So, there's absolutely no hope of you two reconciling?" Lottie asks as we walk slowly around the dog park, our breath visible in the gray and gloomy winter air. "You guys were the perfect match."

I raise my brows at her. "Tell me if I'm wrong, but didn't I mention that, like, a hundred times already?"

"Oh, yeah, you definitely did," Zara replies. "I think the last time you mentioned that you weren't ever going within a mile of Charlie Cavendish again was when you paused the scene where Mindy met that guy in the bookshop on *The Mindy Project* to tell us you would never go to a bookshop with Charlie because he'd double cross the shop owner and they'd end up having to close down."

"No, I think it was when we were talking about whether we should jump on the Eurostar this weekend to go to Disneyland for the day and then eat too much cheese and drink too much wine afterwards in Paris while sitting on a dinner cruise boat on the Seine, and you said that if we brought Charlie, we could chuck him overboard," Tabitha says. "Which totally has my vote, by the way."

"The Paris thing or the chucking Charlie overboard?" Zara questions.

"Both, clearly," she replies.

Lottie shakes her head. "Nope. It wasn't either of those, girls. It was this morning when I offered you a cup of coffee and you said they should ban mistletoe, so people won't kiss under it in elevators and ruin everything."

"What's mistletoe got to do with a cup of coffee?" Zara asks.

Lottie gives another shake of her head, her ponytail bouncing. "It wasn't clear."

I scrunch up my face. "Have I mentioned him a few too many times?"

"Oh, not at all," Lottie replies, as both Zara and Tabitha agree hurriedly.

"Just every now and then. Hardly mentioned him at all."

"Charlie who?"

I know they're only being nice.

"It's natural, babe. You were totally into him, and he let you down in a spectacular way," Zara says.

I let out a heavy breath, my shoulders sagging. "What an idiot I am, right? Falling for your enemy is never recommended." I look up to see my friends sharing a look. "What?" I ask.

"You fell for him?" Tabitha asks.

"As in you've got all the feels, you've caught major vibes, you're...in *love* with the guy?" Lottie's wide, questioning eyes are trained on me.

I look between my friends. Each one is watching me closely, awaiting my reply with a large dose of anticipation. I push out a heavy breath. "We were only together for a few weeks," I explain. "You can't fall in love with someone that fast."

As the logical, rational words leave my mouth, even I don't believe what I'm saying. I fell for the guy hook, line, and sinker. Totally and completely.

I'm in love with the wrong guy.

And worse yet, it's the kind of love you can spend your whole life looking for. The kind of love that fills you up and gives you a deep and wonderful sense of peace. The kind of love you can rely on being there for you, no matter what.

Only Charlie didn't feel the same way, because if he did, he wouldn't have kept this life-changing secret from me.

Lottie chews on her lip before she replies with concern in her eyes, "But you did, didn't you, Kennedy? You fell in love with Charlie."

I press my own lips together, my habitual hurt bubbling

up, tears threatening my eyes. With a lump forming in my throat, I don't trust myself to speak, so I simply nod.

"Oh, honey," Zara says, as she pulls me in for a hug. "I didn't realize it was that bad."

"Love is never bad. It's beautiful," Lottie tells us.

I shoot her a look.

"Not helpful, Lott," Zara says.

"It's not so beautiful when the guy you're in love with keeps a major secret from you that means you lose your job and have to leave your BFFs," Tabitha says.

Zara rubs my arm. "Exactly. Kennedy can't love someone like that."

I scoff through my tears. It sounds weird. "I'd stop loving him if I could."

"How do you do that? How do you stop loving someone who's bad for you? Because I sure as heck don't know how," Tabitha says, her face glum.

Zara shrugs. "I dunno."

"Me, neither," Lottie agrees.

"You girls are a great help," I say with a watery laugh.

Lady M canters back to me, the stick that's twice as long as her little body jutting out either side of her mouth. She drops it at my feet and looks from the stick up to me and back again, her whole body shimmying with each wag of her tail.

I lean down to pick it up and hurl it for her once more, watching as she tears after it. "Wouldn't life be so much easier if we were all dogs?" I question, more to myself than to my friends. "We'd only care about chasing sticks, where our next snack was coming from, and where we were going to take our afternoon naps. Bliss."

"Why don't you stay here for Lady Moo?" Lottie questions. "You love her, and I can totally tell that she loves you."

I watch as Lady M clamps the stick between her teeth,

shakes her head, and immediately drops to the ground to gnaw on it. It's true. Although we got off to a rough start with the frequent Winnie the Pooh disemboweling and that stash of eyes I never want to think about again, the little dog has become an important part of my life. Leaving her will be super hard, even if I know she'll be back with Delphine.

"I'd love to stay for Lady M, but it's not in the cards."

"I'll tell you what is on the cards," Zara begins. "A warming hot chocolate with extra marshmallows at The Black Cat. Say you'll come, Kennedy. You still have a week before you desert us."

"Okay. I'll come."

"Oooh, the hot choc is good there," Lottie agrees. "And we can bring Lady M and Stevie, too. That's the great thing about British pubs: you can bring your dog."

"It's almost the law," Tabitha agrees with a laugh.

I call Lady M and she comes bounding over to me, as though me calling her is the best thing she's ever heard in her life. I click her leash into place, and the six of us walk together down the street. My heart is well and truly warmed by the friendships I've made in my time in London. I know I'm going to miss these friends, this little dog, and this city more than I can ever say.

CHAPTER 23

The tape dispenser makes a tearing sound as I run it over the box, making Lady M's ears prick up.

"It's okay, girl," I tell her with a pet of the warm fur on her back. "You'd think with all the boxes I've taped this afternoon you'd be used to that noise by now." I slump down onto Delphine's living room floor and pat my lap for her to climb into it. As she sits down and gazes up at me, her long pink tongue darting out of her mouth in an attempt to lick my face, I smile sadly down at her.

"I'm gonna miss you, you know that? But your mommy is going to be back later today, and who knows? She'll probably even let you have a go at that closet full of Winnie the Poohs behind me." I scratch her in her favorite spot, right behind her ears, and a look of utter blissfulness claims her squished little face. "You be a good girl for your mommy, okay?"

She's too blissed out to reply. Either that or she's got no clue what I'm saying because, you know, she's still a dog.

There's a knock at the door.

"Maybe that's your mommy now?" I say to her as I pick her up and carry her across the room, trying my best to ignore the stab of pain that saying goodbye to this little terrier elicits.

I pull the door open. It's not Delphine. Standing in the hallway is not one, not two, not even three, but all six of the Ducks. They're all smiling at me, their pearls and spectacles in place.

Lady M wags her tail at them, making one of her characteristic whiny sounds.

"Hello, dear, and hello there, Lady Moo," Barbara says to me with a smile. "We thought we'd pop up and say hello." She reaches out and gives Lady M a scratch under the chin.

"Well, goodbye, really," Winnifred corrects.

"That's what I meant, Winnifred," Barbara sniffs.

"I was going to stop by to say goodbye to you all," I reply. "Delphine's going to be here any minute. Would you like to come in for a bit?" I scan the group and add, "All of you?"

"We don't have to be asked twice," Elsey says, as she bustles in through the open door and the others waddle after her.

"Hello, love," Evelyn says.

"Nice to see you, Kennedy," Maude adds.

"What a lovely view you have up here," Elsey observes as she looks out the window.

"Look at all those boxes." This from Gertie. "Do you think she'll offer us a cup of tea?"

"Oh, I could do with a nice cuppa, myself," Barbara replies.

I put Lady M back on the floor, and she immediately begins to bounce between the Ducks, seeking whatever attention she can get. "I'm so sorry, ladies. I don't have any tea or coffee or anything to offer you," I tell them.

"No tea?" Gertie asks.

"That's right. No tea," Barbara confirms.

"What did you say?" Maude questions.

"She said no tea," Barbara repeats, loud enough for Maude to hear.

"Goodness. How very odd," Maude declares, her eyes wide as she regards me with suspicion.

"She's American," Evelyn explains. "It's all coffee and Jim Beam over there, you know."

Barbara waves her hand in the air. "Don't you go worrying about tea, dear. We're all fine without it. Aren't we, ladies?"

"Absolutely," Elsey agrees.

"I've just had a cuppa, so I'm right as rain," Winnifred sniffs.

"Nice for you. I'm parched," Gertie harrumphs.

"Get your own cuppa when you go home after, then," Barbara scolds. She eyes the boxes dotted around the living room, containing all my worldly possessions, destined for warmer climates. Californian warmer climates, to be specific. "I see it's true, then. You're leaving us."

"That explains *everything*," Elsey says, as she shoots the Ducks a meaningful look.

"That explains what, Elsey? You know you really should be more specific. You could be talking about anything," Winnifred complains.

"She does like to generalize," Gertie observes, as the others nod their agreement.

Elsey lifts her chin. "Thank you everyone for that valuable feedback," she says, clearly *not* thanking them for their valuable feedback. "What I was going to say, before I was rudely interrupted, is that explains why Charlie has been wandering around like a bear with a sore head this past week."

"He looked very down in the mouth when he turned up to our knitting circle on Monday evening," Barbara says.

"Didn't he just?" Gertie agrees.

I blink at them in total disbelief. Charlie actually went to the Ducks' knitting circle? "Charlie was there?" I question.

"Oh, yes. Turned up without any knitting," Elsey says. "It was most peculiar."

"I think he just wanted the company," Gertie offers.

"Oh, no. He was on a fact-finding mission if ever there was one," Winnifred says.

"That's true," Elsey agrees.

"What's true?" Maude asks.

"Charlie wanted to find out about Kennedy," Winnifred explains in a loud voice.

"He did ask a lot of questions," Maude replies. "And none of them were about knitting. Very odd."

Part of me wants to know what non-knitting related questions Charlie had asked—the part of me that still hasn't gotten the memo that he and I are over.

But the rational part of me tells myself that what Charlie does in his own time is entirely up to him and of no concern to me whatsoever. If he wants to go to the Ducks' knitting circle without any knitting and set their tongues wagging by asking questions about whatever it is that he was asking questions about, then that's his business. Not mine.

Barbara raises her brows at me. "Don't you want to know what he was asking about?"

I offer her a pleasant smile. "There's no need to—"

"It was you!" Winnifred declares, before I have the chance to complete my sentence. "He wanted to know how you were and what you were doing and had any of us seen you and were you okay. Didn't he, ladies?"

"Yes, he did," Barbara agrees.

"It was Kennedy this and Kennedy that," Gertie adds.

"*So* many questions," Elsey says.

"It got a little tedious after a while," Evelyn adds.

"We had to ask him to change the subject," Elsey explains.

"Oh, but he did seem very sad," Winnifred says.

"But he didn't even bring any knitting." This from Maude.

My eyes bounce between the Ducks, a heaviness forming in my chest at the thought of Charlie being sad. But it's not entirely heavy. If I'm totally honest, knowing that he went to the Ducks' knitting circle specifically to ask after me gives me a fleeting sense of elation. Until I remember that he could never stand up to his dad and put my needs first, and then think he can fix it all by waving a magic new-job-finding wand.

Yeah, *that*.

"He told us all about what happened," Barbara says.

"All of it. He was quite upset. Wasn't he, ladies?" Elsey says.

"He didn't even drink his coffee," Evelyn observes.

"I prefer a cup of tea, myself," Gertie says, shooting me a meaningful look.

"Oh, I'd love a cuppa," Maude says.

I cut the beverage conversation short. No one needs to go there again. "Look, Charlie and I are over, so there's no need to tell me what he was asking. Seriously."

Winnifred ignores me completely. "He told us that he was doing what his father told him to do, and he hurt you along the way, Kennedy dear. And do you know what I said to him?"

"We all know what you told him, Winnifred. We were all there in the room with him," Barbara complains. "Are you going senile in your old age?"

"She's not old," Gertie snaps. "She's only eighty-two. She's a spring chick."

"Not you, you silly old goat," Winnifred sniffs. "Kennedy. She doesn't know what I said to him."

"Well go on, then. Tell her," Barbara instructs.

"I told him he'd made a total arse of himself. Messed it all up with you. And do you know what he said? He said he absolutely agreed and that he regretted it deeply."

"Deeply," Elsey agrees, as the others nod their heads. "He said you're not returning his calls."

Every eye in the room turns to me.

"I...I didn't see the point," I murmur.

"Why not? The man's in love with you!" Winnifred declares.

My heart squeezes, that familiar sunken feeling claiming my belly. "It's no use."

"Do you love him?" Elsey asks.

I suck in a breath before I give a small nod.

Barbara slaps her thighs. "Well then!"

"You know, I never used to like him," Evelyn says.

"None of us did," Elsey declares.

Gertie shakes her head. "He was very rude."

"Very unsociable," Winnifred tells us.

"But awfully handsome." This from Elsey. "If I were fifty years younger..."

"Listen to yourself! Fifty years. More like sixty," Winnifred scoffs.

"I'll tell you who's getting older this week and that's you, Maude, isn't it?" Evelyn says.

"It's her 95th birthday and we're all going to celebrate with a nice sherry," Barbara tells me.

I sit through the Ducks chatting among themselves, thankful the conversation has moved on from Charlie and me, until my phone beeps with a message.

Zara: *Running late. Be there in ten mins max. Meet me on the street with the first load and I'll send Asher up for the next.*

Me: *Okay. On my way.*

I tell the Ducks it's time for me to leave, and see them to the door.

"I'm really going to miss seeing you around, young lady,"

Barbara says, as she gives me a hug. "It's hard to believe you've only been here for a few months."

"I'm gonna miss you. All of you." I hug them each in turn, and then stand in the doorway and wave them off. As I close the door behind me, I'm instantly plunged back into silence but for Lady M's snoring in her bed, having worn herself out with her excitement at seeing the Ducks earlier.

I heave the last of my suitcases off the bed, pull out its handle, and wheel it across the floor to the front door. I collect a second suitcase and stack it on top. Lady M pricks up her ears at the sound.

"I'll be back soon. Don't worry. I'm just gonna drop this first load in the lobby."

I grab my keys from the hallway table and pull the door open, only to stop dead in my tracks.

It's him, standing in my doorway.

Charlie.

His face creases into a tentative smile. In a pair of jeans, a navy V-neck sweater, and tennis shoes, his handsomeness sucks the air from my lungs.

My heart leaps into my mouth.

"Hello, Kennedy," he says in that familiar, deep voice of his. "Barbara told me you were back here."

Barbara the traitor. Why did she have to do that? And more importantly, why the heck does he have to look so dang good?

He glances at my suitcases. "Can I help you with those?"

Despite the emotional turmoil raging inside, I lift my chin and reply, "I'm fine, thanks. I-I need to go." With as much composure as I can manage, I pull the handle of my suitcase and move past him as the door to my flat closes behind me.

He follows me down the hall toward the elevator, where I press the button and wait.

"Please, Kennedy. I promise I won't bite."

The elevator doors slide open, and I step inside, trailed by him.

My heart is going all kinds of crazy in my chest. It's thudding hard with a mixture of shock, anguish, and terror—but also with hope. Hope that he's come to make it right.

Although how he can do that is beyond me.

"Kennedy?"

I scrunch my eyes shut, my breathing short. "Yup?"

He reaches out and presses a button, and the elevator comes to a sudden, lurching stop.

"What are you doing?" I ask, as I grab onto my suitcase and manage to keep my balance. As the bouncing of the elevator eases, I lift my eyes to his, and my breath catches in my throat by what I see in his eyes.

Love, pure and simple.

"I've been trying to talk to you, to tell you things, but you haven't returned any of my calls or messages."

"I'm meeting Zara downstairs. She and Asher are helping me move out," I murmur, not even sure why I'm telling him this.

"I can see that. I-I need to say something to you, Kennedy. I know you're leaving, and I don't want to miss the chance to put things right between us."

I cast my eyes down. "I'm not sure you can."

"Please, just listen to what I have to say?"

I lift my head and twist my mouth, faking bravado. "We're in a confined space and you just hit the stop button. I think I'm a pretty captive audience right now. Shoot."

His lips curve into a smile that pulls on my heartstrings. Hard. "That's the Kennedy I know." He takes a step closer to me, and I'm immediately struck by how good he smells, how soft his eyes have become, how being close to him makes me want to hold onto him and never let him go.

I swallow, forcing myself to remain composed.

Well, as composed as I can be in a confined space with the man I've so recently loved and lost.

"Kennedy, I'm so sorry for what I did to you. It was wrong. I blindly followed my father's wishes in not telling anyone about shutting *Claudette* down, and I should have disregarded what he said when it came to you. You deserved to know what was happening, and I should have had the strength to stand up to him and warn you."

I bite my lip. "Yes. You should have."

"And then I made it worse by thinking I could fix it by simply offering you another job. That was totally insensitive of me. I thought I was making things right for you, but I was only adding insult to injury. Please forgive me."

"Sure," I tell him, as I hold my lips in a thin line and steady my breathing.

"I've realized something in the last week, and it's because of you."

"Me?"

He nods. "I've spent my entire working life trying to make my father proud of me. Stepping into what should have been James's shoes, I've never measured up. Not in my dad's eyes, and certainly not in mine. James was a natural leader, in a way I've never thought I could be, and Dad has reinforced my failings time and time again by not trusting my instinct, not following my ideas, not giving me a voice. In the end, I gave up. It was easier that way, easier to defer to him, which I've done without question for a long time now. Until you. You've taught me that I can have a voice, that I can take a risk and stand up for what's important to me."

"But...*Claudette*?"

He shakes his head, his mouth turned down. "I wish I could have saved it for you, for everyone who worked there, but it wasn't financially viable for us."

"So, you supported your dad's call to sell it?"

"It was the right decision. But I messed up. I should have warned you about what was happening."

There's an ache in my chest and my throat grows hot from unshed tears. "Yeah, you should have."

He hangs his head before looking back up at me, tears welling in his eyes. "I don't want to lose you, Kennedy. I can't lose you. I know this thing between us is new and I know my lack of action to protect you is wrong, but you mean too much to me to let you slip away without a fight." He reaches for my hand and takes it in his. "Because I'm fighting for you. I don't want to lose you because I was trying to live up to my dad's expectations of me."

My heart is beating out of my chest. I swallow, my throat dry. "I get that your dad is this big driving force in your life. I really do. But can't you see that what you did made me feel unimportant?"

"I put you second, and I made you feel less than you are."

He hit the nail squarely on its head. My belly twists at the painful truth that hovers between us.

He clutches onto my hand as his gaze intensifies, reaching inside of me and clamping hard onto my heart. "I will never put you second again, Kennedy. Never."

"Promise?" I ask, my heavy gloom lifting.

The edges of his mouth lift. "Promise."

As I gaze into his eyes, I'm struck by such a sense of love and acceptance, it almost takes my breath away. "I need to apologize to you, too," I tell him.

"No, you don't."

"I do. I judged you unfairly from almost the moment I laid eyes on you. I expected you to treat me the way Hugo treated me. When you didn't tell me what was happening with the magazine, I automatically assumed it was because I wasn't important enough to you."

"But you are. You are so important to me." He reaches out and places his hand against my cheek. "I still love you."

"You do?" I ask, my voice breathless, as a huge smile bursts out across my face.

"Quite a lot, actually. I love you. I want you. I will do anything to have you back."

My breath is coming short and shallow as my heart threatens to beat out of my chest. "But…your dad."

He takes both my hands in his. His touch sends a jolt through me.

"I told him what had happened, how blindly following his instructions had destroyed the most important thing in my life. I told him I couldn't lose you, that by not warning you what was happening with the magazine, you had lost all faith in me. I've told him I can't ever do that again, That I *won't* ever do that again."

"You stood up to him."

"I did." His intensely blue eyes bore into me, and all the anger, resentment, and sorrow that I've felt since that terrible day washes out of me. It's replaced with a ferocious, burning love for this man confessing his wrongs and seeking my forgiveness, right here in the elevator where it all began.

"I-I love you, too, Charlie," I murmur, as tears pour down my cheeks.

His face creases into his beautiful smile before he closes the gap between us, circling his arms around me and pulling me close as his lips find mine, wrapping me up in the most heartfelt, emotional, and love-filled kiss of my life.

EPILOGUE

We walk hand in hand along the pathway toward the huge white statue, looming at least a hundred feet above us. Wearing shorts, T-shirts, and tennis shoes, we look like every other tourist around us as the early morning sun illuminates the stone, rendering the statue otherworldly in its undeniable magnificence.

"Isn't this incredible?" Charlie says, as he gazes up in wonder. "And that's before we even take in the view from up here."

I give his hand a squeeze and he pulls his attention from the oversized Christ the Redeemer statue to look at me. "Was it worth the wait?" I ask him.

"Are you kidding? It's been ten years since I'd first planned my trip here, but that wait was worth every moment to get to be at the top of Corcovado Mountain with you."

I beam at him, my heart completely full. "Let's go look at that view."

We make our way through the crowds to the edge of the statue and gaze out at the city of Rio de Janeiro below, from the Bay of Guanabana to Sugar Loaf, to the city and the famous beaches, it's like we're on top of the world, gazing down.

"Simply stunning," I breathe. I slip my arm around Charlie's waist, and he hooks his own arm around my shoulders, pulling me close against him.

Since that day we got back together in the building elevator, so much has happened. Right from the moment we started kissing, the Ducks tried to "save" us from the elevator, which they assumed had broken down once more. But then, when they saw us exit together, beaming like the in-love couple we are, they bustled around us in glee, Winnifred and Barbara bickering about who was the one to bring us together again.

Elsey's email on Tuesday tells us the argument still rages.

Charlie helped me move into Zara and Lottie's flat that day, and he and I have been together every single day since. That includes taking Charlie's long overdue trip to the Americas together. We spent a week with my family in San Diego after touring the east coast, and now we're here in Rio, our first stop on our South American adventure.

Charlie's phone vibrates in his pocket, punctuating our moment.

"I know you want to take that," I tell him with a smile on my face.

"You know I've told Dad I'm a work-free zone for all six weeks of our trip."

"But it might be about your new job."

He pulls the phone out of his pocket and his face lights up as he reads the screen. "Will you be really upset if I take it?"

"Of course not. Cavendish Travel won't set itself up. They need their new CEO."

He answers his phone with, "Hello, Hilda. Would you

mind holding for a second? There's something I need to do before we talk." With his phone held against his chest, he slides his hand behind my head, bends down, and brushes his lips tantalizingly across mine. "Happy Valentine's Day, darling," he tells me.

"Happy Valentine's Day."

"I love you. Did you know that?"

"I kinda got that when you announced it to my whole family last week during lunch at the Aldridge Country Club, although gathering the entire staff to hear the announcement was perhaps taking things a little far."

"I wanted everyone to know how I feel about you," he tells me.

I let out a contented laugh. "Go talk to Hilda. Set the world of travel on fire."

He grins at me as he lifts the phone to his ear and turns to leave. "Sorry about that, Hilda. What's the latest?"

I watch him walk away, admiring his broad shoulders, the way his cotton T molds to his muscular back, tapering into a slim waist and that perfect butt of his. I let out my second contented, Charlie-inspired sigh of the morning—and it's still only dawn.

It's hard to believe how much has changed since we officially became a couple once again. Charlie standing up to his dad was the first domino he knocked over, which led to a frank and open discussion with both him and his uncle about the direction he wanted his career to take. Long story short, that conversation resulted in him stepping down as Cavendish Group C.O.O. and instead heading up a business he could be passionate about: the newly minted Cavendish Travel.

Sure, he still works hard. He still gets up at some ludicrous hour of the morning to hit the gym on his way to work. Old habits are hard to break. But the big difference is, he's happy, *truly* happy, and he's doing it all for the right reasons—not trying to fill James's impossibly big shoes to please his dad.

During that time, things have changed for yours truly, too.

Along with the rest of the staff at *Claudette*, we put our all into making the final issue the best it could be, and I bought twenty copies when it hit the stands to give to my friends and family as historic keepsakes.

Only it turned out not to be the final issue of the magazine I'd grown up loving. You see, after the Cavendish Group publicly announced the magazine's demise, another company—one based in my home state of California, no less—offered to buy it out. Most of our jobs were saved, mine included, and the magazine's readership has exploded under the new management.

Not everyone got to stick around, though. Just as Sandra was kicked to the curb, so too was Edina, and now I've got a new boss, a guy named Ted Fairhall, who allows me to write what interests me. And I'm glad to report there have been no more awkward blind dates with random men I met on the Internet at London's themed restaurants and bars, either.

Although I do occasionally wonder how gold-Speedo wearing Carl is getting along with his ex—and his cat with the thousand Instagram followers.

So, I too continue to live my dream as a writer at my favorite London-based magazine. And I've got to tell you, *not* having to keep my relationship with my boss's boss's boss's boss secret at work has been a breath of fresh California beach air.

As I drink in the view of the city and the Atlantic Ocean, stretching out to the hazy horizon, warm arms circle my waist. I turn around and look up to see Charlie grinning at me. "All systems are go when we get back to London in a few weeks."

"That means we'll have plenty of time for our trip to Lima and Machu Picchu before we have to leave."

"And your new place will be ready for you to move into with Lady M, too."

I grin as I think of the little Boston Terrier with the cow-like markings who has well and truly won my heart. "I'm having the most incredible vacation with you, but I've gotta say I've missed the little pooch."

"I'm so happy that flaky Delphine moved to New York and gave you her cow dog, even if it's because Lady M's become 'off brand' with her YouTube viewers."

"Right? She and I are going to be very happy living above The Black Cat, I just know it."

"Are you sure she won't have some kind of existential doggie crisis because she's living in a place named after a cat?"

I let out a giggle. "She'll be fine, and we get to have as much cottage pie as we want, too."

"Music to my ears," he replies. "Now they know you'll be living only a block away, the Ducks will pay you frequent visits, you know."

"Tell you what. I'll come to see them at the next knitting circle at your flat," I tease.

"You do know I only went to their knitting circle once and it was only to glean intel on you, don't you?"

"Sure," I reply with a laugh. "I can totally see you in a string of pearls with thick-rimmed glasses, gossiping with Barbara and Winnifred as you purl and slip stitch."

His low, warm laugh reverberates through me. "Can you now?"

"Totally. Guys who knit are super hot." I push myself up onto tippy toes to plant a kiss on his lips.

This time it's my phone with a notification. I pull it out of my purse. "Message from the London Babes," I tell him.

"What's the latest?"

I scroll through the chain of messages. My girls sure have been chatting. But then, that's no different than usual.

"It looks like Zara and Asher are having an awesomely romantic Valentine's trip to Paris, Tabitha's got another hangover, and Lottie's thinking of giving up on Matt, the guy she's had a crush on at work since for*ever*, although she's being super vague about why."

"So just the usual, then."

"Well, they *are* planning a party for our return, so that's new. Drinks at The Black Cat."

"You won't have to travel too far for that one."

I glance back up at the statue behind us. It's utterly majestic as it glows in the morning light. "I feel a selfie coming on." I hand Charlie my phone and he holds it at arm's length as we press together and grin.

"Okay, tour guide. What's next?" I ask him, as we begin to walk back toward the train that carried us up here.

"Breakfast, followed by Sugar Loaf on the gondola, and then I'd quite like to hit the beach."

"Copacabana or Ipanema?"

"Famous golden sand beach or famous golden sand beach." He weighs the options up in his hands. "Tough call."

I let out a laugh. "Life ain't too shabby for us right now, huh?"

He pulls me into him once more, and as his lips meet mine I breathe in his delicious, unique Charlie scent, happiness bubbling up inside of me. "Not too shabby at all."

This. This is what I was looking for. This is what I was missing.

And who knew I'd find it with the guy I once thought I hated, the guy who reminded me of my ex.

The guy who turned out to be nothing like him.

Charlie Cavendish, my Big Love.

THE END

ACKNOWLEDGMENTS

Kennedy Bennet is one of the most long suffering characters I've ever created. She first appeared as one of the contestants on the reality TV dating show, *Dating Mr. Darcy* in the book of the same name, along with Emma, Sebastian, Phoebe, and the rest of the gang. She didn't get her HEA (happily ever after) in that book, and nor did she get it in the following four titles, either. That's right, poor Kennedy appeared in five books before she got her own story. That's long suffering, for sure, but made writing it all the sweeter for me.

In fact, finally being able to give her the HEA she so deserves has been wonderful, and I hope all the readers and reviewers who have told me that they needed her story *now* have loved reading it. I only hope I met their expectations and gave Kennedy the story they wanted.

As always, I have a bunch of people to thank for helping me with this book. Jackie Rutherford is my long-suffering critique partner whose unstinting support and enthusiasm for my stories gets me through every book with a massive smile on my face. Jackie, your razor sharp intelligence and wit keeps me delivering books I can be proud of, and I love our time together, sharing our passion for writing, dissecting storylines and building characters.

Kim McCann has worked on a few projects with me now, and she's a fast and efficient proof reader who I have come to rely on. Thanks for your hard work, Kim.

My husband supports me and my writing every day of his life, and I know I couldn't do this without him. Thank you for letting me get lost in 'book world' and for being there when I come up for air, my darling.

To my readers, I so hope you loved this book. I've got two more books planned in this series, so even though Kennedy has had her HEA, there will be more to her story yet to come.

ABOUT THE AUTHOR

Kate O'Keeffe is a *USA TODAY* bestselling and award-winning author who writes exactly what she loves to read: laugh-out-loud romantic comedies with swoon-worthy heroes and gorgeous feel-good happily ever afters. She lives and loves in beautiful Hawke's Bay, New Zealand with her family and two scruffy but loveable dogs.

When she's not penning her latest story, Kate can be found hiking up hills (slowly), traveling to different countries around the globe (back when we used to be able to do that), and eating chocolate. A lot of it.

Printed in Great Britain
by Amazon

76888455R00187